FROZEN CHARLOTTE

FROZEN CHARLOTTE

A Martha Gunn Mystery

Priscilla Masters

severn House

This first world edition published 2011
in Great Britain and the USA by
SEVERN HOUSE PUBLISHERS LTD of
9–15 High Street, Sutton, Surrey, England, SM1 1DF.
Trade paperback edition first published
in Great Britain and the USA 2011 by
SEVERN HOUSE PUBLISHERS LTD.

British Library Cataloguing in Publication Data

Masters, Priscilla.
  Frozen Charlotte. – (Martha Gunn)
  1. Gunn, Martha (Fictitious character)–Fiction.
  2. Coroners–England–Shrewsbury–Fiction. 3. Forensic
  Pathology–Fiction. 4. Detective and mystery stories.
  I. Title II. Series
  823.9'14-dc22

ISBN-13: 978-0-7278-8006-2 (cased)
ISBN-13: 978-1-84751-333-5 (trade paper)

All Severn House titles are printed on acid-free paper.

Severn House Publishers support The Forest Stewardship Council [FSC],
the leading international forest certification organisation. All our titles that
are printed on Greenpeace-approved FSC-certified paper carry the FSC logo.

Typeset by Palimpsest Book Production Ltd.,
Falkirk, Stirlingshire, Scotland.
Printed and bound in Great Britain by
MPG Books Ltd., Bodmin, Cornwall.

ONE

There was nothing to mark her out. She sat quietly in the corner of the Accident and Emergency department, in the seat farthest away from the registration hatch. She merged almost perfectly into the background in a dark fleece and paint-spattered jeans, hunched over a small bundle. She could have been a relative or a friend of a patient – even someone who had wandered in, looking for warmth, shelter and safety on this cold night. There are plenty of waifs and strays in and around a hospital and in general the staff are kind, allowing them to sit, even giving them a cup of tea. They realized later, when they had the debrief, that no one had really noticed her. She had blended into the background so successfully that even the nurses, who, like waiters in a busy restaurant, were trained to notice everyone, had not seen her. They were all too distracted and the woman made no demands so did not draw attention to herself. She had not approached the desk to register her complaint, but sat, head down over a pink woollen bundle, crooning softly, rocking it ever so slightly, to and fro, acknowledging no one.

All around there was the usual noise of a casualty department in a district general hospital on a freezing Saturday night. The snow had brought in the usual slips and tumbles, sledging collisions and car crashes. The air ambulance had been ferrying casualties to the hospital all day long so there was a line of trolleys and people waiting to be seen by the overworked staff. There was heightened tension that night. This was a hospital and a town still traumatized by the explosion on the previous Sunday afternoon which had tested out the hospital's Major Incident Policy for only the second time in ten years. It had worked well but they were all still twitching from the effect. So tonight the bustle under the bright lights appeared particularly frenzied: the shouts of patients louder and more querulous, the screams of children shriller, the

metallic clash of trolleys coming and going more discordant.
Bleeps and telephones, shouts of instruction and everywhere
people hurrying, a sense of urgency, of quickness, of life and
death. There was colour, movement and bright lights everywhere, except in this one dimly lit far corner where a woman
sat hunched over a pink blanket, isolated in her own quiet
pool.

Staff Nurse Lucy Ramshaw was getting married in eight
weeks' time so she was working long shifts to earn much
needed extra cash. All the time she worked that evening,
carrying out the hundred and one tasks that were expected of
her, she was distracted, her mind floating up the aisle to the
strains of Wagner's 'Bridal Chorus' to become Mrs Werrin.
She was mentally making lists of Things To Do Before The
Special Day: checking flowers, cars, times, lifts, accommodation, final fittings of the dresses and worrying about the
iceberg of her credit card bill which seemed to have grown
exponentially. On top of that were other worries: seating
arrangements, potential hostility between a divorced couple –
her brother and ex-sister-in-law meeting up after years. Lucy
was looking forward to the Great Day but she wished that
somehow she could be transported there right now with the
list ticked off completely. There was too much to think and
worry about and these long shifts at work were a kill. She
was dog tired. She sighed as she searched the computer for
a blood result that would make the difference between
admission to the Coronary Care unit or a patient being
reassured and sent home. It was negative.

She stood up ready to speak to the patient and felt slightly
uplifted. After all the stress of the wedding there would be
the honeymoon. She smiled to herself. Rob Werrin was quite
a catch. A fit, smart guy who worked in a car showroom and
knew how to make her very happy. She adored him and he
her. So for the early part of that evening Lucy Ramshaw was
happy in her work.

7.30 p.m., The White House

Martha was decorating what had been Martin's study. In over-
alls and with a shower cap protecting her red hair from the
paint spots, she was making very slow progress. It had seemed

as though it would be a simple, quick job, splashing emulsion over the walls but, as with many DIY jobs, it was taking a lot longer than she had anticipated, which was frustrating. Sam was home for the weekend and she would have preferred to spend more time with him, particularly as he was more subdued than normal. He was suspended from playing in any of the junior league matches because of a tendon strain and the inactivity had made him grumpy and a little reflective about his future as a football player. Martha looked at her freckle-faced son and wished she could find the right words to console him, maybe even direct him towards more positive thinking. The worst thing was that since he had been signed up for the Liverpool Football Academy his erstwhile local friends had drifted away into their own lives. Now when he came home he was largely alone, his friends now being the Liverpool gang. She wasn't much good. Mothers rarely are when it comes to sporting chit-chat. The entire clannish football world was foreign to her and after a few attempts at describing matches, goals, runs, passes and so on, Sam had given up. She dipped her roller in the paint tray. She had long grown out of the habit of wishing that Martin was here to help her through this or even believing that he would have dealt better with the situation. He hadn't been a great football fan either. It was a mystery to her where Sam had got this talent from. Riding on the back of this puzzle was the knowledge that Martin had never known this Sam, this teenager with the complicated life, this emerging man. He had left behind three-year-old twins. A little boy and a little girl.

Sukey, in a white towelling dressing gown, wandered in, frowning. 'Mum, have you seen my white top?'

'In the wash?' Martha ventured.

Sukey looked impatient. 'It'll want ironing.'

Martha turned around and gave her daughter a straight look. Agnetha, the au pair, was leaving in a month. From then on she would only have Vera, the daily, for a couple of mornings a week. And Vera, famously, did not like ironing. In the future if Sukey wanted something ironing she was going to have to do it herself. She may as well get used to it. But instead of answering her daughter's very indirect question Martha countered with one of her own.

'Where are you going tonight, Suks?'

It is the question every teenage girl resents. Sukey's scowl deepened. 'Out.'

'You know the rules,' Martha said quietly. 'Where?'

Sukey flushed and looked evasive. 'With a bunch of people.'

Martha put the paintbrush down with exaggerated deliberation. 'You know the rules,' she repeated. 'Where are you going, who will be with you and—'

'What time will you be home,' Sukey chimed in with a squeaky, mocking voice.

Martha ignored the cheek and smiled. 'Precisely,' she said.

Sam decided it was time he contributed to the discussion. 'As I'm home I'd have thought you'd have wanted to stay in,' he said grumpily. 'I'm hardly ever here, Suks, specially at weekends.'

Mercurial as ever, Sukey's face changed. She gave them both a wide, warm smile, each in turn. 'I'm going out with Sally, Emma, Feodore and Rumilla,' she said carefully, spoiling this innocent statement of intention by slipping in, 'and some of the sixth-form boys are tagging along too.'

In spite of the warning bells alarming in Martha's head, she forced herself not to over react. 'And where are you going?'

'To the new club that's just opened in town. It's a sort of disco/coffee shop. Don't worry, Mum', Sukey said quickly, 'Feodore's dad is being taxi driver tonight and he promises to have me home before eleven. And as for you, little brother,' she said, turning to Sam, 'as penance for abandoning you tonight for the fleshpots of Shrewsbury I shall spend all day tomorrow listening to your utterly boring football talk.' She diluted the insult by rumpling her brother's hair and they exchanged a small, secret smile, one that perhaps only twins can share.

'All right, Suks,' he said, good-naturedly, then eyeing the decorating with resentment he continued, 'I suppose I shall have to help Mum paint this room.'

Both mother and son looked around them with a distinct lack of enthusiasm. 'It seems to be taking an awfully long time,' Sam tagged on disconsolately.

'Mmm.' Martha wiped her face, smearing emulsion across her right cheek and privately she agreed. Perhaps she had bitten off more than she could really chew. The ceilings in this room seemed particularly high and full of nasty small cracks that would all need filling with Polyfilla. She'd never done much decorating and now wished she'd summoned a professional. She was not enjoying this, particularly as tonight was a rare occasion. She would have her son all to herself. It seemed a waste to spend it doing something so mundane as decorating. As Sukey left the room, presumably to see if Agnetha would iron her white T-shirt, Martha put the paint tray down. 'You know, Sam,' she said, 'I don't much feel like doing this tonight. How about we do some cooking and watch a film or something instead?'

His answer was a wide grin. She and Sam shut the door firmly on the chaos, took the brushes out to the laundry and started rinsing them through.

But now she had dealt with one problem her mind focussed on Sukey's deliberately careless words. Sixth-form boys?

A mother might see her daughter every day but the moment is still sudden when she realizes her little girl has become a woman. Martha watched the paint-stained water swirling down the plughole. It had happened so fast.

When Sukey came downstairs fifteen minutes later Martha and Sam were rifling through the kitchen cupboards, trying to decide what to cook. Sukey walked into the kitchen and Martha realized that her daughter had the poise of a woman twice her age. She shook her head almost in disbelief and watched her. When had Sukey turned from sweet schoolgirl into something so resembling a super model? As she eyed the tiny black skirt around boyish hips, long, slim legs and blonde hair swinging almost to her waist and noted that she was wearing the newly ironed T-shirt – ironed by whom? – Martha felt a snatch, not only of apprehension, but also of pride. Was this really her own daughter?

'You look lovely, Sukey,' she said. 'Really lovely.' She sighed. 'Nothing like me or your father. I don't know where you get it from.'

Sukey gave her a grin. 'Neither do I,' she said cheekily. Behind her Sam chortled and for a brief, precious moment, they were a family of three, undamaged by grief or un-happiness.

'What do you think, Mrs Gunn?' Agnetha had appeared in the doorway. 'I am glad I ironed the shirt so she could wear it. It looks so good on her.'

One question answered.

'She does look great, Agnetha. You're going to miss her when you leave to get married.'

'I am. But maybe you will allow her to come over to see me?'

'Yes, of course.'

'That would be lovely. My family will like her so very much.' She and Sukey looked at each other and smiled conspiratorially. In the years since Agnetha had been their au pair they had built up a close friendship.

Uninterested in Agnetha's impending wedding, Sam had stayed silent during this girlish exchange. He was still rooting through the fridge to see what he could find to cook. He waited with unaccustomed patience as the three women chatted about clothes and fashion and the forthcoming wedding in the summer.

The conversation was cut short by the ring of the doorbell. Sukey jumped up and kissed her mother's cheek. 'Bye, Mum,' she said. 'Don't worry. See you later. Bye, Sam. Bye, Agnetha.' And she was gone leaving Agnetha a free evening to watch the television, surf the Internet and chat with her fiancée and Martha and Sam to enjoy cooking fish pie, once they'd defrosted some cod steaks.

As they steamed the fish, grated the cheese, peeled and cooked the potatoes, Sam began to unburden himself.

'It's sort of unsettling, Mum,' he said, his face looking troubled. 'I mean – you're never really on an even keel, you know. One minute they're calling you a god, the next they're throwing shit in your face and calling you a dickhead.'

'Sam.' She was shocked at how cynical he'd become so very quickly. Her daughter might have the poise of a woman twice her age but her son had the cynicism of someone twice his age. He'd only been at the academy a little over a year and he'd changed completely. She felt a sudden anger. What the hell did they teach boys there? She studied his face. He'd always been a gritty little character, biting his lip when he'd fallen and hurt himself, determined not to cry. In that way he had not changed at all. He was still her tough son, wiry and determined, yet vulnerable, but this newly acquired cynicism made him appear older, much wiser, than his almost fifteen years, even a littler careworn. She watched him with concern until he started forking in the food, energy and enthusiasm increasing by the mouthful. She smiled and relaxed. It turned out a pleasant evening.

Saturday night is 'drunks night' which always keeps the staff busy. But this night was different. After the initial rush of casualties during the day and early evening, the department gradually emptied out as the snow was obviously keeping people to their own homes and encouraging those who were out to return earlier than usual. By a little after 9 p.m. the department was clearing, the chairs slowly emptying.

Dr Jane Miles wiped some hair out of her eyes and looked at Staff Nurse Ramshaw. 'How're we doing, Lucy?'

Lucy grinned back and rotated her shoulders to loosen them up. 'Not bad. We should manage a cup of—'

This was being a little over optimistic. The bleep interrupted her. 'Dr Miles to Resus. Dr Miles to Resus.' Jane picked up the number and started running.

There is a particular atmosphere which surrounds a cardiac arrest. Noise and stillness, activity and a lack of movement. Quiet words of direction and finally a decision. Screens are put round, relatives ushered away and anyone who does not have an active role keeps on the periphery, to act as messenger. It was a young road-traffic victim, a youth of twenty who had been walking along the road because the pavement was icy but a car coming in the opposite direction had struggled to maintain control and had smashed into him causing multiple injuries. The team worked on him for an exhausting half hour before their eyes met and they made the decision to stop resuscitating. There is nothing more defeating than this moment. But it is not only a time of grief. It is the moment of decision. Tragedy for some can be the ray of hope for others. There is the question of organ donation which has to be hurried past already traumatized relatives.

And so, amid the bustle and noise of the A&E department on this Saturday evening, the woman continued to sit with the pink woollen bundle on her lap. She was not so much ignored as sitting at the bottom of the department's priorities. Finally, at half past ten, it was left to Staff Nurse Lucy Ramshaw, to deal with her just before she finished her twelve-hour shift. First of all she went to speak to Sarinda, the clerk on the registration desk. 'Do you know anything about the lady sitting in the corner?'

The receptionist leaned over to peer over Lucy's shoulder. 'No,' she said. 'She hasn't registered here. Maybe she's waiting for someone. She doesn't look like a down-and-out.'

That was when Lucy started to feel just a little uneasy. 'The cubicles are empty,' she observed. 'The weather's keeping most sensible people indoors.' She pushed open the door into the waiting area. 'I'd better find out what she's doing here.'

She threaded her way through the rows of now-empty chairs. 'Hello,' she said. 'I'm Staff Nurse Lucy Ramshaw. Can I help you?'

The woman looked up, a polite, questioning smile on her face.

It seemed a slightly odd, inappropriate expression so Lucy sat down beside her. 'Have you been here a while?' she asked. 'I'm sorry if you have. We've been really busy.'

The woman seemed to understand, even to sympathize. She put a hand out and touched Lucy's arm. 'It's all right,' she said in a soft voice. 'I'm in no hurry.'

'Are you waiting for someone?'

The woman shook her head.

'Do you need medical attention?'

The woman appeared not to understand her. She looked confused. Stared at the nurse, her face frowning as if trying to comprehend. She said nothing. Her lips didn't even move to begin to form a reply.

Lucy felt further prickings of disquiet as she glanced at the woollen bundle in the woman's arms. 'Is that a baby?' she asked sharply.

The woman's eyes dropped sentimentally to the contents of the pink blanket.

Fuck, Lucy thought. Babies were meant to be seen by a medical person within half an hour of arrival. This woman had probably sat here for hours.

'Is it the baby who needs seeing?'

At last there was a vocal response. 'Yes, yes,' the woman said, still in a soft, polite, rather formal voice. 'I thought I'd better bring Poppy here.'

'But you haven't registered her.'

The woman stared back, again without responding to this

statement. Lucy was torn. This promised to be 'an incident'.
A baby who needed medical attention had not been registered
at the desk and therefore had been ignored for what could
have been hours. She didn't want to leave this loose end for
the night shift to sort out but she was dog-tired. She wanted
to go home and this woman seemed strange. They always
took the longest to sort out. Already she was wondering who
the duty psychiatric social worker was.

'If you or your baby needed to be seen by a doctor or a
nurse you really should have registered at the front desk otherwise how would we know you were here?'

The woman thought about it and then apologized. 'I'm
sorry, I didn't know.' She looked around her. 'I don't think
I've ever been in a place like this.'

'There are notices – everywhere. That's why you've ended
up waiting for so long.' Lucy tried out a smile. 'We always
try and see babies really quickly.'

The woman's eyes were wide open, somewhere between
grey and hazel with dilated pupils. They remained focussed
on a spot behind Lucy rather than on the nurse herself, but
there seemed no real comprehension behind them. No
reason, no intelligent thought. They were blank, curiously
devoid of emotion. Yet she had brought an ailing baby to a
hospital and sat for hours without being dealt with. It made
no sense.

Something clicked in Lucy's mind. A premonition, some
panic, some warning that here everything was even farther
from the norm than she had first realized.

'Can I take a look at Poppy?' Lucy put out a hand to draw
the shawl away from the child's face but without warning the
woman's expression changed. She glared at the nurse with
unmistakable hostility, clutching the bundle tighter to her
breast, fastening her arms around it and interlocking the fingers
so Lucy couldn't grab at it. She thought quickly. The woman
appeared in her early forties. She was around five feet four
and probably weighed around ten stone. She was not going
to be able to take the baby forcibly from her. Lucy glanced
at the adjacent chairs for clues as to the woman's character
but could not see a handbag, purse, mobile phone or car keys.
Possibly they were in the pocket of her fleece.

She sat and waited, still making observations. The woman

was wearing little make-up, a smear of lipstick, some mascara. That was all. She had a good complexion and her hair, though sprouting a few grey hairs, was short and professionally cut. She was wearing little jewellery except a platinum wedding ring, pearl studs in her ears and a gold watch. And rather incongruously, almost hippy-like, purple glass beads around her right wrist.

Again Lucy tried to lean over to take a peek at the baby. Just to check it was all right but the woman responded by leaning back and tucking the blanket even more firmly around 'Poppy'.

Lucy glanced up at the clock. A quarter to eleven. She should have gone fifteen minutes ago. Inwardly she sighed. She couldn't go home and leave this mess. She must keep trying. 'What's *your* name?'

A drip of saliva appeared in the corner of the woman's mouth. She loosened her hold on the infant to wipe it away. 'Alice,' she said. 'Alice Sedgewick. Mrs.'

'OK, Mrs Sedgewick.' Lucy gave one of her bright smiles. 'You know you're in a hospital, don't you? In Shrewsbury.'

Alice Sedgewick nodded. 'I thought it was the right place to bring Poppy,' she explained.

Oh, bugger!' Lucy thought again. She's been here for ages. No one took care of her. We all left her. We didn't notice her because she was sitting in the corner, quiet. And now?

The feeling was creeping down her spine, like an icicle. In the ten to fifteen minutes since she had noticed the woman she had not heard the child cry. Neither had she seen it move. No stretch or yawn, whimper or grunt. From the bundle of pink blanket she had seen absolutely no sign of movement. No sign of life. Again she looked around her. There was no nappy bag nearby with a bottle or change of clothes, none of the paraphernalia that surrounds a live infant.

'I'm really sorry,' she said, 'that you've had to wait, Mrs Sedgewick. We'll see Poppy now. This very minute.'

Alice looked straight into Lucy's eyes and touched her arm timidly. 'It's all right,' she said. 'Don't worry. We didn't *mind* waiting. There's really no hurry, you see.' She gave a bright smile and spoke down, to the baby, this time. 'We can wait all night if need be, can't we, Poppy?'

From the bundle there was no response.

Lucy felt a real chill now. But she could not simply grab the baby. It was not allowed. She must persuade this Alice Sedgewick to hand the child over voluntarily. And to do that she must gain the woman's trust. Somehow.

She glanced at the clock again. Ten fifty.

'How old is Poppy, Mrs Sedgewick?'

Alice shrugged. 'I don't really know exactly,' she said.

Lucy felt sick now. 'She's not *your* baby then?'

Tears appeared in the woman's eyes. 'Not my baby?' Her eyes were brimming with tears. 'Not my baby? How can you say that? It's not true. I look after her. I love her. She's mine. She has to be mine. Who else's could she be?'

Lucy felt a further sinking feeling. It was an abduction. They'd had one of those last year from the post natal ward and the police had kept the staff on tenterhooks, interviewing, re-interviewing, interviewing again. They had all felt guiltily responsible and the hospital had spent months running an enquiry and finally tightening up on the security arrangements in all areas where babies and children were treated. It had upset and unsettled them all and writing statements had taken up a lot of time. Time they simply didn't have. Particularly her. Not just before the wedding.

She held out her hands towards the woman and child. 'Can I take a look at her, please?'

Alice peered down at the bundle. 'She's asleep now,' she said. 'You shouldn't try and wake her when she's so nicely settled.' She looked up. 'Babies need such a lot of sleep, don't they? You must know that – as a nurse.'

'I won't wake her,' Lucy promised.

Alice scrutinized her as though wondering whether she could trust this nurse with her precious child.

'I'm due to go off duty now,' Lucy said. 'But it would be nice if I could see to Poppy before I go.'

Alice nodded. 'All right.' She loosened her grip on the bundle but did not hand her over.

It was going to take more coaxing. 'Why did you bring her to the hospital tonight, Mrs Sedgewick? Is she ill?'

The woman's eyes dropped. She swallowed and her eyes moistened. 'Don't take her away from me,' she whispered. 'Not again. I couldn't bear it this time. She *is* mine. Don't take her. Please.'

'Alice,' Lucy said, 'you need to give Poppy to me so I can help her. Make her better.'

The expression in Alice's eyes changed now ever so slightly. They still looked frightened and guilty but there was a flickering light. Something was humouring her. 'I don't think so,' Alice said, smiling now. 'I don't think you'll be able to make her better. It's a little late for that.'

Lucy's hands reached out. 'She'll be safe with me,' she promised and at last, at long last, Alice Sedgewick handed the bundle over.

It was very light, was Lucy's first thought, as she grasped it. She drew back the blanket, peered inside and almost dropped *the thing*, making a sound of utter revulsion, as though she was retching. Members of staff came running then from all directions as Lucy Ramshaw held the bundle as far away from her as she could, her face shocked and revolted.

TWO

The hospital slipped straight into Correct Protocol, there being one for every single situation. Almost.

The priority is to isolate, to keep dramas away from the public gaze and minimize disruption and upset. Dr Jane Miles and a couple of porters ushered Alice Sedgewick into the nearest available private area, Sister's Office. Lucy Ramshaw took the bundle and placed it in an empty cubicle with hospital security keeping guard. They had expected Alice to make a fuss when she was separated from the baby but she was surprisingly quiet.

Sarinda rang the police.

A squad car was usually marauding somewhere in the vicinity of the hospital A&E department. If it was a quiet night outside the police could, if they wished, find customers in here. Drunks, druggies, people who'd been in fights. Then there was the other side of the coin, the victims, the rape-or-not cases, the prey of minor thieves who'd got a black eye for trying to defend their possessions and tonight there were plenty of people who'd been in slips and slides or prangs and bangs in their cars, slithering around on the icy roads. All in a night's work on a Saturday evening for an average Shropshire copper like Police Constable Gethin Roberts. So after cruising round the town, picking up waifs and strays, he'd stuck round the hospital casualty department and was waiting for customers to roll in. If they didn't, there were consolations; the nurses were generally friendly and generous with cups of coffee and chit-chat. A&E departments had been the birthplace of many a romance between copper and nurse or copper and doctor. Police Constable Gethin Roberts had been sitting outside, watching the sliding doors open and close and wondered which nurses were on duty tonight. So within minutes of Lucy Ramshaw uncovering the child's face and Sarinda's desperate call, his size elevens were striding towards Sister's Office. Tall and thin with a large Adam's apple that was bobbing up

and down his nervous neck, he hardly knew what to do. This
was not in the police manual. He had a quick word with Dr
Miles who filled him in with the bare details. He followed
her into the cubicle, peeked at the contents, wished he hadn't
and spoke quickly and nervously into his phone.

'Roberts here. Yes. I'm at the A&E now. I've got a woman
here who . . .' He ran out of words. 'She turned up with a
bundle wrapped up in a blanket. She'd been here a while, I
think.'

He paused, listening.

'Staff don't know how long exactly . . .'

There was more talk on the other end.

'It's a baby – or it *was* a baby.'

Dr Jane Miles could well imagine the next question.

What do you mean it was *a baby?*

'It's in a state of decay.'

How long's it been dead for?

'I don't know.' Roberts's response this time was truculent.
'I'm not a pathologist, am I?'

Have a guess when it died.

'A long time ago, I think. Anyway. It's definitely dead now
and I could do with some backup.'

He listened for a while to the invisible voice before adding,
'Well – I'm going to need a police surgeon because I'm going
to have to bring *her* into custody.'

He folded his phone back into his pocket and spoke to Dr
Miles. 'OK then,' he said, with a cheerfulness and confidence
he definitely did not feel. 'Let's take a look at her.'

As he approached the door he glanced through the glass at
the woman who was sitting bolt upright, staring into space in
front of her. 'A psychiatrist wouldn't be a bad idea, surely,
doctor?' he commented.

'Possibly,' Jane Miles said briskly. 'It's hard to say how
disturbed or psychotic she is. And until you or we do a bit of
delving we won't know her psychiatric history. At times she
appears composed and lucid and at others . . .' She gave the
bony police constable a friendly grin, 'Well, to use a well
known medical phrase, "barking".'

PC Roberts pushed the door open. His instinct had been to
interview the woman somewhere that seemed less like a
fishbowl . Sister's Office was a little too public with a glass

window which overlooked the entire cubicled area. He'd thought there were rooms set aside for grieving relatives but Jane Miles explained that it was already taken by the girl-friend and parents of the road traffic victim who were trying to come to terms with the idea that their loved one wasn't coming home tonight. Not only that but he had suddenly become a valuable collection of spare parts. So PC Roberts had to make do with the distraction of a ringside seat which overlooked all the dramas being enacted in the department. It was hardly private. Not only could he look out but others could look in. And they did. Peering in like the people who suddenly find themselves on the television when an inter-viewer walks the streets. He would have had curtains drawn or screens put around, but curtains and screens had been banned from the hospital a few years ago by the Infection Control Team. As he entered the room the first person he noticed was Lucy Ramshaw who was sitting, white-faced, her chin in her hands, staring ahead of her with a shocked expres-sion on an already tired and pale face. Perhaps they both needed a psychiatrist, was Roberts's next thought. A doctor too. And a nurse. Staff Nurse Lucy Ramshaw looked as though she was about to be sick.

He was glad when one of the night nurses came to sit with her, filching a cardboard vomit bowl underneath her chair. He had sympathy with Staff Nurse Ramshaw. He knew exactly how she felt. He too had been horrified at the sight of that tiny, wizened face with its parchment, blackened skin and hollowed eyes.

Alice Sedgewick was sitting in the corner, looking at the floor. Gethin Roberts sat down next to her and introduced himself, flicking his ID card in front of eyes that were completely uninterested in her surroundings. He drew out his notebook

'What's your name, love?'

The woman stopped staring at the floor and looked him straight in the eye. 'Alice Sedgewick,' she said. 'My name is Alice Sedgewick. Mrs.' Her accent was not what he had been expecting. It was middle class. Almost posh. And her voice was soft and polite. So how come she had wandered into the A&E department of the local hospital, carrying a long-dead child, Roberts thought? What was going on?

He wrote the name down, trying to make sense of the situation and failing completely.

'Where do you live, Mrs Sedgewick?'

'The Mount. Number 41.'

No sign of her being 'barking' so far.

Roberts looked up, his pen lifted off his pad. The Mount was a smart road, one of the nicest in a very smart town, a row of large Victorian detached and semi-detached houses. He looked again at the woman and noticed for the first time that although her trousers were paint-spattered and she was wearing a dark fleece, she was also wearing expensive-looking black patent leather shoes with a small, neat heel. And when she moved her arm he also noticed a gold watch that looked understated rather than flashy and whispered 'money' to him. It matched her voice, which was low and controlled. Not hysterical. She seemed detached. A bit unreal but not barking. All the time he talked he would be revising his judgement of her, moving up and down stops, changing as many times as the picture when you look through the end of a revolving kaleidoscope.

Roberts frowned. So she was not an escapee from the local psychiatric unit then. Or an ex-con from the prison but a local from a smart area in town. And yet somehow a long dead baby had come into her possession and instead of ringing the police, which would have been the normal thing to do, she had come here – to a hospital. What on earth could have been her motive in bringing the child here, nursing it for what could have been hours instead of handing him or her over to the nursing staff?

'Can you tell me anything about . . .' He let his gaze drift out of the window, towards the space where the curtains were tightly drawn round the cubicle, the security officer standing guard, arms akimbo, legs apart, like the coppers who stand outside 10 Downing Street. Alice Sedgewick followed his gaze and momentarily lost the blanked-out expression. Now she frowned and looked confused. Then she turned her gaze back at the gawky policeman and looked at him as though she had only now seen him properly. Her eyes drifted around the room, passed straight over Lucy Ramshaw and then her body gave a great shudder and appeared to actually recoil as though she had suddenly realized what it was she had been holding. She gave a little shriek of revulsion, as if she had woken up from a nightmare. PC Roberts witnessed the change open-mouthed; luckily for him that was the very moment when Sergeant Paul Talith arrived and took over.

To them all Talith's bulky presence was reassuring. He had a quick word with Roberts who led him outside into the cubicle. With a gloved hand Talith twitched back the blanket and peered down. 'Bloody hell,' he said, his face contorted. 'What the heck is that?'

Roberts shrugged and tried not to think too much about it. He certainly did not even attempt to answer the question.

Talith recovered himself. 'Right. We can arrange for this –' he couldn't quite keep the loathing from his voice or face – 'to be removed to the hospital mortuary and take it from there. We'll inform the Coroner's Officer first thing Monday morning. She'll instruct us further. There'll have to be a post-mortem, though God knows how long it's been dead for. Looks to me like one of those Egyptian mummies. All shrivelled up and black.'

They left the cubicle. Talith glanced through the window at the woman who looked so very ordinary, sitting quietly, her hands folded on her lap. 'Whatever she's got to do with it I don't know,' he muttered, 'but we're going to have to question her down at the station, preferably with a solicitor present.' He looked across at Gethin Roberts. 'She's married?'

'I think so. She's wearing a wedding band.'

'Better wake her husband up and tell him then.' Talith grinned. 'He's in for a shock.'

They were both wondering the same thing. Was it her child? His child? What was the story?

'Perhaps she had it years ago,' Roberts mused, 'and because she didn't want her family to find out she buried it.'

'Then dug it up, Roberts?' Talith's voice was mocking. 'Why? Why now?'

'I don't know.'

They still didn't enter Sister's Office but stood outside, talking quietly. 'It's just a baby,' Talith said. 'Probably a newborn. Why bring it here?' he mused. 'Tonight? Look at the state of that thing. It's been dead for years. Kept some-where. Not buried, I don't think. More like kept somewhere. What was the point of bringing it to a hospital? What did she think they were going to do?'

Gethin Roberts shrugged. 'It's where you would naturally go. Or perhaps . . .' he ventured, then found inspiration from somewhere. 'Sanctuary?'

Talith sighed. 'Well, whatever, it's going to be a long night. I'd better go in and talk to her.'

He went into the room. Lucy Ramshaw was sitting still, her face as white as chalk. Talith touched her shoulder. 'You'd best go home, love,' he said kindly. 'You look knackered. We'll take a statement from you some other time. All right?'

She looked up and nodded.

'Do you want someone to drive you or shall we get your bloke to come and pick you up?'

She gave a weak smile. 'No. It's OK. Really. I'll be all right. Better in the fresh air. Rob's probably had a drink or two. I don't want to drag him out at this time of night. I'll drive myself.'

'All right, love. We'll be in touch.'

Paul Talith sat himself down opposite Alice Sedgewick and introduced himself. 'Mrs Sedgewick,' he said, 'we're going to have to question you down at the station about this baby you brought in, I'm afraid.'

She nodded, even gave him a faint smile, subtly condescending. 'That's all right,' she said.

The words 'gracious' and 'a lady' came into Paul Talith's mind. He studied her carefully. Mrs Sedgewick seemed well mannered, contained and old-fashioned. It seemed appropriate to use these conservative words about her.

'We'll just wait for the police surgeon to make sure you're in a fit state to take in, Mrs Sedgewick.' Talith deliberately avoided the use of the terrible word 'detain'. It might send her back over the edge. 'Is there anyone else – family – you'd like us to contact? They might be worried about you. It's late and it's a nasty night.'

Alice simply shook her head.

They waited in awkward silence until Dr Delyth Fontaine appeared. A large, untidy woman with straggly, greying hair, she cared little for her appearance. All her energy was focussed on her career as a police surgeon (or Forensic Medical Examiner, as they were now called), and the smallholding she had to the south of the town where she bred Torddu sheep, a rare Welsh mountain breed. Both Gethin Roberts and Sergeant

Talith were relieved that it was she who was on duty tonight. Her no-nonsense approach to her work was exactly what they needed in this situation. She gave them each a broad smile. 'Nice of you to drag me out on such a snowy night.'

They didn't respond. They knew she didn't mind really. 'I suppose,' she said, 'I'd better take a peek at the infant first?'

They led her into the cubicle. Slipping on a glove she took a swift glance. 'OK,' she said. 'Looks like a neonate. A newborn,' she explained to the two police officers. 'It's been dead for a number of years. I can't say how many but at a guess more than five. I won't undress it,' she said. 'There's no point. It'll be better if the clothing is removed at the post-mortem.'

'Natural causes or . . . ?'

She looked at the pair of them with amusement. 'You really expect me to hazard a guess?'

Talith waited.

'Not a clue,' she said. 'Now. Lead me to Lady Macbeth.'

She regarded Alice Sedgewick with interest before sitting down opposite her.

'Mrs Sedgewick,' she said, 'I'm Dr Fontaine. I'm a police surgeon. I've been asked to come and see you because the police want to question you, preferably down at Monkmoor Police Station, about how you came to find yourself here, tonight, with the body of a child who is long-since dead. Can you tell me anything about it?'

Alice looked at her. 'No,' she said politely. 'I'm afraid I can't.' she said. 'I can't tell you anything.'

'Is this because you don't want to or because you can't remember?'

'I can't remember.' A pause. 'It's possible that I don't know.'

Interesting, Delyth Fontaine thought.

'What *do* you remember?'

Alice turned puzzled eyes on her. 'Sorry?' she said, still in the same flat but polite, social voice.

'Well – you know your name and you know your address.'
'Yes.'

'Do you remember how you got here tonight?'

'I think – I don't know. I'm not sure.' She frowned. 'I don't know. I really don't know.'

Jane Miles was standing behind her looking sceptical. Like

most doctors she thought that amnesia could be just a little too convenient for people who had not quite worked out what to say.

Delyth Fontaine met her eyes, gave the slightest hint of a very cynical smile and continued. 'Do you drive a car, Mrs Sedgewick?'

Alice nodded. 'But I sometimes use the bus.'

Delyth Fontaine asked the next question deceptively casually. 'You can't remember which you did tonight?'

'I think I would probably have driven.'

It was *almost* an admission.

In which case the car would be outside. Delyth looked up and met Paul Talith's eyes. It wouldn't take the police long to home in on the registration number and search the hospital car park.

'Do you feel unwell at the moment?'

A shake of the head.

'Do you take any pills?'

Alice's eyes looked bright. 'I take something for my blood pressure,' she said, in a reassuringly normal voice. 'It's a little high –' the words were accompanied by a small, tight smile – 'so my doctor tells me.'

'Who is your doctor?'

'I belong to the group practice on the Ellesmere Road.'

Delyth made a note of it.

'Do you know where you are now?'

Alice nodded. 'I'm at the hospital, I think, in a room at the accident and emergency department.'

It was all very precise and lucid – with significant bits missing.

'Do you remember what you were doing earlier on this evening – *before* you came to the hospital?'

'Decorating.'

Which explained the paint spatters on her clothes.

'Do you mind if I just check your pulse and blood pressure?'

'Not at all.'

Apart from a rapid pulse – 120 a minute – all the readings were normal as the police surgeon had anticipated. Except, of course, that no one in their right mind would call this a normal situation.

'Mrs Sedgewick,' she continued, 'you seemed very upset earlier when the nurse looked at the baby you were carrying, wrapped up in a shawl.'

Alice's shoulders drooped.

'Do you need something to calm you down?'

Wearily she shook her head, bowing it in submission.

'Do you have any objection to going down to the police station, Mrs Sedgewick?'

'No.'

'OK then.' Delyth sighed and stood up, then left the room, followed by Roberts and Talith. 'Fit to detain,' she said. 'I'll ring Martha first thing Monday morning. You may as well take the infant straight to the hospital mortuary.' Her eyes met those of both Roberts and Talith and she smiled. 'It'll at least free up the security guard.'

She paused then turned to speak only to Paul Talith. 'I don't want to tell you how to do your job,' she said in a low voice, 'but if I was the investigating officer in this case one of the first questions I'd ask would be how long she's lived at her current address.' She paused. 'Assuming, that is, that the corpse was found somewhere near there. It's a snowy night. The blanket was dry. I doubt she'd have been wandering in the country-side somewhere and stumbled across it. From the condition of the body the baby was been mummified – that is kept in warm, dry conditions. I would assume then that this body turned up in her own house. Oh and by the way, I don't know where the blanket came from. It is a baby's blanket but that hasn't been with the baby's body all this time. It's too clean and in too good condition. If it had been wrapped around the body it would have deteriorated. Got stained, eaten by moths, rotted.'

Roberts and Talith both nodded. 'Thanks, doc.'

'Under the McNaughton Rules,' she added, 'I'm not absolutely certain whether she has a full and complete under-standing of what's going on around her. I suspect she's working on two levels. Part of her mind is aware of her surroundings and part is somewhere else.' She glanced back through the window at Alice's calm face. 'God only knows where. But wherever it is it doesn't appear to be troubling her.' Almost to herself she added, 'I would dearly love to know how all this came about.'

Roberts nodded, with relief. Delyth Fontaine had taken charge, done her job and now they could take this weird woman down to the station and question her, which was what he and Talith were dying to do. A porter brought the mortuary trolley and loaded up the pathetic little bundle, zipped now in a forensic body bag, then trundled along the corridor to the hospital mortuary. The security guard was summoned to another part of the hospital where a confused patient had just assaulted a nurse, while the police were left to focus on their side of the job. Though she patently wasn't a threat to them they both felt uncomfortable with her. She was unpredictable. They wondered whether she might ask to see the infant again and if they denied her request whether she would 'flip'. One of the problems with having no blinds or curtains in Sister's Office was that the trolley in which the infant's body was encased was clearly visible through the window. There was nothing they could do about it. Sister's Office was designed to have a goldfish view of the entire department. It ensured smooth running.

Paul Talith hadn't always had the best of manners with the general public. He could be brusque but this time he made a real effort to do it properly. He hunkered down on his meaty thighs and spoke very gently to Alice. 'I'm really sorry, Mrs Sedgewick,' he said in his most polite and apologetic voice, 'but we're going to have to take a statement from you about . . .' He jerked his head towards the window. 'Down at the station. Is there anyone you'd like us to telephone?' He gave a swift glance at her gold wedding band. 'Your husband, perhaps?' He ventured a friendly smile. 'He must be wondering where on earth you are.'

All he got back was a guarded, panicked look. 'I'd rather you didn't,' she answered tightly. 'He's away on business. Abroad. I don't want to drag him from his work. He's going through a difficult time.' She met his eyes. 'Like many people.'

Certainly like you, Talith thought, then realized none of this had sunk in. He sensed an aura of unreality around this woman and indeed the entire situation was surreal. How could she act with such normality having delivered a rotting corpse to the local hospital? Did she have no idea what was going on? Could she not see how abnormal this situation was, to be talking about 'her husband being away on business' when she'd arrived at the hospital nursing a long-dead baby?

He needed some anchor.

'Well perhaps a family friend or a solicitor?'

Alice was silent for a while, frowning, thinking. Then her face cleared. 'Both,' she said, with a bright, social smile. 'Let's kill two birds with one stone.' Then, equally unpredictably, she burst into tears. Talith straightened up, shot Roberts a despairing look and waited for the sobs to subside.

'Acantha,' she finally supplied. Roberts and Talith exchanged looks. Was that a name?

Alice Sedgewick finishing her crying with one last, wracking heave of her shoulders and explained. 'Mrs Palk. She's both family friend and a solicitor too. You can ring her if you like.'

I do like, Talith thought. Hope she can make some sense out of this. Then: 'Do you have her number?'

Alice nodded and gave it out.

Roberts dialled the Shrewsbury number right then, using his mobile and breaking hospital rules. It was now after one in the morning. He didn't expect much of a welcome and was not disappointed. The phone rang for a while before a male voice, both sleepy and angry, barked, 'Yes?'

PC Roberts explained who he was and why he had rung and without another word the phone went dead while he heard an urgent, whispered conversation. Then another voice came on the line.

'Hello?' A calm, intelligent, sane voice. One which would take control. Thank goodness for that.

'I'm PC Roberts from the Shrewsbury police.'

'Yes?'

'I'm speaking from the Royal Shrewsbury Hospital. We have a friend of yours here, a Mrs Sedgewick, in some rather strange circumstances.'

'Alice? Is she hurt? Has she had an accident?'

'No. She isn't hurt but she's in a bit of difficulty and we're going to need to interview her down at the station. She has requested that you be present both as a solicitor and a friend.'

There was a moment's silence than Mrs Palk said slowly, 'What sort of difficulty, Constable Roberts?'

She'd made a note of his rank and name. Gethin Roberts swallowed. 'I'd rather not say,' he said. 'It's better we speak face to face.'

There was another moment's silence before Mrs Palk said,

'OK. I'll be down at the station in twenty minutes. Monkmoor?'

'Yes.'

'I'll see you there then.'

'Thank you. I'm sure Mrs Sedgewick will appreciate it.'

Too late. The phone had been put down.

Roberts returned to the room with his news. 'She'll meet us at the station in twenty minutes,' he said. Mrs Sedgewick looked up, grateful.

'Shall we go then?'

They had also anticipated that Mrs Sedgewick might react to her removal from what Roberts had termed her 'sanctuary' but she seemed almost to have forgotten about it. She didn't twitch or turn her head as they left the department but thanked the waiting doctor almost as if she was on some social visit to the place. It was as though she was on autopilot and her polite, well-mannered self had taken over. Talith and Roberts felt distinctly uncomfortable.

The journey took less than fifteen minutes at that time of night. There were a few stray roisterers about but the night was too cold to loiter so the town was largely quiet and deserted. The Welsh bridge had been closed since the explosion less than a week ago. They turned into the Harlescott Road then took a right, soon reaching Monkmoor Police Station.

They ushered Mrs Sedgewick into an interview room and asked her again, 'Are you sure you don't want us to contact your husband? He might be worried about you.'

It provoked the same violently negative response as before. 'No,' she said. 'Please.'

Paul Talith felt even more concerned. This response was unbalanced. Too vehement. He glanced at his watch and wished the solicitor would hurry up and arrive.

A couple more minutes ticked away. Talith tried again. 'Son? Daughter?'

This time even more violent shaking of the head. Talith gave up and waited in silence for the solicitor to arrive.

At twenty five to two a.m. Acantha Palk made an appearance. She was a big woman – impressive – almost six feet tall and of mixed parentage at a guess. She had black frizzy hair which she had attempted to control with a hair clip, skin an attractively dark shade of olive and expressive big black eyes and was wearing an orange kaftan underneath a long black woollen coat. Alice seemed to come to life as her friend entered the room. She stood up. 'Thank you for coming,' she said. 'I'm so sorry to get you . . .'

The big woman enveloped her in a bear hug. 'Alice,' she scolded, 'what *have* you been up to? Too many gins behind the wheel?'

Alice simply shook her head.

Roberts and Talith exchanged glances.

Acantha Palk immediately took command. 'If you wouldn't mind,' she said in a deep, booming voice, 'I'd like to speak to Mrs Sedgewick alone for a few minutes.'

They would have loved to be flies on the wall. What story was Mrs Sedgewick telling her friend?

After about fifteen minutes the door opened and Ms Palk met their eyes.

'A strange business,' she commented.

It was that.

'Mrs Sedgewick is very tired and upset,' she continued without waiting for a comment. 'I'd appreciate it if you kept your questions to a minimum for now. She's not going to walk out on you or disappear. I'll vouch for her.'

Talith spoke up. 'All we want to know,' he said heavily, 'is how come she walked into the Accident and Emergency department holding what looked like the body of an infant that had been dead for years. Where's it come from? We don't know yet how the infant died, whether of natural causes or . . .' He left it to the woman to fill in the gaps. 'We'll have to wait for the post-mortem so we don't know how serious an offence has been committed. All we want is a little bit of enlightenment.'

'True. I understand.' She hesitated. 'I'm not sure . . .'

I'll bet you're not, both Talith and Roberts thought.

Alice seemed calmer as they re-entered the room, sat down and switched on the recorder. They checked her name and details.

'At some time last night you entered the Accident and Emergency department of the Royal Shrewsbury Hospital carrying something. Can you tell us what you were carrying?'

Alice gave a strange smile. 'It was Poppy,' she said clearly.

Ms Palk looked both startled and confused.

'Who is Poppy?' Talith asked.

Alice Sedgewick's eyes dropped to the floor. 'I'd rather not say,' she whispered, 'at least, not at the moment.'

'Why did you take her to the hospital?'

'Because she was ill.'

The two policemen and solicitor exchanged surprised glances. If they hadn't seen the body for themselves it would have been a sane and logical answer. But . . .

'And you thought one of the doctors or nurses would see her?'

'Yes.'

'But the nurses tell me that you didn't register your arrival.'

'I don't really know how the system works,' she confessed. 'I thought they seemed so busy that they'd get around to me eventually and they did.' Again it was a credible response.

Acantha Palk lifted her shoulders in a gesture of confusion.

Alice spoke again. 'I didn't think there was any hurry. She was so quiet, you see.'

Indeed.

Mrs Palk spoke up. 'Is there any point in continuing this interview? My client is obviously not well.'

Talith stood up. 'Can I have a quick word – outside?'

She nodded.

They closed the door behind them.

'Has Mrs Sedgewick any record of mental disturbance?'

'Not that I know of.'

'She's never been depressed?'

'Again – no. Not that I know of.'

'Do you know anyone called Poppy?'

'No,' Mrs Palk responded stiffly. 'She has a daughter called Rosie. She lives in London. She's a barrister. She's going to be very angry about this. Most inconvenient. The publicity, you know.'

Paul Talith felt as though his head was spinning. *Publicity? Inconvenience?* Not exactly the words he'd have used.

'Might it be an idea to ask Rosie to come and stay with her mother?'

Mrs Palk looked awkward. 'I wouldn't have thought so. They're not particularly close. I think Rosie will want to distance herself from this. Besides – I did mention that to Alice. She is vehemently opposed to it. She doesn't want Rosie to know anything about this business.'

'It's going to be hard keeping it from her,' Talith ventured.

'Yes, I know, sergeant,' she said impatiently. 'But those are her wishes. We can only respect them.'

Talith heaved a long sigh.

'Look – I have a suggestion. Let me take her to my house. I'll keep an eye on her. She'll come to no harm.'

Talith was frowning. 'Does she have a son?'

Acantha Palk gave a smile. 'She won't want Gregory around. She adores him. He lives in Turkey anyway. Let her tell him in her own way.'

'What about her husband?'

Mrs Palk's face changed as though a storm had blown across it. 'Aaron Sedgewick is a very *exacting* man,' she volunteered. 'Exacting and probably the most self-absorbed person I have ever met in my entire life. He will only mind about this if it affects him either directly or indirectly.'

'Where is he now?'

'I don't know. Probably on some business trip abroad. Maybe Germany. He goes there quite a lot. If she doesn't want him to know about this . . .' She left the sentence unfinished, hanging in the air.

'He's going to have to know at some point.' Talith spoke bluntly. 'For a start we're going to have to make a search of the house – if that's where the body was kept.'

Acantha shivered. 'I wouldn't like to be around when he finds out. He'll worry it'll affect his business and he has a hell of a temper too. He can fling things around with the best of them,' she finished dryly.

Talith shrugged. 'She didn't give you any idea how this dead infant came to be with her?'

'None.'

'Do you have any idea who the child might be?'

'No.'

'Does the name Poppy mean anything to you?'

Acantha shook her head. 'Look,' she said awkwardly, 'I'm sure this has nothing to do with it but Alice and Aaron quarrelled over Gregory years ago. I don't think father and son have spoken since. Alice goes over to see him for a few weeks every year. Mother and son have remained close.'

'What did Mr Sedgewick quarrel with his son about?'

'I don't know. Something silly in all probability. At a guess it would be more to do with Aaron than Gregory. Aaron is a very forceful personality.'

'A control freak?'

She smiled. 'If you want to call him that – yes.' She seemed to want to say more but pressed her lips together tightly, containing whatever she had been tempted to say.

'I don't want to sound unkind or patronizing,' she said finally, 'but Alice is a very ordinary woman, very much in awe, enthralled by her husband's wealth and status and Aaron drinks this up like nectar. Alice's world is husband, son, daughter, home – in that order. This is completely strange and out of character. I've never known her do anything bizarre like this before. She always seemed nice. Ordinary.'

Paul Talith was floundering. 'Her daughter, Rosie, is she exacting too?'

'Oh yes. A chip off the old block all right. She's a high flyer – a barrister with an eminent firm in London. Alice won't want any scandal near her.'

'Right,' Talith said. 'Well, it's already been a long night. I'm happy for Mrs Sedgewick to go home under your care.' He fingered the spot on the top of his head where he was just beginning to go bald. 'We're going to need a psychiatric assessment and wait for the result of the post-mortem. And how all this came about I really don't know.'

Acantha almost smiled. 'It's going to take some unravelling, I agree. But not tonight, sergeant. And if it's any help I would stake everything on the fact that Alice had absolutely nothing to do with the child's death or the concealment of its body.'

Both Talith and Roberts resisted the temptation to ask the obvious question: so what was she doing nursing the corpse?

They watched the two women leave the station with a feeling of unreality. Had these events really happened or had they been one of those inexplicably strange and disturbing dreams?

THREE

Martha woke feeling troubled and couldn't understand why for a minute or two. Then she remembered. Last night, Sukey had arrived home at eleven, driven by her friend's father, as promised. Martha had been just about to go to bed herself when her daughter had 'rolled in', in a state that people describe delicately as being, a little 'the worse for wear'.

Martha had always subscribed to the idea that youngsters should be treated liberally and make their own rules for 'responsible drinking'. Goodness – she'd had a hangover or two herself. She'd never made a big thing about alcohol. Sukey and Sam had had sips of wine with meals from around ten years old. Neither had liked the taste so they had reverted to smoothies, fruit juices and Coke so Martha was a little disappointed that this social experiment had patently not succeeded. Cigarettes yes, she had made a thing about those. She'd watched too many friends struggle to stop the habit and read too many post-mortem reports on smokers to believe they were anything but vile, smelly and harmful, but she really had hoped that both Sam and Sukey would develop a mature and sensible attitude to alcohol. Have a drink without necessarily having to get 'pissed', 'ratted', or any other of the words which were usually accompanied by a giggle or two. So she had watched her daughter stagger up the stairs, clutching at the banister with a feeling of dismay and it was this that was hanging, like a dark cloud, over her this morning, even though she had her family all together under one roof. It was at times like this that she missed Martin most. She wanted – needed – to have someone to talk this over with. She could have done with his common sense and sense of humour. But he had died when the twins were three years old so she had to make the decision herself whether she should play it down, ignore it, or make an issue of it. She lay in bed and couldn't make up her mind. She frowned at herself. She wasn't generally so indecisive. If she couldn't bring up her own daughter properly – well – there was no one else.

Sukey was coming up to fifteen and Martha sensed she had a few turbulent years ahead. She herself had been a high-spirited teenager but she had had to work so hard to get into medical school that she had had little time for high jinks. She had the sinking feeling that her daughter's path through the teenage years would be different.

Lying back in bed she reflected that for once it wasn't Sam who was the focus of worry and attention. Even allowing for maternal pride she knew her daughter was exceptionally beautiful with a natural, long-legged, fine-skinned radiance. Perhaps when Sam had returned to the Liverpool Football Academy she should spend some 'quality time' with Sukey before her daughter slid further along the path of womanhood. Now Agnetha was going they would be together, largely alone in the White House.

And now she had made her decision. She would ignore last night.

Sergeant Talith began the day with a phone call to Detective Inspector Alex Randall. The phone rang and rang in his house until finally it was picked up and Talith heard his inspector's voice. 'Sorry to ring so early, sir.'

'That's all right.'

But Talith had the feeling it was not all right. Something was wrong. He listened out for background noise and heard none. No wife asking him what was going on, no children, no radio, no television. All was eerily quiet in the Randall household.

He outlined the drama of last night and Alex listened silently until his sergeant had finished, then advised him. 'You'd better get a warrant to search her house. Presuming that's where she found the infant's body.'

'Yes, sir.'

'I wonder if there's anything else there. And Talith.'

'Yes, sir?'

'Whatever Mrs Sedgewick *says* her husband is going to have to know all this as well as the rest of the family. This is bound to get out and make headlines. Better give the house a ring and forewarn him.'

'She says her husband's abroad on business, sir.'

'Well – maybe he is. Best find out before you break in, though I presume Mrs Sedgewick has a key to her own house so you won't need to batter the door down.'

'Yes, sir.'

'Keep me informed, Talith. Let me know if there are any developments and I'll speak to Martha in the morning and interview Mrs Sedgewick myself.'

'Yes, sir.' Talith put the phone down and wondered. There was usually some camaraderie between officers – Christmas parties, social occasions. He knew most of his colleagues' spouses, even a few of their children. But Alex Randall? He was married. He mentioned a wife sometimes, in a vague sort of way. But he'd never met her; neither had anybody else from the Monkmoor station. There were no invitations to barbecues or family parties. No one he knew had ever been to Inspector Randall's home and he never talked about children, so presumably there were none.

Strange.

Sam was full of football talk as she prepared the breakfast and though Martha was happy to hear him chatting away she wished that for just ten minutes a day Sam would talk about something else. Instead of that he was always either on the phone, talking to his old friends about Life in The Club, or sitting in the kitchen, telling her about people she did not know or incidents she did not understand, at least, not with an insider's understanding. She realized with dismay that the inevitable had happened. He had grown away from her, into another world and she felt a pang as she watched him. Had it been the wrong decision to allow him to move to Liverpool? But, she argued, he had wanted it so very much. She and Martin had decided that they didn't want to lose their children to boarding school, but surely this was different? Had he not taken up the chance to attend the Liverpool Football Academy it would have passed him by – and with that the chance at least to become a professional player. She shouldn't be a selfish mother, keeping her son at her side and deny him such an opportunity – but oh, this was hard. She watched his eager, freckled face as he talked on the phone to some pal or other. 'Yeah but did you see the tackle in the second half?'

There was talking on the other end and Sam interrupted hotly. 'It *was* a foul. Definitely.'

She resisted the temptation to ruffle his spiky red hair which appeared to be getting redder by the day. He could thank his mother for that, she thought, touching her own copper curls with regret. All her life she had wanted black hair. The blacker the better. Raven locks. Silky curls. She dreamed about having black hair.

She sighed. It wasn't going to happen even if she could have persuaded Vernon Grubb, her hairdresser, to conspire with her.

Back to Sam. She had known one or two widows who had needed to keep a hold over their sons as some sort of perverted substitute for their dead husbands, but it was not her way. She boiled the kettle to brew a cafetière, surreptitiously watching him with a smile on her face. His top incisors still crossed. He still had his freckles and the angry-looking hair which he complained acted as a beacon on the football pitch. Not only because of the bright colour but because it stuck up all over the place in spite of the gel which he plastered on it. He still had the same jerky way of talking as he hung up the phone and proceeded to try and educate her in the finer points of the game and for the nth time explain the offside rules and the point of the intense training. 'See, Mum, you just *have* to do weights and things to get your strength up and keep your tendons supple or you get injured and that's bad news.'

She turned around. 'Is it a fault of the training then that you have this problem?'

'Well, yes and no,' Sam said seriously. 'I kind of meant to kick one way and hadn't quite decided how to play the ball. My mind went one way and my knee the other. See?'

'Ye-es.'

'Then we have to so some really weird exercises, stretching and things, a bit like ballet and they're supposed to help too.'

She took the box of eggs out of the fridge and wondered how long it would be before Sukey and Agnetha appeared. Her son was hungry.

'How long are you going to wait for, Mum?'

'Have a bowl of cereal to start,' she said. 'I thought it'd be nice if we had breakfast all together this morning. It's not often we can do this, Sam.'

Her son grunted and helped himself to some Shredded Wheat, still keeping up the running sports commentary. 'Half the trouble is, Mum, that if you miss a ball, a really import-ant ball, people don't forgive you. They keep on and on about it and reputation's important. This is a very important time for me. Michael Owen was not much older than me when he played in the World Cup. The clubs are starting to pounce on guys my age.' He didn't even realize that she was only listening with half an ear. 'Paul Driscoll – well – he's been transferred to Stoke. He'll be playing full games next season. Fantastic.' She noticed that his eyes were shining and his crooked grin was stretched wide as he polished off the bowl of cereal. What she failed to notice was the surreptitious glance he aimed in her direction.

Sukey appeared just before ten o'clock, yawning and pushing her white-blonde hair out of her eyes. 'Morning, Mum. Morning, Sam.' To Martha's relief she looked relatively normal.

'Did you have a nice time last night?' Though she'd tried to keep the edge out of her voice Martha could hear the censorious tone all too clearly.

Sukey gave a deep sigh. 'OK,' she said. 'It was all right.'

'You don't sound very sure.'

Sukey gave her a smile, turned to the fridge, poured out some apple juice and took a deep swig. 'Sometimes,' she said, 'I find the whole thing a bit boring. I mean you can't talk or anything. The music's too loud.'

'You're very young to have reached this cynical point,' Martha said, deciding that her decision to say nothing about alcohol had been the right one. Sukey wouldn't be the first or last person to drink too much because she had, in fact, found the evening unsatisfactory. She'd done the same herself, particularly in the early months just after Martin had died when social occasions had been really tough, friends awkward, not knowing what to say and she'd hated being introduced as a 'widow'. She hated the word.

'I know I'm cynical, Mum.' Sukey gave another deep sigh, took a second swig out of her glass and Martha sensed her daughter wanted to talk.

She waited.

'What was it like when you met Dad?'

'It was at a party – at someone's house.' Martha smiled to

herself. 'The music was really loud. Blasted our eardrums out. We spent a few minutes screaming at each other, unable to make out a single word then we went outside, although it was pouring with rain. We just found an old brolly in the hall and stood under it. We talked and talked and talked.'

She closed her eyes, remembering the rain splashing off the edge of the umbrella, the wetness of the driveway, the sound of water everywhere, the eagerness in both their voices because they had both known they had met someone on the same plane.

Sukey's eyes were bright. 'I wish he was still around, Mum. I wish I could remember him.'

Martha nodded. Sam was looking across. 'Me too,' he said gruffly. 'I wonder what he'd think of me being a footballer.'

Although Martha couldn't know she gave the right answer, the one Sam needed to hear. 'He'd have been very proud of you.'

'Sometimes,' Sukey said dreamily, 'I think I can remember things, a snatch of a laugh or fingers tickling me.' She closed her eyes as though struggling to conjure up these faint and elusive memories. 'I so wish I had a dad.'

Martha stood back from the Aga. 'I know,' she said. 'I just have to concentrate on being very glad that I have you,' she said. 'Both of you because it's all I have of your father.' She smiled at Sam. 'You're so like him, you know, in many ways. You look like him. Apart from . . .'

'The hair,' Sam said, smiling at her. 'Thanks, Mum.'

Sukey was quiet for a moment, too motionless not to be forming some other thought. 'Mu-um', she said at last, 'does it always happen that the guys you fancy don't fancy you?'

Martha laughed. 'Mostly. In my experience anyway.'

'Did you fancy Dad right away?'

She needed to be truthful. 'Not at first, no. He wasn't the most handsome of men. It was later, when I talked to him, that I realized what a very nice, kind and intelligent person he was. That was when—'

'So he fancied you first.'

She nodded. 'He said he thought I looked different.' She smiled. 'He said later on that he'd been right.'

She laughed then realized Sukey was watching her, needing something from her. 'Darling,' she said to her daughter, 'you're very young. You will meet people you think you love and find out you were wrong and you'll meet people who don't initially attract you but interest you and quite often they turn out to be the really good things in your life. Now then,' she said, wiping her hands down her apron, 'enough chatter. It's time to get the breakfast on.'

'What about Agnetha?'

'She'll be down when she smells the bacon.'

Martha enjoyed herself cooking the huge breakfast for the family. Perhaps it was the Irish in her but it felt so normal, the house filled with the scent and sound of bacon frying. A warm, comfortable, greasy, sizzling, winter's smell. As they sat around, munching toast and the fry-up, sipping juice and coffee, Agnetha appeared, already dressed in tight skinny jeans and a scarlet sweater. Sam and Sukey were teasing each other.

'So how *was* last night,' Sam asked his twin as he crunched on a bit of crispy bacon.'

Sukey shrugged. 'Oh, you know. OK, I suppose. You ought to come out with us one evening.'

'Maybe I will,' Sam grunted, 'though it's not really my scene.'

'Not sure it's mine either.' Sukey sighed loudly. 'But I must have a "scene" otherwise there's no point being a teenager. Dire. Let's change the subject. How long do you think you'll be injured for?'

'I've got to have a check-up with the doctor next week,' Sam said. 'But really I feel absolutely fine now. One hundred per cent so I think I should be playing again by next weekend.'

'Don't you ever get fed up with football?'

'Never,' Sam answered fervently, as though she had asked a devout Christian whether he ever got fed up with God. 'But . . .' He stopped abruptly and they all looked at him, his mother, sister and Agnetha. He went red. Almost red enough for his face to clash with his hair.

'What is it,' Martha prompted gently.

Sam coloured even more. 'It's only been *mentioned*.'

They all waited.

'It's just a possibility,' he said carefully, 'that I might be lent to Stoke too – just for a season.'

Martha's heart leapt but it was Sukey who said it. 'You could live at home with us?'

Sam grinned at them all. 'Except Agnetha. You won't be here, will you?'

'I will be a married woman,' she said primly, 'back in Sweden.'

'But it would still be good,' he said uncertainly, 'wouldn't it?'

Martha raised her glass of juice. 'Certainly would,' she said. 'We'll drink to that.' She gave the slightest of glances in her daughter's direction. 'Won't we, Suks?'

Her daughter went only ever so slightly pink.

'I was wondering,' Agnetha continued tentatively, 'if you would allow her to be one of my bridesmaids possibly?'

'Yes. Yes, Agnetha. Of course, provided she'd like to. You know Sukey.'

Sukey was beaming. 'I'd love to, Mum. My friends at school will eat their heart out. A Swedish wedding. Wow.'

Talith had had to apply to the magistrate for a warrant to search the Sedgewick abode. It was granted without demur. He then tried the home telephone number Alice had given him but, as he'd expected, no one picked up. Instead the call was diverted straight to answer phone. He left no message. Perhaps Aaron really was abroad, as his wife had claimed, though surely he would have a mobile phone? Practically everyone did these days. He rang the number Acantha Palk had left him and explained that they needed access to the Sedgewick's house.

She seemed unsurprised. As a solicitor she would have anticipated this request. Maybe had even warned her client/friend of this likelihood. There was no 'I'll have to check'. Instead she responded calmly. 'That'll be fine. We'll meet you there in half an hour to let you in.'

'How is she this morning?'

'Calmer.'

He wanted to ask so much more, whether Alice had said anything about how she had found herself at the hospital with her bundle, but instinctively he knew all this would have to be done formally, according to the book and on the record, so he arranged to meet them both at The Mount in half an hour.

*   *   *

At eleven, as she was putting on her make-up, Martha was surprised to have a telephone call from Simon Pendlebury. Simon had been married to her friend Evelyn but Evelyn had died of ovarian cancer almost a year ago and since then they had shared the odd friendly dinner every couple of months or so. It was uncharacteristic for him to ring her early on a Sunday morning and when he spoke she quickly realized that this was not the only uncharacteristic thing about his telephone call. He sounded agitated – a little nervous. Almost unsure of himself. He was a strange man, who had been a great friend of Martin's in their university days, an accountant who seemed to have made an awful lot of money in a very short space of time. Martha didn't quite trust him. There was a dangerous aura around him but she did enjoy his company – perhaps because of this. He spoke urgently. 'Martha,' he said, 'I'd really appreciate it if you could spare me an evening. This week?'

'Of course, Simon. Is Wednesday any good?'

'Yeah. Yeah. I'll see you at Drapers'. Eight o'clock?'

'Fine.'

'Thanks, Martha, I appreciate it,' and he put the phone down, leaving her to wonder what on earth was going on? She had never heard him so unsure of himself, or so grateful for her company. It was all odd. She smiled at herself in the mirror. She was going to learn something new about this man she'd known for almost twenty years. In the meantime, she looked out of the window and watched a few flakes of snow swirl outside. What were they going to do today?

It was midday by the time Talith had gathered his team together. They arrived at The Mount in a large van and a police car. Talith looked up at the property. It was imposing. A three-storeyed Victorian house with black and white gables in perfect condition and well tended gardens. The snow lay thickly on the roof giving it a Christmas card air. Talith had to remind himself what he was here for – nothing like a Christmas card, more like a horror film. His policeman's eye registered the oblong shape in the snow where a car had recently stood and the skid marks in the drive, presumably where Mrs Sedgewick had driven out – in a great hurry by the look of the gravel spewed up and slushy. He indicated the marks to the police photographer who snapped them obediently. Beneath a thick blanket of snow lay another car, a white Mercedes with a personalized number plate. AS 10. Aaron Sedgewick's presumably? This car had obviously sat here for the last few days, which gave further credence to the 'away on business' claim. In fact there was no sign of life around the property at all. No lights, no roar of a central heating boiler. The front curtains were tightly drawn. The Mount looked abandoned.

Mrs Palk pulled up minutes later, in a blue Mazda. She climbed out, smartly dressed in a fur-trimmed black anorak, tight black jeans and Ugg boots. Alice followed her, still in the same shabby clothes she had been wearing the night before. She still looked pale but perfectly composed and avoided meeting Talith's eyes. From her coat pocket she drew a Yale key on a small chain and silently unlocked the door.

Behind her Talith sucked in a deep, apprehensive breath, a little ashamed of the fact that he was so nervous at entering. There had been something so morbid, so ghoulish about the remains of the tiny child, and a woman who nursed it as though it was a live infant baby had upset him. It took him back to a moment he preferred to forget, a time when he was eight years old and he and his dad (who was a great fan of Hammer Horror movies) had watched a black and white Boris Karloff film, *The Mummy*. Though it had been an old film and he could see now that the special effects had been clumsy and Boris Karloff's movement jerky and unrealistic, it had scared the pants off him at the time. Even now he felt silly thinking it had so terrified him but his dad had been a film buff and had laughed when his son had spent at least half of the movie cowering behind the settee. Talith still felt ashamed of himself.

And he felt exactly the same now, entering this House of Horror. Except that he was a detective sergeant now and could not cower behind the sofa any more. He must face up to this.

He shook himself, but it was still there, that icy finger creeping up the spine.

What else would he find? How many more dead babies?

The hall felt chilly and smelt very slightly musty.

He must take charge. 'Do you want to show us where you found the ummm baby, Mrs Sedgewick?'

She nodded towards the staircase ahead. 'Upstairs. We're

thinking of using the loft for an extra bedroom and bathroom. I thought I'd better take a look up there.' She gave a half smile, both vague and vacant. 'I wasn't sure how feasible – or pleasant – it would be as the water tanks are all up there.' Another smile. 'I thought it might be noisy – and a bit cold. And I wasn't sure how the windows would work.' She could have been showing someone over the house and trying to put them off, Talith thought, not pointing where she had discovered a baby's rotten corpse. He took charge. 'Let's take a look, shall we?'

He glanced into the rooms as they passed. They were, as he had expected, luxuriant and well-ordered. There were cream carpets, coordinated curtains, smart, polished antique furniture. And yet it felt little used. It was very tidy and impersonal. Apart from comfortable wealth there was no clue as to the Sedgewick's characters and interests. Talith wondered whether Alice did her own cleaning. Probably not, he decided. She was more likely to have a 'daily'. He followed her up a wide, mahogany staircase with a narrow strip of dark red carpet anchored by brass stair rods and then towards an extending loft ladder on the landing. Acantha drew up in the rear, saying nothing, but she kept a suspicious eye on the white-suited forensic team ahead of her, as they clambered, noisily bouncing up the ladder. Perhaps she too, was apprehensive at what they would find at the top.

'How long have you lived here?' Talith asked the question conversationally but Alice Sedgewick wasn't fooled. 'Only five years,' she said deliberately, turning around and reading his eyes.

His next comment was equally polite but probing. 'It's a very big house for a couple whose children have flown the nest.'

Alice turned around again with that perceptive and unsettling stare. 'My husband likes big houses,' she said, adding to herself, 'even though he isn't here that much.' There was resentment in her tone and Talith wondered whether she shared her husband's enthusiasm for living in big houses.

They reached the top of the ladder. Alice Sedgewick put her hand out to the left and flicked a light switch on illuminating the entire loft space with four swinging light bulbs. Talith made a mental note of even this small action. She'd remembered to turn the switch *off* then last night as she'd left the roof space, even though she must have been holding her grisly burden. Not someone in a panic then but a woman calm enough to carry out an action of economy. So she had either been in control of herself, had acted automatically or maybe, just maybe, it was possible that someone else had switched the light off.

Already Talith's policeman's mind was starting to look at scenarios, possibilities and ask the relevant questions.

The loft was neatly boarded. There was plenty of headroom and four bare electric lights so they had a good view. Now they could see how huge the roof space was. Big enough for a couple more bedrooms and bathrooms. Talith straightened up and looked around. It held the usual loft contents: a couple of suitcases, a few boxes stacked neatly to one side, beams and spiders' webs, insulation against the roof. There was a soft, urgent scrabbling in the corner. Mice? Bats? Rats?

It was easy to see where Alice had found the infant. In the far corner stood a hot water tank partly boarded in. Behind it and to the side was a pile of dust and rubble. Talith and the team approached the area. In the rubble was a small piece of tattered woollen cloth so smothered with the dust it was hard to tell what colour it had once been. So, as Delyth Fontaine had suggested last night, Alice must have found the infant partly covered, unwrapped it, taken it downstairs and found the blanket in which she had wrapped the child to bring it to the hospital. She had provided the newer pink blanket herself. From where? It had been no larger than a cot blanket – nowhere near adult sized. But it was surely a long time ago that a baby had been resident here, in number 41. Alice Sedgewick's children were in their twenties.

As though reading his mind, she followed his gaze. 'That's where I found her,' she said very quietly. 'I – there was some plasterboard around the hot water tank. I thought I'd take a proper look to see if it should be moved. I pulled off some of the boards surrounding it.' Alice was walking towards the spot very slowly, in a trance, speaking softly to herself, as though she had forgotten they were there. 'Then I found her, waiting for me. She was wrapped up.' Her eyes were wide open now but unfocussed. 'She'd been lying there all that time. Not buried at all. Just stuffed behind an . . . ' There was a look both of grief and horror in her face.

'Hey.' Acantha put her arm around her friend's shoulders. 'Hey.'

It looked as though Alice Sedgewick was beginning to lose the plot again, Talith thought. And yet, though the content of her tale was enough to tip the sanest mind into hysteria, there was, around Alice Sedgewick, a complete lack of drama. She had simply related the story in a flat, quiet voice.

The SOCOs had already slipped on their gloves and were stepping towards the spot ready to bag up the tattered woollen rag, but not before Talith had seen some staining on it, dark and rusty. As a policeman he'd seen enough of this particular mark before to know exactly what it was.

Acantha saw it too and intervened quickly. 'Don't you think it would be better if all this was continued back at the station while your people look around?'

Talith nodded slowly. The team would work better un-hampered anyway.

He took a quick sweep of the area, frowning. He couldn't really see why Alice Sedgewick had investigated the area around the water tank. If he had been considering converting the loft into further living space it wouldn't immediately have struck him as that important.

He had a quick, quiet word with Roddie Hughes, the scene of crimes investigator. A sharp-eyed Essex boy who had moved up to Shrewsbury a few years ago because he'd visited the town for a weekend and liked it so much he'd decided to stay rather than go home.

'Take a quickie round the house,' Talith said. 'I'm wondering where that little kid's blanket came from.' He thought for a minute. 'Unless she's got grandchildren, of course.'

As they trooped downstairs, he was already adding that to the list of questions he wanted answers to.

As they reached the hall he made his decision and spoke to the two women. 'I can't see any point dragging you down to the station today,' he said. 'The senior investigating officer, Detective Inspector Alex Randall, will take over tomorrow. It'll be up to him how he conducts the case.' He omitted to mention that how things proceeded would also depend on the results of the post-mortem. Talith wasn't sure whether he was glad or sorry he would be handing over responsibility for the case. It promised to be interesting but probably frustrating

too. He had the feeling that winkling out the truth would prove
to be a challenge equal to any police officer's talents. Even
Detective Inspector Alex Randall. A time lapse between what
might have been a crime and the discovery of a body always
made a case harder to solve and it might be hard to determine what exactly the time lapse had been. The SOCOs would
be looking for other clues as to how long the child had lain
concealed. But there was no doubt about it. DI Randall would
be taking over the investigation in the morning and probably
he, Sergeant Paul Talith, and definitely PC Gethin Roberts,
who was right at the bottom of the pecking order, would be
relegated to the Second Division. Talith was a fan of the 'beautiful game' and whenever possible he liked to use sporting
jargon to describe his work. It made his job sound dangerous,
exciting, energetic, and besides it made him feel better.

Acantha looked vaguely surprised at their release and Talith
had the feeling she had expected a long grilling of her client
most of the afternoon, so he explained his reasoning. 'I've
done what preliminary work is necessary, Mrs Palk.' He
glanced at Alice. 'This is quite a strain on Mrs Sedgewick.'
A further quick glance at Alice confirmed that she was looking
wan. 'I think we should leave her alone for now until DI
Randall takes over, the examination of the house is complete
and we've done some further investigations.' He gave a ghost
of a smile. 'I take it you'll vouch for her.'

'Yes,' Acantha said, a little stiffly.

'Have you contacted Mr Sedgewick?'

'No.'

'So you don't know when he'll be back?' He addressed the
question vaguely to both women. It was Acantha who
answered.

'Not a clue,' she said airily. 'Aaron rather makes up his
own rules, doesn't he, Alice?'

This elicited a vague nod.

'He rarely tells Alice exactly when he'll be home but always
manages to arrive unexpectedly,' Acantha explained then gave
a wide, slightly mischievous smile. It transformed her face,
melted away the severe expression and replaced it with a soft-
ness and humanity that made her look instantly attractive.
'When she was younger I used to think he imagined he'd walk
in on her doing something she shouldn't.'

Both Alice and Sergeant Talith were startled. Alice stared at her friend.

Talith pursued the comment. 'You mean another man?' He gave a sceptical glance at Mrs Sedgewick.

'Oh no,' she said hastily. 'No. Nothing like that. All the other things Alice wasn't allowed to do. Eating chocolate, having a glass too much red wine. Talking for too long on the telephone. Wearing shoes in the house, not rinsing out coffee cups before putting them in the dishwasher. Having a Chinese takeaway or even worse a pizza delivery. There were a hundred things she wasn't allowed to do. The children not in bed when they should have been, watching soaps on the television.' She gave an amused grimace. 'You don't know what control is until you've met Aaron Sedgewick, sergeant.'

Alice was round-eyed with incredulity at Acantha's forthrightness but she stayed silent, not defending her husband or contradicting her friend's opinion.

'I can hardly wait,' Talith responded dryly.

He kept his last question back until they had walked outside into the freezing air. 'Does Aaron Sedgewick have a mobile?'

Again it was Acantha who answered for her friend. 'Probably. Everyone does these days, don't they? But I don't know the number. Alice,' she said, 'do you?'

'Yes,' Alice answered politely, 'I've got it written down by the telephone in the kitchen but I'm only supposed to ring it in an emergency.'

Talith felt stunned. What on earth constituted an emergency in the mad Sedgewick household?

It struck him then that Alice Sedgewick was bobbing in and out of reality like a boat whose tether is loosened by a gentle but insistent current. At some point she might well drift all the way downstream.

FOUR

Sunday afternoon

Martha had solved the problem of what to do. The day was bitingly cold but bright and the weather quite beautiful. She was fond of photography and Bobby needed a good long walk. She chose her favourite route, knowing that plenty of people would be sledging on Lyth Hill this afternoon. Mary Webb had had a house there and she was one of Martha's favourite authors. She had studied *Precious Bane* and had loved the book ever since.

They set out, well wrapped up in gloves, scarves and anoraks, laughing in the sparkling air and the challenging cold and Bobby straining on his lead, barking and panting. Martha had thought they might take their sledge but Sam was worried about making his injury worse and Agnetha and Sukey said they preferred to walk and chat in their easy, friendly way. Martha decided she would cut a lone figure. One needed a child present to justify this juvenile sport. And there was always the chance that she would bump, either literally or metaphorically, into someone she knew professionally. The thought of the coroner whooping with joy and exhilaration as she sledged down Lyth Hill was perhaps not quite 'the thing', so reluctantly she'd slammed the garage door on the red plastic sledge.

Talith also had worked out what to do with his afternoon. He decided to visit the staff nurse who had been on duty the previous evening and take a proper statement from her. It would be less traumatic, he had decided, if he went to her house rather than summoning her to the station and he wanted to minimize the impact of the events of last night. She'd had a late night as well as a shock.

Lucy Ramshaw lived with her boyfriend on the Gains Park Estate. It was an area popular with the nurses because it was so close to the hospital – within walking distance. That meant they didn't even have to battle over the scarce parking spaces and run the gauntlet of the vigilant and quite merciless parking attendants who slapped their fines and warnings on anyone, whether staff or patient. Lucy answered the door herself, looking very different to the harassed and upset nurse he had encountered the night before. She was wearing tight jeans and a low-cut blue sweater, which showed a neat, strong, slim figure, Paul Talith noted approvingly.

She recognized him at once and showed him into a small dining room, passing the sitting from where he could hear football on the television. He wished he could have been watching the Premier League game instead of working.

Lucy made them both a coffee and they sat around the small dining table.

'I don't think I've anything to add really,' she said. 'I mean I saw the woman but she didn't seem to want anything. We were really busy what with the snow and everything. She just sat there. I mean she could have been waiting for a relative or someone,' she finished lamely. 'I didn't realize she was holding a baby. It just looked like a blanket. If I'd known it was a baby obviously we would have dealt with her much quicker. But she just sat there,' she repeated.

Talith knew she felt guilty. 'It wouldn't have made any difference, really.'

The nurse nodded. 'I know that but I still feel bad that I didn't at least go over to her and speak. To tell you the truth I was relieved she wasn't one of the more demanding patients. Some of them can be quite difficult.'

Talith looked at the nurse. She had one of those open faces, honest and true. 'It really wouldn't have made any difference, I promise.'

She looked mollified at that.

'Now then. At what time did you first notice her?'

'Eight, I think.' She looked uncertain. 'I can't be sure.'

'And she was simply sitting quietly in the corner?'

'Sort of crooning. She was looking down at her lap, tucking the blanket round her. She looked sort of . . .' Lucy fumbled for the word and found it: 'Serene. Contented.'

'And when you spoke to her, later?'

'She seemed startled, a bit shy.' Lucy Ramshaw thought for a moment. 'As though she didn't want anyone to bother with her.'

'What time was that?'

'Nearer ten thirty. Things were beginning to quieten down and I wondered about her.'

'OK,' Talith said. 'Did you notice anything else?'

'Well – she was dressed fairly shabbily.' Lucy frowned. 'There was paint on her jeans.'

'She said she'd been doing some decorating – well – more investigating a proposed loft conversion.'

Lucy nodded. 'Right – well – she was one of those people who faded into the background. I think she would have sat there all night if I hadn't gone over to her.'

'And when you did?'

'She was in a sort of trance. She appeared vague. When I spoke to her she seemed startled almost as though she didn't quite know where she was.'

'And she let you take the baby from her?'

Lucy looked distressed. 'Not at first. I didn't realize what it was.' She closed her eyes against the creeping horror she had felt when she had realized that in the blanket was an infant who had not moved or cried in the entire time it had been in the department. 'When I realized it was a baby I asked her to hand it to me and she did. Then I looked . . .' She was stricken at the memory. 'It was horrible. Those eye sockets. That blackened, papery skin. Awful. I don't think I'll ever forget it. It felt so light in my arms. Then I saw what it was and – I almost dropped it.' She went pale.

'Then what?'

'I must have shouted out. People came running.' She fixed a pair of large blue-grey eyes on him. 'I'm a bit hazy. It all happened so quickly. Someone must have taken the baby from me because I wasn't holding it. That's about all I remember.'

'Thanks,' Talith said. 'I'm sorry to have to question you like this but I thought better here than in the station or at work.'

Lucy Ramshaw gave a deep sigh. 'Thanks. I suppose there'll be an enquiry at the hospital,' she said gloomily. 'Just what I need with my wedding coming up.'

'That's up to the hospital,' Talith said. 'Not us. I would imagine they'll want to play it down rather than make a big issue of it.'

'I hope so,' Lucy said, with feeling. Then: 'Do you know

anything about the circumstances? Was the baby hers? She looked a bit old for that. A grandparent?'

'We don't know yet.'

'Or did she just find it?'

'I can't really discuss the case with you,' Talith said kindly, 'but don't worry about it. No one blames you for anything. Anything at all. You acted just fine.'

Lucy smiled then, a broad, wonderful smile which made Talith warm to her even more. 'Would you like another coffee,' she offered.

'Thanks.'

The walk was brisk which kept them warm. They parked at the bottom and threaded up the hill, passing Spring Cottage, which had been Mary Webb's home, Bobby, their Welsh Border Collie, giving little yaps of delight and straining on his lead. They climbed until they could see the Stretton Hills, Stiperstones and the distinctive, conical shape of the Wrekin. As she had anticipated Lyth Hill was full of sledgers and she watched them whoop and scream with a tinge of envy. Oh, for just one trip down the hill. They walked for a couple of hours, Sam striding ahead, Agnetha and Sukey arm in arm, chatting so vivaciously they hardly noticed where they were going, even taking a wrong turn a couple of times until Martha and Sam shouted them back. Martha took a few photographs, both of the snow scenes and her family and then they all trooped home to a Sunday roast, Sam sitting at the table, extolling the virtues of football and bemoaning all the games cancelled because of the freezing weather, Sukey and Agnetha being more useful, helping to peel the potatoes, lay the table and open a bottle of wine. It was a warm family day, always with that one person missing, but Martha was finishing with regrets now. It had taken her a long time but she was very much back to her old self.

Talith detoured on the way back to the station to inspect the hospital car park. Alice was the owner of a Vauxhall Zafira. He'd checked the number plate on the PNC and drove towards the back of the hospital to the A&E entrance, easy to spot because of its red signs. Alice's car was also easy to spot. Slewed across two parking spaces and with a ticket already on the screen, warning that the car must be removed – or else.

Talith added one of his own: 'Police Aware'. He'd get it taken in to forensics although he doubted they'd find much there. He tried the door. The car was unlocked, the keys still in the ignition. Lucky it was the Shrewsbury Hospital. Had it been Telford it would have been gone by now. He pocketed the keys and peered in. As he'd thought it was neat and tidy and there was nothing on the floor except . . .

He slipped a glove on and picked up a child's plastic rattle. The colours were pale and slightly faded. It didn't look new. He shook it and heard little bells jingle.

Jingle all the way, he thought, before replacing the rattle on the floor and locking the door. He had the feeling that no child had played with this for a while. It would have to be officially found – again – by the SOCOs but it posed another question. Had the rattle been found with the child? Or was it a contribution from Alice? Talith realized that in his mind he had all but solved the case. However long the child had been dead for, the estate agents could let them know who had lived there then and, 'Bob's your uncle, Talith,' he muttered to himself.

He made a quick call to the station to organize removal of the car and climbed back into his own. Talith was not normally a reflective man but this case was a learning curve for him. As he leaned forward and started the engine he mused that most cases were reduced to a random collection of odd, un-connected objects.

Like the rattle.

He returned to the station in time to see the recovery lorry setting out and gave them the keys.

Wheels in motion, he thought with satisfaction.

Two hours later he had finished his reports and was ready to go home to his own Sunday meal and put his feet up in front of the television.

In the Palk household Justin and Acantha were finding it hard not to talk to their house guest about the subject which was occupying their minds.

The trouble was that Acantha couldn't seem to find a neutral subject. All topics led straight back to the one the three of them were struggling to avoid. Even if she asked a polite, innocuous question, like what exactly her daughter was doing these days, it always seemed to lead back to 'Don't tell her, Acantha. Don't tell her.'

In the end Acantha gave in. 'Then tell *me* what happened.'

'You already know what happened,' Alice insisted plaintively. 'I went up into the loft to see about the conversion that Aaron wants to do.'

'Yes?'

'I wondered about moving the hot water tank. Then I noticed . . .'

'What?'

'I saw what I thought was a bit of old blanket stuffing up a hole. I thought there might be mice – rats even – so I pulled it out and *it* came out as well.'

'That isn't quite the story you gave the police,' Acantha said.

Justin, very wisely, was saying nothing.

'I've had time to think about it.' Alice was more rational, defiant even. 'Remember it properly.' Acantha couldn't rid herself of the feeling that her friend was defending something.

'You must have realized there was no point in taking it to a hospital.'

'I didn't know where else to take her.'

'How did you know she was called Poppy? Was her name stitched on the blanket?'

'I don't remember. There's no point you pushing me. I don't remember everything.'

'OK,' Acantha said resignedly. 'But when you got to the hospital you simply sat there?'

'I didn't know the system.' Alice was sounding aggressive now.

Her friend could have pointed out that she had had a broken night's sleep as well as acting as both her lawyer and her guarantor so the least she owed her was a truthful explanation, but she had the feeling that if pressed Alice would hide behind the 'I don't remember' explanation. It could be a very convenient way of avoiding the truth.

Acantha watched her drink her coffee, butter her toast, spread the marmalade. On the one hand she realized her friend was stressed and she must allow her some leeway. On the other hand she had been a solicitor long enough to know that when criminals couldn't conjure up an explanation they frequently hid behind the excuse of a poor memory or amnesia.

Alice burst out suddenly, 'Why do you keep asking? Why do you keep pressing me for answers, answers I don't have. I don't have the answers,' she repeated. 'You know that I was trying to work out the loft conversion and I came across . . .'

'Yes, yes,' Acantha prompted impatiently. 'I know that but I don't understand when you found the body why didn't you just ring the police? And you –' she looked directly at her friend – 'haven't even come near giving me a good reason.'

Alice looked confused and a little vulnerable. 'There's a lot I don't remember and a lot I don't know. I . . .' It was as though the spark of an idea came to her. 'I suppose,' she said brightly, 'I was temporarily insane.'

It all seemed a little too convenient. Acantha bit her lip, gave her husband a swift look across the table and knew his thoughts were very close to hers.

So she decided to press Alice. 'Look, Alice,' she said, 'you may as well try and think up some answers other than that you don't know, because at some point you're going to have to answer all these questions to the police satisfactorily and if you can't do that it may well be that they charge you.'

Alice looked alarmed. 'What with? What on earth could they possibly charge me with? I haven't *done* anything.'

'I don't know but I do know what the police are like. I've worked with them for enough years,' Acantha said dryly. 'They like answers, Alice, to their questions. Answers that make sense. And if they don't get the right answers they get suspicious. It'll be the worse for you, I can promise you, so you'd better start thinking and remembering.'

Her friend looked at her with dismay. 'But I can't remember.'

'Can't you?'

'No.' The two friends looked at each other and Acantha suddenly thought that though she would have called Alice Sedgewick one of her best friends she was realizing now that she didn't really know her at all. She looked at her friend through new eyes. Her lawyer's instinct was whispering to her that there was much more to this episode than met the eye. To her the entire story was unconvincing. Alice Sedgewick was holding something back. She could read it in her eyes.

Monday morning, 7 a.m.

Martha was woken by the alarm radio. She stretched out her hand to still it. She couldn't cope with the news at this hour. She ought to retune it really so she was wakened by Classic FM or Radio Two but somehow she never quite got around to it. She had enough to think about. Work. Sukey to school. Another couple of days and Sam would be returning to Liverpool for a medical examination by the team's doctor. Agnetha had offered to drive him back which suited Martha. She anticipated a busy week ahead with the poor weather. She expected plenty of slips and spills which in the elderly or vulnerable could so easily prove fatal. As a coroner she could never forecast what the week would hold and sometimes, on a Monday morning, she lay in bed for ten minutes and wondered, even sometimes tried to see into the near future. Hers was an interesting role, her job to tidy up after death. It wasn't always possible and that was where her work could become difficult. But when she did ease suffering for the bereaved she could honestly say it fulfilled her.

Detective Inspector Alex Randall was at his desk by eight thirty a.m. A tall, spare man with a craggy face and deeply penetrating hazel eyes which normally were grave and serious, sometimes even a little sad. But occasionally they could light up with amusement and transform him into an attractive man in his early forties. He spent half an hour reading through Talith's preliminary reports then put in a call to the coroner's office.

Martha arrived at her office at a little after nine. And the first thing she noticed was that Jericho Palfreyman, her assistant, was waiting to ambush her, wearing what she called 'that look' on his face. A sort of suppressed excitement which told her some drama was afoot. He was a grizzle-haired man, Dickensian both in his looks and demeanour, even down to the habit he had of rubbing his dry palms together when intrigued. Jericho was one of those souls who had probably looked old from the age of thirty and hadn't aged for the last twenty-five years. Martha simply couldn't imagine him as anything but grey-haired, with slightly bowed shoulders which meant he usually looked up into people's faces, giving him a slightly creepy look. He took a ghoulish delight in his job and squeezed out every last detail of sensational cases. His pleasure was exponentially increased if he learned of them before Martha so *he* was the one to inform *her*.

And this was just such a case.

'Good morning, Jericho,' she said and waited, deliberately not prompting him.

Jericho rubbed his hands together. 'I've just had a call from Detective Inspector Randall, ma'am,' he began then paused, wanting her to ask him what the inspector had wanted. It was a sort of cat and mouse game, a procedure he wanted to follow.

Martha sighed. 'Yes, Jericho?'

'He's investigating a most strange and mysterious case,' he said, pausing for a fraction of a second to extract the maximum satisfaction before he spilled the beans. As usual he spared Martha no detail, adding a few extra twirls of his own. 'She'd wrapped the little girl in a pretty little pink blanket and then drove all the way to the hospital with it on her lap.' His eyes gleamed. 'On her lap, mind.'

She couldn't resist a little leg-pull. 'Really, Jericho, and how did they know all that?'

Jericho was unperturbed. 'She must have done, mustn't she, ma'am. I bet she didn't have a car seat.'

'Well, we'll soon find out,' she said. 'Thank you very much for all that, Jericho,' she said. 'So the body is now at the hospital mortuary?'

'That's right, ma'am,' he said. 'They're waiting to do the post-mortem. Detective Inspector Randall wants you to ring him the very minute you arrive.'

'Then I must do so, mustn't I? I'll have coffee in my office,' she said, then remembered something. 'Oh, by the way, Jericho, do you know the number of a painter and decorator? I want to revamp my study and I'm terrible at decorating. It'll take me from now right up to next Christmas.'

'As it happens, ma'am,' he said, 'I do. I can give you the number of a very reliable person who can be trusted to do a neat job honestly.'

'Thank you.'

Of course Jericho would know someone, she reflected. He knew everything. She copied the number down, resisting her assistant's offer to set the whole thing up for her and went into her office to ring Alex Randall.

She knew the number off by heart. She and Detective Inspector Randall had worked together on a number of cases. She liked him very much. He was professional, polite, private. An enigma.

She dialled his office number. 'Morning, Martha,' he said.

'From what Jericho has already told me this sounds a very odd case, Alex.'

'I agree,' he said. 'Odd and puzzling. Not least what this woman's part was in the drama.'

'Alice,' she said slowly. 'Alice Sedgewick. Have you met her yet?'

'No. Sergeant Talith has and thinks she's very strange. A bit weird and disturbed.'

'But presumably not a child killer? Does he think she's responsible for the child's death?'

'Well, apart from a few points which have puzzled him I can't see how she could have been. It really depends on how long the baby has been dead for and I have the feeling we won't be able to pin the pathologist, Mark Sullivan, down to a precise number of years. Alice has lived at The Mount for five years. Delyth Fontaine's opinion is that the baby has been dead for longer than that. So, if Mrs Sedgewick was responsible for the child's death, she would have to have brought the body with her when they moved into The Mount. I suppose the body would have to have been kept in the same environment or its condition would have deteriorated.'

'Delicately put, Alex.' She wanted to ask what points exactly had puzzled Paul Talith but knew she would have to wait. 'If she had done that why suddenly would she lose her rag and come up to the hospital with it?'

'I don't know. Maybe something she had hidden from her husband? Something to with the proposed loft conversion?' He gave a dry chuckle. 'There are plenty of questions to be answered.'

Martha agreed. 'Well whatever we'll have to have a post-mortem if only to find out whether the infant was born dead or alive. Can we see if Mark Sullivan is available to do a post-mortem? Today if possible.'

'Do you want to attend, Martha?'

'I think I ought to, although I've a ton of work ahead of me. Winter really is the season of death, isn't it? Luckily,' she added hastily, 'most of them from natural causes. But I have a nasty feeling that this will become a cause célèbre. It's just the sort of sticky mystery that makes a good headline – better than the economy or the deaths of our troops abroad. And definitely better than the secret date of the election. If the press start sniffing around let me know, won't you? And let me know as soon as you have a time for the PM? I'm available all afternoon.'

'Will do.'

'As the A&E department at the hospital is such a public place we're not going to have a hope of keeping this quiet. It *might* be an idea if you made a brief statement to the press and kept them informed. It'll at least minimize their tendency to make up an entire story. Let's try and get them to stick to the facts.'

'Of course.'

'It strikes me that behind this little drama is a tragedy, some woman in desperate straits. Let's not make it worse for her whoever she might be.'

'Right. I agree.' He paused. 'Family well?'

'Yes, thank you. Yours?'

It was something she'd never done, made any comment about his family, enquired about them. She didn't even know whether he had any children. She knew there was a Mrs Randall but he never mentioned her name or said anything about her at all. It was almost as though when he was at work she didn't exist. Martha had been to his office on a number of occasions and observed that there were no pictures on his desk. In fact nothing personal at all. He was an enigma who seemed to want to remain so and she hesitated to intrude but she had known him for years now and her question had been no more than a polite response that had slipped out before she could check it.

'Aah,' he said, which could have meant anything at all.

Alex rang back at lunchtime. 'PM at three,' he said cheerfully. 'Can you still make it?'

'I'll be there,' Martha said grimly. 'Is Mark Sullivan going to perform?'

'Yes. He's working today and has agreed to do it.'

'Good. There's no one better.' She could have added a few words more but discretion and all that.

Provided he's . . .

I hope he's . . .

The missing word was 'sober'.

In the end she said nothing except: 'See you later then, Alex.'

As she drove to the hospital mortuary she worried about Mark Sullivan. It was no secret that Sullivan, one of the cleverest pathologists she'd ever worked with, had a drink problem. A serious drink problem which affected his work at times. She had watched him perform post-mortems with shaking hands, bloodshot eyes, an uneasy gait and seeming to exhale pure, neat alcohol. At those times she was glad that his subject was not a living person. And yet, when he was good, sober and alert, as a pathologist he was very, very good, like the girl with a curl in the middle of her forehead. He seemed to be one of those pathologists who could tease out information from seemingly invisible marks, find evidence deep inside the tissues, of trauma or an assault – or even some-times the other way round when a death appeared suspicious and a suspect held, he had the talent to find a clot or a haem-orrhage or some other natural cause of death. And as every law enforcer knows it is as important to free the innocent as to convict the guilty. For the sake of what would almost certainly prove to be a very delicate case she hoped that today Sullivan would be at his sober best.

Her wish was granted. Sullivan himself opened the key-padded door with a sweeping gesture and a wide grin.

'Martha,' he said. 'A challenge ahead.'

'Yes indeed.'

He looked bright and clean and – yes as she scrutinized him she knew he was – sober. Absolutely stone cold sober. He smelt of coffee and vaguely of a spicy aftershave. His teeth looked bright and white, his skin clear. Best of all he looked confident, sure of himself. Happy. She hadn't seen him look this good for years. It was a puzzle. What had wrought this change? He bounced her scrutiny back with a mocking defiance and she was sure he knew exactly what she was thinking.

'Alex will be here in a minute,' he said.

She followed him down the corridor and Sullivan continued talking. 'I have the poor little scrap ready and waiting. A newborn male infant. Superficially I'd say the child's cord was cut but not properly ligatured and he bled to death.'

Something struck Martha. 'Did you say he?'

'That's right.' He made a face. 'Even I can sex a child, Martha.'

She was sure Alex had mentioned something about a little *girl* in a *pink* blanket. But when Alex Randall arrived a few minutes later the sex of the baby wasn't foremost in her mind. If Martha thought Mark Sullivan looked well Detective Inspector Alex Randall looked simply terrible, as though he had hardly slept for weeks. His eyes were puffy and he looked strained and exhausted. Whatever was going on in his life it must be something quite dreadful to have this awful effect on him. She'd never seen him look quite so bad. He avoided Martha's searching, enquiring glance as though he knew he looked rough and was embarrassed for her to see it too, resenting both her cognizance and her concern. He passed a hand over his face wearily, pressing his fingers into his eyelids almost with pain. Something was patently very wrong. Martha felt concerned. She was fond of Alex. They were not only colleagues but friends – even though she could not say she had got to know him well. She had always suspected there was tragedy lurking somewhere in his life but he had never confided in her and she had never asked.

But now they had important work to do. It was not the time to tackle him.

They moved into the post-mortem room.

Even Martha could see that the child was a newborn, a neonate. Stripped naked this was easy to see. There was a stump of an umbilical cord. Blackened and shrivelled but quite unmistakable. Its head was still elongated from its birth. Its skin was dark and papery; the bones looked soft. They stood around and looked at it, the remains of a pathetic infant who had never had the chance to live either at all or for more than a few hours. And Sullivan was right. It was a little boy.

'Well,' Alex said. 'Talith's statement clearly says that Mrs Sedgewick called the child Poppy, and referred to her as a girl. Wrapped her in a pink blanket.'

The blanket was neatly folded to the side. In a forensic bag was another blanket, tattered and partly eaten by moths or rodents. They all glanced over at it.

'Was it wearing any other clothes,' Alex asked.

Sullivan answered. 'No. Just that.'

'No nappy, no Babygro?'

'Nothing,' Sullivan said again. 'Which supports the theory that this is a neonate and died round about the time of birth. I've had a quick look at the blanket the baby was wrapped in. There's some staining which I think is meconium.'

Alex looked puzzled. 'Sorry? I wish you wouldn't use these medical terms.'

'When a baby is born the first motion it passes is meconium, the liquor or water it's swallowed whilst still in the womb.'

'Thanks,' the detective said.

Mark Randall held his finger up. 'And there's something else,' he said.

'Our little boy wasn't exactly perfect. He has a harelip.'

'Really?' Martha was again reminded of *Precious Bane*.

'Yes. Look.' He inserted a finger behind the shrunken lip of the infant so they could see a distinct gap.

'Good gracious,' Martha said then narrowed her eyes. 'But you don't die of a harelip, Alex.'

'No. Nor of a cleft palate which he also had.'

'So who is the mother?' Alex asked.

Sullivan met his eyes. 'That,' he said, 'is the million dollar question.'

The mortician measured the crown to heel length.

'Obviously,' Alex said a little stiffly, 'the big question is whether the child was born dead or alive.'

'Yes,' the pathologist agreed.

Sullivan worked without speaking, examining the lungs in great detail, taking tiny pieces for analysis under the microscope and scraping samples.

Then he spoke. 'The whole thing hinges,' he said, 'on whether the lungs ever inflated. It looks to me as though there has been some partial aeration. It's very difficult as the body is in this state of decay. Suffice it to say that I can't see any wadding down the larynx or any sign of suffocation. I can't see any obvious trauma.' He looked up, at Martha this time. 'To be honest, Martha,' he said, 'because of the advanced decay of the child I couldn't say with any certainty whether it was born alive or dead. I couldn't swear what exactly happened in a court of law. All I can say for certain is that I see no evidence of infanticide.'

She glanced at the row of pots. 'Would your tissue samples show whether the lungs had ever expanded?'

'Possibly. I think the child probably lived for a few minutes. Its lungs are partially expanded. It looks as though the cord was cut but not properly ligatured and the baby could have bled and died, even from shock. The mother – or we assume the mother – tried to wrap it up in that shawl.' He indicated the scrap of material. 'Then she concealed it.'

'Time scale?' Alex asked delicately.

Mark Sullivan again looked dubious. 'Again I can't be absolutely certain – somewhere between five and ten years or thereabouts.' He started peeling off his gloves. 'And even then if someone said categorically that it was eleven years or even four years I couldn't argue. Not with certainty. Was there any collaborative evidence,' he asked hopefully, 'newspaper wrapping or something?'

'Not that's been unearthed so far.'

'And the lady herself, can she throw any light on this?'

'I haven't spoken to her yet but from what Sergeant Talith tells me she's calling the child "Poppy" and seems to thinks it is her responsibility. I'm not even sure she's quite sane.' He hesitated. 'Was the child moved at any point?'

'No, I don't think so. There's no evidence of that.' He glanced again at the pathetic remains of the child. 'It probably stayed where it had initially been put, in the space behind the airing cupboard, somewhere warm and dry, which is why it has been preserved in this particular way.' He untied his apron and hung it up. 'And that is all I can tell you for now. He was a full-term infant. The X-rays will prove that. He was born relatively healthy and without any obvious defects. DNA will isolate his race but he appears Caucasian. I can't tell you why he was not born in a hospital, as I can't tell you why his corpse was concealed. His DNA should give us his mother and father, if we ever find them.'

Martha looked at Alex. 'You've enough to go on?'

He nodded, apparently recovering from his initial state. 'Plenty.' He smiled at her. 'We've got a few leads and, of course, the fact that it was found in The Mount. We should get to the bottom of this.'

'Good. Then to work.'

FIVE

Alex Randall returned to the station and met up with Paul Talith. They spent a while together and were ready by five o'clock to face the press and make a statement for the six o'clock news. It was always better to give the press a considered statement. Otherwise they tended to write their own story.

Randall spoke in a slow, clear voice, sticking to the bald fact that the body of a newborn infant had been brought into the hospital on Saturday evening.

It wasn't going to wash.

The inevitable questions followed. Firstly from a ginger-haired reporter sitting right at the back, speaking loudly, so everyone heard his question.

'I understand that a woman brought the child in to the hospital. Is there anything to connect her with the dead child?'

Alex Randall kept his voice steady and calm. 'We are keeping an open mind but it seems unlikely.'

The next question, from a tenacious blonde-haired woman from the *Shropshire Star* he had also anticipated.

'Did the baby die from natural causes, inspector?'

'I'd rather not say at this stage in the investigation. There has been a post-mortem but the results so far were inconclusive. We are awaiting the results of further tests.' This would buy them some time.

The ginger-haired reporter at the back again: 'I understand the baby had been dead for quite some time?'

'That is correct.'

The reporter looked up. 'How long, exactly?'

'It's hard to be exact but a number of years.'

All eyes were on DI Randall. The reporter seemed to be staring straight at him, frowning. The next question was the one he had hoped would not be asked.

'Why did she take the body of a child who had been dead for a "long time" to a *hospital*? Why not just ring the police?'

Alex said again that he was not prepared to comment

specifically but they could surely understand that the woman had been understandably distressed by the discovery.

The press then tried to badger him for the exact location. They could find it out fairly easily, but Alex trotted out the usual statement about respecting people's privacy. He finished with a pledge that he would keep them informed of developments.

There was a lot of muttering and the press finally dispersed.

The last thing Alex did before going home that evening was to set up a meeting with Mrs Sedgewick and her solicitor on the following morning.

Then he went home, feeling his spirits sink as he turned into the drive of his house.

Martha cooked shepherd's pie for tea. It was one of Sam's favourites and he would be leaving in the morning. She hoped he would pass his medical examination and be pronounced fit to play again but she was also holding in her heart that throw-away comment about possibly playing for Stoke and living at home. She was trying not to get too excited about it, but oh, how she wanted him back here. She missed having a male around the place. She loved this cooking for a hungry lad, the washing of muddy clothes and dirty boots. She loved the noise of the place when he was around because, unlike his sister, who seemed to move around silently and whose only noise was her beloved pop music, Sam could do nothing quietly. He always made a noise, stumping around in his boots, clomping up and down the stairs. And his voice, again, unlike his sister's silky tones, was gruffly masculine. While the pie was browning under the grill she rang the number Jericho had given her and arranged for the painter and decorator to come round on Thursday evening to give her a quote for the study. She felt content.

Only one thing happened that evening to disturb the domestic heaven. At around nine o'clock the telephone rang. Martha picked it up and heard the song playing. It was one which was becoming uncomfortably familiar to her. The slow beat of Adam Faith's 1964 hit 'Message to Martha'. Martha listened for a minute then spoke. 'Hello, hello.' As she had expected there was no response except that the phone was put down softly and she was left with that creepy feeling that someone was out there, watching her, with some intent.

She dialled 1471 and again, as she had anticipated, the caller had withheld their number.

She sat still for a minute. She had been bothered by these vague messages for a couple of years now. Flowers had been left at her door. There had been an occasion when a mouse had been dumped on her doorstep. She had, at first, thought it must be Bobby until Alex Randall had drawn attention to a ligature tied around its neck. The record itself, 'Message to Martha', cracked and dirty, had also been left on her doorstep. This was an isolated house. Three women lived here. At times she had felt threatened by these approaches but they had never become more threatening. It was less a physical assault than someone whispering in her ear, insinuating that she should understand. Understand what? She was less frightened now than frustrated. If someone had a message for her why didn't they just come out and say it instead of this subversive, cloak-and-dagger approach which was so obviously meant to disturb her?

Sukey came in and found her sitting in the dark. She put her arms around her. 'Mum,' she said. 'What's the matter?'

Martha didn't want to tell her. Sukey wasn't quite fifteen years old. Mature for her years but still a child. She might not be frightened for herself but she was worried about Sukey. When Agnetha left Sukey would be alone in the house from when she arrived back from school to when Martha came back from work, and that could be late. Frequently after seven. There was the half-a-mile walk up a rough tree-lined track to the house. There was no other house within calling distance of The White House. Then there were the school holidays. Long days when her daughter would be here, alone.

She chose her words carefully.

'Suks,' she said, 'this is a very lonely house. Would you prefer to live in the town?'

She didn't mention that she, personally, would hate it.

It was unnecessary. So, it seemed, would her daughter. 'Absolutely not,' she said with vigour. 'We've got the woods here to walk Bobby and lots to see around. Oh no, Mum. I'd hate it. Why do you ask?'

Martha hid behind a half-truth. 'It's just that next month when Agnetha leaves you'll be here quite a bit on your own.'

'I won't be on my own,' Sukey said stoutly. 'I'll have Bobby. And maybe even Sam if this Stoke thing comes off.'

'That would be nice.'

Sukey slid into the chair next to Martha. 'Mum,' she said in the wheedling tone that daughters use when they want to get something out of a parent. Usually a father.

'Yes?'

'Would you hate it very much if I became an actress?'

'What?'

Martha was astonished. She had never really thought about what career Sukey would pursue. But the stage . . . ?

Keep calm, she lectured herself. Keep calm.

It helped that she knew exactly what Martin would have done in this situation. He had been tolerant, happy to allow life – his own and that of his wife and children – to work itself out. Whenever he had been faced with a conflict he had invariably chosen the easiest way out. So she followed this maxim.

'You must do as you wish,' she said. 'It's your life – not mine – but find out a little about the real acting world before you embark on that as a career. Don't believe all you hear in the tabloids and glossy magazines. As I understand it most actresses spend a lot of time waitressing or scrubbing floors because—'

'I know,' Sukey interrupted impatiently, 'but I was good in the school play last year, wasn't I?'

The school had put on *Abigail's Party* the previous year. Sukey had played the part of Abigail and yes, even allowing for maternal pride, Martha had thought she had been good. Very good. Her daughter was very determined. There was no point in opposing her but Martha had a feeling of dread. It wasn't what she wanted. She gave the softest of sighs. Neither had she wanted Sam to become a footballer. She had hoped they would go into a profession. Medicine, the law, teaching . . .

Dream on, she said to herself.

She looked at her daughter's anxious face. 'OK,' she said, 'as long as you know what you're letting yourself in for.'

Sukey gave her a cheeky grin, bounced out of her seat and was gone, leaving Martha alone again, unable to resist humming Noel Coward's, 'Don't put your daughter on the stage', substituting Mrs Gunn for Mrs Worthington.

She drew in a deep breath and felt powerless to influence her children's lives any further. But now her daughter had skipped out of the room Martha's mind returned to the anonymous phone call.

Alex Randall had told her if she received any more obscure contacts from the 'Message to Martha' person to inform him and he would investigate. She decided then that she would – if only for Sukey's safety and her own peace of mind.

She would speak to him tomorrow.

Tuesday morning

And now it was time for Alex Randall to speak to Alice Sedgewick himself – with her solicitor present. After Talith's descriptions he was curious to meet both of them and determine in his own mind what part Mrs Sedgewick had played in the fate of the infant. He spent the first hour of the day reading through Gethin Roberts's initial statement and the notes made by his sergeant. He read through Talith's comments with approval. He'd wondered about him when he had first joined the force. He had seemed abrasive, not good with the general public. He'd ruffled a few feathers with his lack of subtlety. But every now and again an officer learned his job, acquired unexpectedly good skills and changed to become something of real value to the force. This new sergeant would go far. He had become intelligent and perceptive, had matured as a police officer. Randall noticed as he read through Talith's report that he had a great eye for detail, mentioning the fact that even in her confusion Mrs Sedgewick had remembered to turn the attic light switch off even though she must have left the loft in something of a panic. He smiled as he read through PC Roberts's report. The poor lad had had a shock – not the first – and with a long career ahead of him in the police force it wouldn't be the last either.

The two women arrived promptly at ten. Quite a contrast was DI Randall's first impression. The large, overpowering Mrs Palk and the mouse-like Alice Sedgewick, who looked frankly terrified.

He led them into an interview room and sent for coffee.

'You do understand,' he said, addressing them both, 'that I shall be recording this interview?'

'Yes.' As he had expected Acantha Palk answered for both of them, tossing her thick hair around as she spoke.

The detective studied Alice Sedgewick very carefully while handing them both their coffee, switching the tape on and introducing the 'persons present'. Alice, he decided, was rather a colourless woman. With mouse-brown hair streaked with grey she was neatly and soberly dressed in a dark suit which looked suspiciously like it came from M&S. Her face lacked expression except a certain apprehension in the grey eyes. Her mouth, carelessly outlined in a nasty pink lipstick, which didn't suit her otherwise pale visage, stayed firmly pressed shut whenever she was not speaking as though she was worried what words would escape through them. Her eyes seemed drawn to him but whenever he looked straight at her they quickly flickered away as though she was frightened if they connected for too long he would read something deep within them that she was anxious to keep secret. He found her a disturbing woman.

He glanced at Acantha and again reflected on the sheer contrast between the friends. She was magnetic, her face full of colour, her hair dyed very dark for a woman of her age but it did not make her look haggard or a witch, but merely emphasized her latent power. Had Alice opened up to her or not? How much did she really know about her friend's current predicament?

He glanced again at Alice and fishlike she opened her mouth, as though she wanted to say something but before even a sound was uttered she snapped it closed again. Clamped it shut. He watched her curiously and worked out his line of questioning.

'Right,' he said now the introductions were over. 'Why don't you start by telling me exactly what happened on Saturday evening – before you arrived at the hospital?'

Alice gave a swift, almost panicked, look at her friend but Acantha was not looking at her. She was watching him coolly. Alex Randall met her eyes without flinching and knew she would prove a worthy adversary as, he suspected, she could probably also be a staunch friend in a time of trouble. Staunch enough to lie and deceive for her client?

Possibly.

'I was on my own,' Alice said timidly. 'My husband was away.' She paused. 'On business.'

Now would have been an ideal time to pursue the subject of the missing Mr Sedgewick but Alex let it roll, for now.

'Aaron has been talking about doing a loft conversion so I thought I'd climb up, have a poke around and see what I thought.' She was starting to relax. The muscles around her mouth were loosening and her voice was gaining confidence. 'There are good lights up there but I thought the hot water tank was in the way. It would spoil things. I noticed it was sort of packed around so I started to pull the plaster board and the slats away. Then I saw a tiny bundle.' Her voice was just starting to falter. 'I thought it was some old cloth – wool, wadding or something. But something was *in* it. I shone the torch down and picked it up.' She gave a convulsive shudder. Even her hands shook. Her friend noticed and covered them immediately with her own. 'I knew it was a baby. I could tell that from the feel of it but it reminded me more of the mummies I'd seen in the museum in Cairo, all dried up, bones sticking out. I nearly dropped it. I didn't know what to do with it. I decided I must bring it out of the loft.' Her voice was quickening, the tone rising, threatening hysteria.

Alex prompted her delicately. 'You wrapped it up in . . . ?'

'I had a blanket,' Alice said. 'A little baby's blanket.'

'Where did it come from?'

Alice's face changed again to become secretive. 'I just had it,' she said baldly.

Oh, yes? Alex thought.

The change of tone affected Acantha too. She gave her client a long, questioning stare but said nothing.

Alex thought. Already he was tossing a few points around in his mind. He had seen the blanket. It was no more than a few years old. Alice's children must be well into their twenties.

'Have you grandchildren?' he asked.

Alice shook her head.

So this blanket had not been bought new for them. So for whom? A friend's child? Then why hadn't she given it? He squirreled the questions away. Now was not the time to interrupt. He needed to let Alice Sedgewick roll on without working out too much detail. So he left the question of the blanket, knowing he would return to it later on in the investigation. In such a puzzle he needed an explanation for every single anomaly.

'Do you know anything about the child, Mrs Sedgewick?'

Acantha opened her mouth as though to speak, but said nothing, only giving her friend an encouraging look.

'No,' Alice Sedgewick said.

'You know nothing about a baby being born in your house?'
She shook her head.

'Or anyone who has been to your house who was pregnant?'
'Not that I can think of.'

Acantha Palk spoke. 'Do you know when the child died, inspector?'

'Not exactly. We have a rough time scale.'

He returned to Alice Sedgewick. 'How long have you lived at The Mount?'

'A little over five years.' Which was well within the time line.

'Where did you live before you moved to The Mount?'

'In Shawbury. Aaron was employed by the RAF so we lived there, in the village.'

Alex frowned. 'This was before he went into business?'

Alice looked uneasy. 'I'm not really sure about my husband's business dealings,' she said. 'I only know he does a lot of travelling.' Alice Sedgewick looked positively guilty now.

Unexpectedly this was another fact to be tucked away. Something about her husband's business dealings made Alice very uncomfortable indeed.

Alex consulted his notes again. 'When you were in the hospital and the sergeant took the baby from you, you said the baby's name was Poppy. Why did you assume the child was a girl and where did you get the name, Poppy, from?'

Quite unexpectedly Alice's eyes pooled with tears. She was almost too upset to cry properly. This was sheer, terrible, sniffing misery. Alex looked helplessly at Acantha who was looking equally confused.

'I think we'll have a bit of a break now,' he said, keeping back the ace card that the baby had actually been a little boy. There was no need to tell her – yet.

While they were having a break he thought he'd give Martha a ring. He'd always known that she was more than super-ficially interested in some of the cases which came before her, particularly puzzling ones like this. If she had had her way, he knew that the coroner's role would have included wearing a deerstalker, carrying a magnifying glass and doing part of the investigation herself. In fact he couldn't absolutely swear that on occasions she hadn't done a little sleuthing herself. He'd always had his suspicions that she had met some of the schoolchildren in the Callum Hughes case before they stood in front of her in the court. But he had said nothing.

Martha was sifting through an even bigger pile of paper than usual. A cold January, swine flu and Norovirus had resulted in a doubling of her usual workload. She listened, intrigued, as Alex spoke. 'So you're saying that the name, Poppy, meant something to her?'

'It would seem so.'

'The child she brought into the hospital was a boy,' Martha observed. 'Kind of lets her off the hook rather, doesn't it?'

'I thought that.'

'But you say the name upset her?'

'Without a doubt.'

As she spoke Martha was scribbling herself a list of things to do.

'One,' she wrote, 'find out who Poppy was.'

Underneath she wrote, 'Pink blanket?'

'You think there is a connection between this Poppy and the pink blanket?'

'You're rushing me, Martha,' Alex said and she could tell that he was smiling.

She asked her next question very softly. 'Do you think Poppy is a real child?'

Randall was reluctant to answer but he knew he must. 'Yes.'

'Alive or dead?'

'Dead,' he said.

'Has the husband shown up yet?'

'Not a sign – nor of either of her children. Mrs Sedgewick is having her wish granted that the family be kept out of this.'

'So far,' Martha said. 'Does she have grandchildren?'

'No.'

'Have you asked her why she took a dead child to the hospital?'

'Not yet. That's on my list.'

'How long have they lived there?'

'Five years.'

'Ah.' He could hear the excitement in her voice. 'And do you know who the estate agent was who sold them the property?'

'Martha.' Again she could tell that Alex Randall was smiling. 'Stop telling me my job.'

'Sorry, Alex.' She waited a moment. 'Actually,' she said, 'I was going to ring you today.'

'Yes?'

'I had another of those odd phone calls last night. You know, the "Message to Martha" one?'

'I thought they'd died down.'

'So did I. I hoped they had but it seems someone is still trying to make me uneasy.'

'And does it?'

'Not so much for me, Alex,' she confided. 'I'm made of tough stuff. It's Sukey I worry about. It wouldn't be so bad if Sam lived at home though . . .'

She didn't want to say it yet. Saying it would turn it from a hope to a certainty. And it wasn't.

Alex must have picked up on her reluctance to finish the sentence. He cleared his throat.

'I'll come round later,' he said, 'and talk to you. Is this evening any good?'

'At home?'

'Yes. Is that a problem?'

'No. No. Look – why don't you come to supper? Sam's gone back to Liverpool so I don't have a male to cook for.'

'No,' he said abruptly, almost rudely. 'No. I'll come round after supper if that's all right.'

'Fine,' she said, a little hurt. 'I'll see you later then.'

She wanted to ask him how he was but the opportunity hadn't seemed to have arisen so she said nothing but hung up telling herself he had sounded perfectly well in control.

Her eyes lighted on the framed photograph of Sam that stood on her desk and she smiled. He was so very like Martin. He had the lot, hair that always stuck out, irregular teeth, an absolutely wonderful smile which seemed to encompass all the good things in life. Sam's smile was exactly like his father's, slightly hesitant, tentative, completely open, very, very happy, 100% genuine and complex. Six months ago she had guiltily removed Martin's photograph from her desk and placed it in the drawer. After all these years, she'd had to say goodbye to him as she had to his son only that very morning, and she was still feeling a bit shaken, a bit bereft.

*   *   *

Alex returned to the interview room, thoughtful after the telephone call. He could tell the two women had had a chat, exchanged confidences and he could also sense that Acantha didn't know all yet. Her face still held questions and a certain amount of frustration.

Alex sat down. 'Right,' he said. 'You know, Mrs Sedgewick, that at the moment we're not charging you with anything. We simply want to find out where the baby came from.'

Acantha spoke. 'Was the baby killed or did it die of natural causes?'

Alex responded quickly. 'I can't give you any details yet. All will be made public eventually. Now then. Shall we crack on with just a few more questions?'

'Why were you so upset at the name, Poppy, Mrs Sedgewick?'

She gave an embarrassed laugh. 'I don't know,' she said, fully in control of herself now. 'It sort of brought it all back to me.'

'Brought what exactly?'

Acantha answered for her. 'I would have thought that was obvious. The discovery of the body – the entire incident.' She gave a self-confident smile which probably stood her in good stead in her work as a solicitor but rather irritated the detective.

He continued smoothly. 'I need to know which estate agent you bought the house through.'

'Huntley and Palmers.'

'The name of the people you bought the house from?'

'Mr and Mrs Godfrey. They were moving to Spain, Aaron said. I think they'd made quite a lot of money.'

'Did they have any children?'

'I don't know. I don't remember.'

'Were there children's things around the place when you viewed?'

'I didn't view.' She spoke baldly and with a hint of challenge in her tone.

'You didn't see the house before you bought it?' Alex struggled to keep surprise out of his voice.

'I didn't see the house before my *husband* bought it.'

Practically feudal, Alex thought.

'Did you ever meet Mr and Mrs Godfrey?'

'No.' Said almost sullenly.

'So you've no idea how old they were?'

'Sorry. Obviously no.'

'OK.'

Alex came to a decision. 'One last question and then you can go.'

The look of relief on Alice's face was tangible.

'Why did you take the baby to the hospital rather than simply ringing the police?'

'I don't know.' It was at least an honest answer. 'Instinct, I suppose.'

'Instinct?' It seemed an odd explanation.

'It's where you go when you're in trouble, isn't it?'

It was an explanation – of sorts.

'OK. We'll leave it there. Do you mind if we contact your husband?'

For the first time he saw Alice Sedgewick's smile, the light of humour touching her rather sad eyes. 'That's two questions, inspector,' she said archly. 'But I'll answer. As I've already said I don't want you dragging him back from his business trip. There's no point. There's nothing he can do. However it so happens that he's left a message on the answer phone to say he'll be back tomorrow. You can speak to him then.'

Alex wasn't even tempted to quip that he would look forward to it.

Martha found it hard to concentrate that afternoon. Her mind kept flitting back to the subject of the dead baby. Boy, girl, pink, blue. It had lain there, slowly desiccating over the years. Whose baby was it? Who was its mother? Where was its mother? How had it died? Why had it died? Had it been wanted or unwanted? A teenager's embarrassment? A married woman's shame? How could a baby disappear if the mother had attended antenatal classes? What was the story behind it? Who was Poppy? Another baby? Another dead baby? What was Poppy to Mrs Sedgewick? Why had the name upset her so very much? Why had she driven to the hospital with a dead child? What had really triggered this bizarre action?

Martha felt her face twitch with curiosity.

Somehow she managed to sift through a reasonable amount of paperwork and take a few calls from doctors which would save post-mortems and an overworked team of pathologists including the newly reformed Mark Sullivan. She spoke to some relatives who had concerns about the residential home their mother had died in and promised to look into it. By six she was ready to go home. Her desk was cleared except for one envelope and her stomach was rumbling. Agnetha had promised to cook supper, salmon, new potatoes and a fresh green salad. Martha couldn't wait.

The supper lived up to expectations and a little over an hour later she was sitting across the room speaking to Alex Randall.

As she had surmised from the phone call he appeared a little better than yesterday. Still tense around the mouth but his dark eyes sparkled as he shook hands with her.

She poured them both a drink and he got straight into it.

'This is the first contact your mysterious person has made since . . . ?' He looked up questioningly.

'It's been months, Alex,' she said. 'I haven't heard anything for ages.' She smiled. 'All quiet on the Western Front. But then there was the phone call and today this arrived in my post.'

He studied the typed address on the envelope: *Martha Gunn, Coroner, Coroner's Office, Bayston Hill, Shrewsbury, Shropshire.* No postcode. Then he slipped on a pair of latex gloves and slid the card out. 'It'll have my prints on it,' she said, apologetically. 'I didn't know what it was.'

Alex Randall studied the card. It was the sort of note one might leave on a colleague's desk. 'Martha,' it read, 'please pick up your messages.'

He frowned. 'It has to be someone who has had dealings with you professionally.'

'I thought that. But where would I start? I meet upset relatives, angry relatives, grieving relatives every day of my life. Plenty of them. By the very nature of my job I deal with unexpected tragedy.'

Alex gave one of his oddly attractive, twisted smiles. Even in that there was still some residual sadness. 'I suppose you do, Martha,' he said gently. 'I never really thought about your work like that but it is all about death. And I suppose in the wake of that does come anger and sadness. Have you had anyone blame you for something?'

'I suppose so but I can't think of anyone or anything specific.'

Alex leaned back in his seat. 'Well I can't really justify having you watched, Martha, but we can put a check on your phone calls if you like.'

'That might be an idea but . . . I worry. I'd prefer a phone call to him coming out here. Maybe it's better to . . .'

'I'll ask the patrol cars to drive up here when they go round,' he said eventually. 'No harm in that. We'll keep an eye out for you. I think for now that's the best course of action.' He stood up. 'Keep me informed and if you feel more vulnerable I'll have to reconsider.' He gave a boyish, attractive smile. 'We can't have our coroner under threat.'

She saw him to the door. 'I suppose,' she said as they parted, 'I'm worried this will escalate.'

His eyes were on her and she felt a sudden shock. He had a job to do. She knew that. But the concern in his eyes had been more than that. It had been quite personal.

'Thank you,' she said and held out her hand. He took it but it was less of a formal shaking of hands than a touching. She stood in the doorway and watched until his car tail lights disappeared down the track.

SIX

The day started badly. A snow storm had made Alex Randall late for work. It didn't help matters that as he was hanging up his coat he heard shouting and a blustering, bullying tone from outside his office. Aaron Sedgewick was back and was making his presence felt.

His door was pushed open and a tall, spare man with a hooked nose wearing a crumpled, expensive-looking suit stormed in. 'What the hell is going on?'

Alex faced him, trying to bury the fact that his temper was slowly rising. 'Mr Sedgewick, I presume?' His tone was icily polite. 'I'm the senior investigating officer, Detective Inspector Alex Randall. Why don't you sit down and I can fill you in on the details of the case and your wife's involvement.'

Aaron Sedgewick bumped down suspiciously on the chair, watching Randall through hooded, hostile eyes.

Alex crossed the room to close the door behind them with deliberation, then returned to his chair. 'Right,' he said. 'It'll probably make things easier and save time if you tell me what you already know.'

His calm manner had an effect on Aaron Sedgewick. He looked at Alex with grudging respect, rubbing his thin wrist with bony fingers as though his cuff was chafing him. 'I know that my wife found a dead child in our attic and that she took it to the Royal Shrewsbury Hospital,' he said steadily, 'on Saturday night.'

'Correct.'

'I can't see that this is a crime,' Sedgewick said tightly. 'She didn't do anything except her citizen's duty.'

Alex leaned forward. 'Is your wife under arrest?'

'As I understand it, no.'

'Has she been charged with anything?'

'No.'

He was practically having to squeeze the answers out of

him. 'So what's your problem, Mr Sedgewick? We've merely
been trying to find out who the child is, how it came to its
death and who concealed it in your attic.' He faced the man
with a stony face. 'What else would you expect us to do?'

'Alice does not know anything,' Aaron said with tightly
reined control. 'She does not know.'

'She might not,' Alex returned, 'but there are certain anomalies in her story, small inconsistencies, which have worried
us and which need explaining.'

'Such as?' He barked out the words.

'Mr Sedgewick,' Alex said politely. 'This is an ongoing
police investigation. We need to find out who the child is and
whether your wife has any involvement—'

Aaron Sedgewick practically exploded. He half stood up.
'You cannot believe my wife . . .' His voice trailed away.
Something had caused him to have a sudden loss of confi-
dence. He snapped his mouth shut.

'We simply want the truth,' Alex said sternly, adding more
softly, 'it's imperative.'

Aaron Sedgewick sat back in his chair, his eyes still bulging
with fury, but he had lost some of his bluster.

Alex spoke again. 'I take it you deny any knowledge of
this incident?'

Aaron Sedgewick frowned and nodded. 'Absolutely
nothing,' he said tightly.

'Well. There are a few ways in which you can help us,'
Alex said in a conciliatory tone.

'Such as?'

'I understand that you bought your house around five years
ago?'

'That's correct.' Aaron Sedgewick had recovered some of
his equilibrium. His tone now was sarcastic.

'From a couple called Mr and Mrs Godfrey?'

Sedgewick nodded.

'Tell me about them?'

'They were in their early forties. They'd made a lot of money
and wanted to go and live in Spain. They were nice people.'

'Did they have any children?'

It was obviously something Sedgewick hadn't considered.
'No-o,' he said, 'at least I don't think so. I don't remember
any.'

'Were there toys around the house?'

Sedgewick shook his head. 'Not that I noticed.'

'Were any of the rooms decorated in children's wallpaper?'

Another shake of the head.

'Bikes, prams, pushchairs – anything like that around?'

'No.' Said resolutely. 'At least – not that I remember.'

'And Mrs Godfrey wasn't pregnant?'

'Not noticeably.'

'Right. Do you have a forwarding address for the Godfreys?'

'No.'

'Did any mail come for them?'

'No. I assumed they had made an arrangement with the post office to have their mail redirected. It's what we did. All our dealings were through the estate agent.'

Aaron Sedgewick was calming down.

'Do you know how long they had lived in number 41?'

'Not that long, I got the impression. A couple of years.'

'I don't suppose you know who they had bought the house from?'

'Not a clue.'

'Which estate agent did you use?'

'Huntley and Palmers.' For the first time since he had arrived Aaron Sedgewick smiled, though it was more of a grimace. 'Always reminds me of the biscuit people – you know?'

Alex smiled too 'Did you ever go up into the attic?'

'Once or twice.'

'Obviously you never noticed anything untoward up there?'

'No.'

'No smell?'

'No. I would have investigated if I had had any suspicions that all was not well.'

'Did you do any building work in the attic?'

'No. None.'

Alex decided to spring something on him. 'Does the name Poppy mean anything to you?'

Sedgewick looked bemused. 'No,' he said, 'it doesn't. At least not that I can think of. I don't know anyone called Poppy. What's that got to do with it?'

'Just one of the many lines of enquiry we're pursuing, sir.'

'Oh.' Sedgewick made a further attempt at conciliation. 'Nice name, isn't it?'

'Yes.' Alex paused for a moment. 'You have two children yourself?'

Without warning the blustering, angry man was back. 'What the hell has that got to do with this . . . ?' A pause while he fumbled for the appropriate word. 'Mess,' he finally spat out.

'Just making conversation, sir.' Alex paused. 'Umm grand-children?'

'No. Look.' Aaron Sedgewick was back in control. 'This is obviously to do with some previous occupant of The Mount and nothing to do with us. I understand the child had died some years ago. Probably years before we came to live there.'

'So it would seem, sir.' Alex was polite and non-committal. 'We will, of course, be having a DNA analysis on the child.'

Aaron's face darkened. 'What are you suggesting,' he asked carefully.

Alex kept his cool. 'Nothing, Mr Sedgewick.' He borrowed a phrase straight out of the police handbook. 'I'm merely imparting information.'

Aaron Sedgewick had no response ready. He stood up. 'So if you've quite finished?'

'For now, sir. Thank you.'

'How long will your team be occupying my house?'

'No longer than is necessary. Another day or two – no more.'

'You will leave my family out of this?'

'As far as we can. I can tell you that we shan't bother them unless it proves necessary to the investigation.'

'Then I would prefer it if you would make your approaches through me.'

'If it's reasonable and possible, I will, Mr Sedgewick.'

Sedgewick shot him a suspicious glance and left, scowling.

Alex sat back in his chair. He knew full well that there were still plenty of reasons why the Sedgewick family might continue to be involved but he let it ride – for now.

Wednesday afternoon

PC Gethin Roberts pushed the door open to Huntley and Palmer's estate agent. It was an upmarket place, with smart offices in Market Street, which tended to deal with properties at the upper end of the market – not anywhere that a police

constable could afford. Gethin Roberts hadn't even bothered
scanning the window for anywhere he might like. Out of his
price range. A glamorous receptionist, heavily made up with
thick black eyelashes, bright red lipstick and wearing a white
polo-necked sweater looked at him, registered the uniform,
obviously decided he was not going to buy one of their 'des
reses' and gave him a patronizing smile. 'Can I help you?'
She hesitated, took in his age, and tacked on: 'Constable?'

Gethin Roberts gave a tentative smile. 'We're investigating
some circumstances around the finding of a baby's body in
number 41, The Mount. You may have read something about
it in the local newspaper.'

The receptionist's eyes flickered across him as though she
was far too posh to read a *local* newspaper.

'I don't quite see what that's got to do with us.'

Roberts pressed on. 'I believe you sold the property a few
years ago?'

The receptionist looked confused. 'How long ago?'

'I believe the property sold around five years ago.'

The receptionist's face cleared as though she was off the
hook. 'I wasn't working here then,' she said with obvious
relief. 'You'll have to speak to Mr Palmer.'

'If you wouldn't mind,' Roberts said, with dignity.

'I'll see if he's free.'

'Thank you.'

She was gone for no more than a couple of minutes. 'He'll
see you now,' she said, with no let-up of her patronizing
manner.

Mr Palmer turned out to be a plump, suited man of around
forty, with a pale, unhealthy complexion and a sweating face.
'Constable,' he said, emerging from the area behind the
reception desk. 'What can I do for you?'

Patiently Gethin Roberts repeated his request and wondered
whether Palmer had read the headlines of the local paper and
if he had whether he'd connected the lead story with the
property he'd sold a few years before. If he had why hadn't
he come forward with the information?

Mr Palmer ushered him into his office. 'It'll be more private
in here,' he said holding open the door for him.

'Now then.' He opened a filing cabinet and consulted some
records. '41, The Mount.' He couldn't resist lapsing into estate

agent's spiel. 'Lovely place, well proportioned rooms, dating from the mid Victorian period.' He looked up and registered that Roberts was a police officer – not a potential customer. He cleared his throat. 'Sold five years ago, in 2005, to Mr and Mrs Sedgewick.'

'The vendors?' Roberts asked stolidly.

'A Mr and Mrs Godfrey,' Palmer supplied, adding, 'they were moving abroad. To Spain, I believe. Lucky things.' He peered out through his window at the drifting snowflakes. 'All that sunshine.'

Roberts didn't take up on the comment. One day, he thought, he would be in 'all that sunshine' himself. One day.

'Do you know how long the Godfreys had lived there?'

'I am not party to that information,' Palmer said, washing his hands of the affair. 'I did not act for them buying the property, only selling.'

'Do you know whom they had purchased the property through?' Roberts was proud of the 'whom'. He had studied English language at school and remembered the rules of subject and object and used them frequently.

'No,' Palmer said shortly. 'It would have been on the deeds, of course, but I have no record of them.'

'Do you have an address for the Godfreys?'

For the first time Palmer looked confused. 'Somewhere,' he said, 'I must have a forwarding address.' Panic seemed to be rising. 'I *must* have one,' He leafed through the file then looked up, 'but I don't seem to have it here.'

'If you wouldn't mind looking,' Roberts said.

'Yes – yes – of course. I'll have a more thorough look on my computer records.'

Palmer sat at his desk and started using his mouse to access files. He tapped a few keys and stared into the computer screen. 'Ah,' he said. 'I knew I'd have it somewhere.' He looked up. 'But I may have a bit of a problem. The address I have is of a hotel in Malaga. As far as I remember they were building their own house over there. I seem to remember them talking about it to me. So . . .' He looked up helplessly.

'If you can give me all the details you have.' Roberts was dreaming . . . A trip to Spain, a trip to Spain. Surely he couldn't be so lucky? He was already picturing himself lounging by an azure swimming pool, bright, hot sunshine, lovely girls in skimpy bikinis, him telling them all he was 'pursuing a murder enquiry'. A cross between James Bond and George Smiley.

He came to with a start. Palmer was handing him a computer printout.

'Here you are,' he said, and as though he had read Roberts's mind, he added jovially, 'expect you'll be flying out to Spain, constable.'

Gethin Roberts went bright red.

That afternoon Alex rang Martha and suggested they meet up to discuss the case. 'Why don't you come here, Alex? Jericho can get some sandwiches in. We can have a working lunch.' She chuckled. 'I'm snowed under – in more ways than one.'

'Good idea, Martha. I'll join you at one.'

'Anything you don't eat?'

'Absolutely nothing.'

Jericho didn't look too pleased when Martha said Alex would be joining her for lunch. He had an almost possessive idea of his role in her work and simply hated it when she had one-to-one meetings with anyone. They should all be through him. So he felt doubly aggrieved that the discussion about a case which was provoking considerable interest would exclude him. He harrumphed and bowed his shoulders with resentment. Martha took no notice. She was used to Jericho's ways and the best way to deal with this attitude was to ignore it, as though he was a two-year-old having a tantrum.

Alex arrived late at a quarter past one and quickly apologized. 'What a morning,' he said. 'So many accidents with all this snow and ice. It's bitingly cold out there, Martha.' He gave her a shrewd look accompanied by a warm grin. 'No more messages from your secret admirer, I hope?'

She shook her head. 'He's not an admirer,' she said, 'I'm not sure what he is but he isn't that. But yes, all is quiet and I feel better having discussed it with you so thank you. As a reward,' she tacked on, 'the sandwiches are on me.'

He laughed. 'I accept,' he said, 'although it really isn't necessary.' His eyes were warm. 'It's all in a day's work, you know.'

'Well, thank you anyway,' she said.

To her relief Alex was looking practically his normal self. More relaxed and he seemed happier. She handed him a chicken and bacon sandwich with mayo and took one herself.

'Now then,' she said, when she had taken her first lovely
bite. She hadn't realized how hungry she'd been. 'What was
it that you wanted to discuss with me? Have there been any
developments?'

'No. Not really. It's how far we take this,' Randall said.
'Mark Sullivan thinks the baby's death was probably a tragic
mistake, even that it could have been born dead. Certainly it
didn't survive more than a few hours. We have, of course,
DNA samples so would be able to match the baby to its mother
and its father. However at best we have a manslaughter charge.
Juries are very reluctant to convict on charges of infanticide,
the assumption generally being that the balance of the mother's
mind was temporarily disturbed. There are very few convic-
tions on record. Certainly when the forensic evidence is so
weak. The CPS will probably not want us to proceed.'

She nodded and Alex proceeded to voice his case.

'In spite of Alice Sedgewick's strange behaviour she's out
of the picture really. She's in her early fifties. It's very unlikely
that she would have been pregnant in the last five years. The
people who lived in the house before the Sedgewicks were a
couple called the Godfreys who apparently had no children and
decamped to live in Spain when they sold the house. I can't
see why they would have felt the need to hide a baby. According
to the deeds of The Mount they bought the house in 2002 from
an elderly widow who had lived there before her husband died
for over twenty years.' DI Randall took a gargantuan bite of
his sandwich and chewed it thoughtfully. 'He'd died in the late
eighties so that covers the entire window of opportunity if the
baby had been concealed by the owner of the house.'

Martha listened and Alex Randall continued. 'It's hard to
imagine that an outsider would have had the opportunity to hide
the child in the loft space. So we're left with this collection of
unlikely people or . . .' He screwed up his face. 'Someone
connected with one of those families. It doesn't make a lot of
sense but I should just speak to the Godfreys.'

'Are you suggesting a trip to Spain, Alex,' Martha asked lightly.

Alex grinned at her hopefully.

She regained her seriousness. 'Well, it seems it's either that
or you drop the case, "The police have decided not to pursue
their enquiries" and all that. If you want my professional
opinion you can probably guess it. You should always pursue

the truth. It may be that the only crime is a case of concealment; the why for now a mystery, but it is just possible that
this is a case of infanticide in which case we must pursue it.
We have no option, Alex. Go to Spain. Speak to Mr and
Mrs Godfrey, find out the truth, if you can. In the meantime
there are other questions, aren't there?'

'Such as?'

'You don't need me to spell it out. Alice Sedgewick is a
disturbed woman for some reason of her own. You've come
to that conclusion yourself.'

Alex nodded.

'There is the name Poppy.' She smiled at him. 'Was there
anything else?'

He shook his head. 'Not for now,' he said. 'Thanks for the
advice. And the sandwiches.'

'Thank Jericho,' she said, smiling. 'He got them.'

'I will.' He eased his long bony frame out of the chair,
stood up and shook her hand. 'I owe you the same back,' he
said. 'Lunch, some time?'

'That would be nice,' she said carefully.

He gave her a smile. And then he was gone.

She was busy all afternoon. The parents of a woman who
had committed suicide wanted to speak to her. They were
upset and disturbed, a devoutly Christian couple to whom
suicide was a mortal sin. She told them to seek reassurance
from their priest but they wanted something she couldn't give
them – an assurance that their daughter had not committed
suicide when she had left a note stating her intention. She
could not lie to them even if it might make them feel
temporarily better. The interview took far longer than she
would have imagined. They had all sorts of questions to ask
her and plenty of issues for her to deal with too. She had just
ushered them out of the door when Jericho rang to say that
a body had been fished out of the river from under the ice
and the police surgeon wished to speak to her. Not Delyth
Fontaine but one of her colleagues.

She spoke to Richard Tamar, the police surgeon in question, and authorized movement of the body and a post-mortem.

Death, she thought. Her work was always to be in that position, sitting on the shoulders of the Angel of Death, trying to
form order out of disorder, trying to make some sense of it all.

For one brief moment she allowed herself to dream the completely impossible, that she was on that flight to Spain, wearing scarlet espadrilles and a floating, white cotton dress, plastering her arms with factor 30, in deference to her pale skin and red hair, wearing a large straw hat and armed with paperbacks. Adventures and romances. It seemed years since she had had a holiday like that.

She stared out of the window at the gloomy arctic landscape. Maybe, she thought, she and Sukey and even Sam if he could, would embark on such a holiday soon. Time to look at the brochures.

She was glad to finish work that day and drive home on salted and gritted roads.

Last month she had bought a lovely black dress with a single silver strap on the shoulder but she hadn't worn it yet. It had been too cold over Christmas to wear an off-the-shoulder dress. It was still cold but Simon Pendlebury was a man who appreciated women dressing up and invariably made some comment on her appearance, so she decided to christen the new dress tonight. As she brushed her hair, unruly as ever, coppery highlights looking fearsomely red, she reflected that since Simon's wife, Evelyn, had died, they had become quite good friends. She enjoyed their occasional dinners together. They were infrequent and emotionally undemanding but she knew he respected her opinion and she enjoyed his company for an evening without either of them expecting it to lead anywhere else. So why the note of desperation in his voice when he had rung on Sunday morning?

Well, she thought, she'd find out soon enough.

Sam rang at seven, jubilant because he'd been pronounced fit to play again. She wanted to ask him if he'd heard anything about the Stoke deal but held her tongue, simply congratulating him and saying she was glad that he was playing again.

She left Agnetha and Sukey watching *High School Musical* – yet again – and drove into the town.

There was little traffic around because of the inclement weather. People were staying indoors. She drove gingerly over roads with their treacherous black icy sheen and headed towards Drapers' Hall.

It was one of her favourite places to eat and that wasn't just because of the food. It was the ambience of the place, the interior of the sixteenth-century hall, one of the oldest if not *the* oldest building in a town that was predominantly medieval. Inside was no disappointment. It was panelled, furnished with genuine antiques and ancient portraits on the walls.

Simon was there before her. She saw his Lexus LS already parked and manoeuvred her Audi behind it. Even with the fur wrap she shivered crossing the road. He was waiting for her in the vestibule, a tall, dark-haired man, slim and very elegant in a dark suit. Martin and Simon had been flatmates briefly when they had been students together which was how she had known him and his wife, Evelyn. She and Martin had had many discussions about Simon's strong and devious personality, but they had never worked out how he could have made so much money in a few short years. Evelyn herself, when she had been alive, had never made any comment about their finances. She had kept dumb about their lovely house with acres of woodland and trout fishing pool, their succession of top-of-the-range cars and school fees amounting to tens of thousands of pounds for their two daughters. In fact, Martha had sensed that even Evelyn did not quite trust her husband who was blessed with a sort of roguish confidence as well as a dark secrecy. During the drive into town she had tried guessing at what was causing Simon Pendlebury such tensions and had finally decided on some subversive financial problem. Though why he would want to speak to her on such matters she couldn't even guess. She was in for a surprise. As he bent to kiss her cheek she sensed something very different about him. He'd lost some weight and a little of his confidence. In fact he was slightly nervous, his top lip beaded with moisture. She studied him. This was most unlike the Simon Pendlebury she had known for years. Curious, she sat down and watched him as he fetched her a gin from the bar. As he set it down on the table, next to his glass of white wine, she noticed his hand was shaking.

'Simon,' she said, covering it with her own, leaning forward, concerned. 'Something's wrong, isn't it? Whatever is it?'

He sat opposite her, hardly meeting her eyes but looking downwards. 'You're going to think me such a fool, Martha,' he said. 'Such a bloody idiot. I'm so angry with myself. Evie would have been . . .'

'What on earth have you done?'

He ran his fingers through his hair. 'Let's order first,' he said.

'Fine.'

She could hardly concentrate on the menu, good though it was. The truth was she was seriously worried. Evelyn Pendlebury and she had been very good friends for a long time, right up until Evie's death. Evie had been kind to her after Martin's death, inviting her round over the long weekends that seemed to stretch so far into the distance. When Evie had known she was dying she had more or less asked Martha to keep an eye on her husband.

Martha waited.

They ate their first course hardly speaking, which again was unusual for Simon. He was a natural talker with a wide variety of topics to keep the conversation flowing but tonight he made no effort. He didn't even comment on her new dress – a first for him. He was polite but distracted.

He waited until they were eating their main course before speaking.

His eyes shifted around the room then landed on Martha. 'I've fallen in love,' he said simply.

She was tempted to laugh. 'Is that all?' she said. 'That's good. A happy thing.' Her eyes found his and she wondered. 'Isn't it?'

'Yes and no,' he said. 'Martha, I'm in my late forties. Christabel is twenty-three years old. She works for me. She's a secretary for the firm.'

'That is quite an age gap,' she agreed. 'But doesn't love conquer all?'

For the first time that night Simon gave her one of his rare smiles. 'No,' he said. 'Not all. Armenia and Jocasta are absolutely furious. They're calling her a gold-digger and all sorts of names. It's tearing me apart.'

She was watching his face. 'There's something more to this than simply a man falling for a woman young enough to be his daughter, isn't there?'

He nodded. 'I'm frightened that they're right,' he admitted.

Martha waited.

'It's hard to say this without sounding a snob but she doesn't come from the best of backgrounds. Her father's in prison for a violent robbery. Her mother – well it's hard to know, but just let's say that Chrissie has never had any money and I think possibly she *is* a bit dazzled by the trappings of wealth.'

Martha was watching him carefully.

'The thing is,' he said, 'I don't care. I think it's that that terrifies me. I don't care if she's just professing love for me out of greed or avarice and I don't care that my beloved daughters loathe her. Nothing seems to matter any more except the time I spend with her.'

Now she was worried. 'You *have* got it bad, haven't you?'

'Yes. I wasn't like this with Evie.' His eyes held mute appeal. 'What's happening to me, Martha?'

'I don't know,' she said. 'I don't have a whole lot of experience with stuff like this. I suppose most people would call it infatuation.' She reached out and touched his hand again to soften her words. 'Forgive me but it sounds like a middle-aged man having a crisis. Have the girls actually met her?'

He shook his head.

'You've set up a meeting?'

'Yes, though goodness knows what I expect to achieve through it. The girls have quite made up their minds. I don't even know if it's fair to expose Chrissie to their spite.'

Martha was shocked to hear Simon reject his daughters in this way. They'd lost their mother. He was their only living parent. She didn't know how to tackle this without alienating Simon herself.

'Simon,' she said slowly, 'it's very early days yet. I mean . . .' She searched for something to say. 'Evie's only been dead for a year.'

'And ill for three years before that.'

She nodded, unhappy to cross this boundary into her friends' personal lives.

Simon's dark eyes met hers, appealing for her to understand this. 'It isn't just sex, Martha. It's having someone young, someone light, happy, cheerful, healthy, beautiful to do things with. So alive. As you say poor Evie was ill. I can hardly remember her well any more. Only the shell of the woman she was.'

'Simon,' Martha said tentatively, sensing something else now, 'what do you want from me?'

'I want to marry Chrissie,' he said, 'and I want the girls to accept her. They'll listen to you. Talk to them – please?'

'Why rush into marriage, Simon?'

'Because I want to,' he said simply. 'I love her and I want to be married to her. Please speak to the girls or they will lose me.' She caught the set of his jaw and knew he spoke no more or less than the truth. At the same time she felt a traitor to her once best friend. Evie would have been desperately unhappy at this turn of events but she must help – do what she could.

'I will,' she said, 'if you really want me to but it won't do any good. I know your daughters, Simon. They take after you. They're determined and stubborn. They're very strong characters.'

'Please,' he said. 'Meet Chrissie for yourself. Make up your own mind.'

She reached out and touched his hand. 'Not that it will make any difference to you?'

'No.'

'And then?'

'Speak to Armenia and Jocasta.'

'And if I think Chrissie is what *they* think?'

He smiled then. 'I can't ask you to lie for me.' He hesitated, frowning. 'I suppose,' he said finally, 'what I'm asking you to do.' He looked straight at her. 'I've been lucky in business and I've shown some very perceptive judgements. I suppose . . .' He laughed for the first time that evening. 'What I'm really asking is for you to check her out. I do trust your judgement, Martha. And I think you're fair. I want to know. Am I being a complete fool? Have I lost all sense and reason?'

'You think I can judge that on a brief meeting?'

'I don't know what else to do,' he said simply, 'or who else to trust.'

So now as well as the problem of the newborn infant Martha had this complicated and potentially tragic case to consider and she didn't know whether she was up to it.

She simply stared at Simon. 'All right,' she said.

SEVEN

Thursday

Roddie Hughes and his team were still working their way slowly through the house, much to the irritation of both Alice and Aaron Sedgewick. They made no secret of the fact that they hated them being there but Hughes refused to be hurried. He was a thorough man and knew his job – inside out – and the Sedgewicks could go to hell and back for all he cared. They were not going to deflect him from his job. If there was forensic evidence in this house, which might lead to the truth behind the baby's death, he was going to find it. Once he'd left the property the opportunity would be gone. There was no returning and checking, rechecking. Forensic evidence would be lost or discredited and whatever the finding of the post-mortem, Hughes knew that the house in general and the attic in particular was a crime scene so he was leaving no stone unturned.

It was in one of the upstairs bedrooms, a room that he'd left until almost last, and had planned for the most cursory of examinations, that he made an interesting and unexpected discovery.

Aaron Sedgewick was hovering at the door, watching him resentfully as Hughes stepped inside. The two men looked at each other and for the first time Roddie Hughes wondered what Aaron Sedgewick's role was in this case. As the two men sized each other up, Roddie started to believe that Sedgewick knew a little more than he'd been letting on. He was somehow involved in the baby that had turned up at the hospital on Saturday night. How, even Hughes's mind couldn't work out except there was something. He could read it in the man's eyes. Some sorrow, some duplicity. Something. Guilt?

He spoke first, after he had glanced briefly around the room. 'This looks like a children's room, Mr Sedgewick. Was it *your* children's room?'

'No,' Aaron said shortly. 'As you've probably realized my

son and daughter are in their twenties. We've been here for five years. Ergo,' he continued, 'they didn't live here as children.' He turned on his heel and left, muttering something down the hallway about interfering busybodies and why couldn't they just be left alone?

Hughes glanced around the room again. OK, so why had this room, which looked as though it had been repapered in the last few years, been decorated for children?

Puzzled, Roddie used his mobile to call Alex Randall.

Randall listened without interrupting. When Hughes had finished he finally spoke. 'That's interesting,' he said. 'Very interesting. I'll be round in an hour or so.'

Alex Randall sat for a moment, thinking, then he picked up the phone and dialled the coroner's number. Jericho answered and did his best to wheedle the information out of the detective. But Alex wasn't playing and asked to speak directly to Martha.

'She is in, inspector,' he said disapprovingly, 'but she's very, very busy. The snow and all that.'

'Yes, but I'd like to speak to her, please.'

Jericho was being at his most intransigent. 'If you'd just like to tell me what it is, inspector, I can decide whether to interrupt her work.' While smiling at Palfreyman's Shropshire burr Alex was losing patience.

'Will you just tell her that we've something of interest at the Sedgewick household,' Alex said. 'She might like to come and take a look.'

'I'll see,' Jericho Palfreyman said pompously.

Two minutes later Martha's voice came on the phone and instantly he could hear the suppressed humour. 'Finally got past Jericho, Alex?'

He chuckled. 'Yes.'

'Now what's all this about?'

He related Roddie Hughes's discovery of a children's room and instantly sensed her interest.

'Do you know, Martha,' he said, knowing he was playing right into her hands, 'I think you should come round and take a look for yourself.'

'Why?'

He laughed. 'You'll think I'm soft-soaping you or sucking

up but it's more to do with a woman's intuition.' Martha
almost groaned. After Simon's embarrassing revelation last
night women's intuition was not something she wanted to lay
claim to.

But she couldn't help herself. Her curiosity was overwhelming. 'Go on, Alex.'

'I just want your take on the situation. Besides –' he was
smiling as he pictured her face, eager and inquisitive – 'it'd
be a good opportunity for you to meet Alice Sedgewick
yourself.'

'But you believe she had nothing to do with the baby she
took to the hospital?'

'I know, Martha, but there's something there. I may not be
able to put my finger on it,' Alex insisted, 'but it's there all
right, deceit, concealment, something.' He knew full well that
her curiosity would get the better of her.

He was proved right. After the briefest of pauses Martha
responded. 'OK. I'll be ready in a quarter of an hour?'

'Thanks. I'll come round and pick you up.'

She looked at the piles of notes waiting for her attention
and sighed. She shouldn't really be playing hookey. But she
was very poor at simply sitting at a desk and working, hour
after hour. Periodically she needed to leave it simply to
maintain her concentration.

Twenty minutes later, through the window, she saw Alex's
car slide in beside hers and didn't wait for him to run the
gauntlet of Jericho again but went downstairs to meet him.

'I thought you'd be in Spain by now,' she jibed as she
climbed in beside him.

'I've asked the Malaga Guardia Civil to see if they can find
a location for the Godfreys,' he said. 'I thought I'd better start
there otherwise it could be a wild goose chase. They might
be anywhere. All Roberts got out of Huntley and Palmers was
a hotel address from five years ago. Apparently they were
building their own villa. At first the Spanish police weren't
too helpful but when I told them it was a case of a dead child
they were full of sympathy and anxious to help. You know
what the Spanish are like about children,' he added.

The throwaway comment brought a bitter pang to Martha.
She and Martin had gone to Spain for a quiet, sunny week,
early in March, years ago, when the twins had been almost

one year old. She remembered the twin buggy and the scores of people who had stopped them to pore over the babies and tell them that in Spain twins were very, very lucky. *Mucho mucho afortunado.*

'I have to say,' she said as they drove around the ring road, 'quite apart from anything else I'm very curious to meet Alice Sedgewick after all I've heard about her. She sounds so odd.'

'Well,' he said, pulling up, 'your wish will be granted in minutes.'

The house was as she'd imagined it, helped enormously by having seen the picture in the newspapers. Once the reporters had sniffed out every available detail they had wasted no time filling their pages with the case. A photograph of the house, looking mysterious in the snow, had taken up a quarter of the front page of the *Shropshire Star.*

Number 41 was a stately, Victorian, mock-Tudor place, detached, with a short drive which led to a gravelled area right at the front. Two cars stood there and a large white forensic van.

Alex gave her a swift glance just before he raised his hand to the knocker. 'Don't expect Aaron Sedgewick to give you an easy time,' he warned.

The door, however, was answered by Alice who looked even more wary than usual. 'He's upstairs,' she said, presumably meaning the SOCO team rather than her husband. Martha decided she should introduce herself.

'I'm Martha Gunn,' she said in her precise voice. 'I'm the coroner for this part of Shropshire. It's my job to investigate the death of the child you brought to the hospital on Saturday night, Mrs Sedgewick. Inspector Randall thought it might be helpful if I came to the house to see where the baby was found.'

Alice regarded her silently for a moment then nodded, a sad smile contorting her face. 'I don't suppose I've much choice,' she said flatly. 'I'm learning that.'

Martha didn't answer the obvious but smiled and shook her hand.

Roddie Hughes was waiting for them upstairs. He greeted Martha warmly. They'd met before and worked on more than one case together. 'Before you go up to the loft,' he said, 'I just thought you might like to take a look in one of the bedrooms.'

They followed him through the open door and immediately saw what he meant. It was a small, square room, bright and sunny but with the chill of a room which is used infrequently – if at all. It was prettily papered in pale yellow with sprigs of lilac. It was a child's room. There was a single bed in the centre. But what drew the eye was a beautiful doll's house standing on a painted chest of drawers. It was a fine Georgian place, almost four feet high, three-storeyed, with sash windows. Over the front door was painted its name – *Poppy's House*.

Confused, Martha glanced at Alex and saw that he was as surprised as she was.

Roddie Hughes spoke. 'I found a couple more baby's blankets and other such stuff in here,' he said, pulling open the top drawer of the chest. 'I'd lay a bet this is where she pulled the little blanket from. There's more stuff. Toys and things, a rattle. It's as though she decorated the room ready for a child.'

The three of them looked at each other. *A child?*

Roddie frowned and scratched the side of his mouth. 'Funny thing is,' he said, 'there's lots of pictures of her kids, growing up around the place, but I can't see any sign of the dolls house in them. This room was done up recently, four, five years ago, probably not long after they moved here.'

'And there are no grandchildren,' Alex said. Something twigged at the back of his mind. He had asked Aaron Sedgewick when they had moved in to number 41 whether any of the rooms had been decorated ready for a child. At the time he had been exploring whether the Godfreys had had children. Sedgewick had replied no. But this room was patently a child's room. The Sedgewicks had only lived here for five years. So this room had been decorated *by them* for a child. Which child? Who was the child?

Back came the answer, whispering into his consciousness, clear as sunlight. *The child is Poppy.*

Was it possible then that Mark Sullivan had made a mistake about the age of the mummified baby? Was it after all connected with the Sedgewicks?

Randall had to force himself to recall. Mark Sullivan might have been a year or two out on the age of the child's body but no one could possibly be mistaken as to its sex. The child who had been found in the attic had been a little boy. Not Poppy.

Another unbidden answer swam into his mind. *Then Poppy is someone else. Somewhere else.* So now there were two children. Poppy and the little boy.

They heard a sound in the doorway. Alice Sedgewick was watching them. 'What are you doing in here,' she asked steadily.

Alex spoke for them all. 'We wondered where the blanket that you had wrapped around the child had come from. Mr Hughes here was under instruction to investigate.'

'Why didn't you simply ask me?'

Randall swallowed. It was always the simplest of questions that tripped him up. 'I don't know,' he said, trying to laugh it off. 'For some reason I didn't think of that.'

Alice said nothing but eyed them warily.

Martha broke the silence, stepping towards the doll's house. 'This is lovely,' she said. 'How old is it?'

'Only a few years. It's a hobby of mine. There's a shop that sells doll's houses in Shrewsbury. They also sell all the little bits and pieces to go inside. I enjoy decorating them.' She looked up apologetically. 'Aaron calls it "playing with dolls". He thinks it's incredibly childish.' She gave a smile which was both naive and confiding at the same time.

'Did you decorate this room?'

Alice Sedgewick nodded. 'When I was a little girl I had my grandmother's doll's house. It had been made out of an orange box. It wasn't nearly as fine as this. But it had genuine Victorian pieces in it.' Alice smiled to herself, a smile both dreamy and vague.

'It had a tiny dining table and chairs, even some plaster of Paris hams and food. Bread. A dresser.' She smiled. 'An upright piano. In the nursery,' she said, 'were some dolls. They were stiff, porcelain, made of one piece, no separate limbs.' She looked up. 'They're called Frozen Charlottes. Actually the name comes from a poem, I found out. An American poem about a girl who froze to death on her way to a party because she was too vain to wear a woollen shawl.' She smiled. 'So there you are. Frozen Charlotte. It reminded me.' Her eyes met Martha's. 'The child I took into the hospital was that way. Stiff. No limbs. Lifeless. Look . . .'

She slipped the catch at the side of the doll's house and opened the door, which was actually the entire front wall.

Inside was divided into six rooms. There was a staircase which led from the ground floor right to the top. It was quite exquisite. The furniture inside looked old but might easily have been reproduction. Alice Sedgewick drew a tiny porcelain doll from the cot in what looked like the nursery, rocking horse, toy bricks, a train with four carriages, an abacus. The doll was an inch long, moulded in one piece, naked, of white porcelain with painted black hair, spots of blue for her eyes, a thin red line for her mouth. She placed the doll in Martha's palm and gave her a long hard look. 'Frozen Charlotte,' she said.

There was something in that look, as though Alice was trying to tell her something. The trouble was that Martha didn't have a clue what this rather strange woman was trying to convey. 'Alice,' she said, 'who is Poppy? Why did you call the house "Poppy's House"?'

Alice's face changed. In the space of minutes it turned from cunning to upset to unhappy. She was at the same time Lady Macbeth and tragedy personified. Villain and victim. Tears spilled down her cheeks and then Aaron Sedgewick was standing in the doorway. 'Look what you've done,' he said furiously. 'Just look – what – you've done.' He wrapped his arms around his wife and left the room.

The three of them looked at one another, no nearer understanding what they'd just seen.

'I think I'd better speak to Mark Sullivan again,' Martha said.

'But first, shall I take a look in the attic?'

They ascended by the ladder.

The site was well lit by naked electric lights suspended at intervals from the joists. Roddie Hughes pointed out the planking around the hot water tank and the floorboards. 'They don't look as if they've been disturbed for years,' he said, 'which fits in with Dr Sullivan's theory.'

'But not with the way Alice Sedgewick is behaving,' Martha observed. 'She is recalling something more recent and personal.' Neither Alex nor Hughes made a comment yet Martha felt they did not disagree with her, only that they had no comment to make.

She looked around her for some clue, some idea. 'Alex,' she said, 'do you think it's a bit of a flimsy story, this business of the tank being in the way of the loft conversion?'

He glanced around. 'Not really,' he said. 'It does sort of stick out in the centre a bit. I mean if it wasn't there you'd have a huge clear area. Enough for a couple of bedrooms and *en suites*. If that was what you wanted.'

'Mmm,' she responded. 'Anything else up here?'

'Not really.' Roddie Hughes stepped back towards the loft access and the retractable ladder.

Apart from the signs of the SOCO team there was little else of interest on the top floor but she was glad she'd taken a look.

It was as she was descending the ladder that ideas began to take shape. Sergeant Paul Talith had said something about Alice switching the electric light back on when he had taken her upstairs to show him where the baby's body had been. From Talith's statement, most of which had been relayed to her by Alex, Alice had left the house with the child's body and not returned until the following morning, when she had been accompanied both by her friend and, more importantly, Sergeant Paul Talith.

As she descended the ladder, Martha noticed that she was having to use both hands to cling on to the frame of it. No mean feat if she'd also been carrying a dead baby. And then to be practical and lucid enough to attend to that one small detail of switching off the light? Something else struck her. When the baby had been found, it had been wrapped in a tattered woollen blanket which, according to the SOCO's report, had been recovered from here, in the loft. So Alice had unwrapped the body which had underneath been naked. Surely she must have seen that it was a boy, not a girl? Why this insistence that the baby was a girl? Where had the name Poppy come from? Had it come from the doll's house or had Alice put the name on the house because of some other child?

While Alex was driving her back to her office Martha relayed all these thoughts to him.

'I'll need to speak to Mark again,' she said, 'check up on the age of the corpse. See how flexible he can be but I agree with Roddie. The planking Alice removed did look years old. At least five years.' She frowned as she left the car and was still frowning as she climbed the stairs to her office.

Jericho was ready with some coffee, having watched the

police car turn around on the gravelled drive. 'I'll have it in my office. Thanks,' she said. 'I've a call to make.'

Sullivan sounded just as jaunty as when she had last seen him and responded quickly to her questions.

'Are you sure that the baby has been dead for more than five years?'

'Well – yes. The condition of the child indicated this, together with the condition of the blanket, which was tattered and fragmented. Roddie Hughes brought in a piece of the planking which encased the tank. There were rust spots around some of the nail heads. No, Martha,' he continued, 'I stick to my guns. I think the body had been sealed up in a warm, dry atmosphere for years – maybe as many as eight years but certainly more than five.'

'Is it possible,' she asked delicately, 'that the baby was moved in that time? Could it be that when the Sedgewicks came to live in number 41 that she or her husband brought the body with them?'

Mark Sullivan thought for a minute or two before answering. 'Unlikely,' he said. 'Not impossible but unlikely. They would have had to mimic the exact conditions in which the child had been held for the previous five or so years. Besides that, Roddie Hughes showed me the photographs of the planking around the child. There's no evidence that it's ever been removed and then replaced.' There was a pause while Sullivan gathered his thoughts together.

'As I see it,' he said firmly, 'the most likely scenario is that the baby died almost at the point of birth, whether from natural causes or not is too difficult to tell as the state of decomposition is far too advanced to ascertain. If you want,' he said slowly, 'I could come over but it's getting late and . . .'

'No thanks, Mark,' she said. 'It's all right. I've got someone coming round to the house at six so I can't be late. I'm having the study decorated. He's calling in to give me a quote.'

'OK, I'll be in touch. Just get back to me if you have any more questions.'

She put the phone down and fiddled with her pen. This case was proving quite a puzzle. But Sullivan appeared adamant that the child's body was more than five years old and hadn't been moved from the time when it was initially sealed up by the water tank in the loft of number 41. That let the Sedgewicks right off the hook. Had this happened a year or two ago when Sullivan had been drinking heavily she might have suspected he had made a mistake in his conclusion, but this new, sober Mark, was a different person. She didn't think he was likely to make errors at all.

She pulled up outside the White House at ten to six. Just a few minutes later Agnetha was showing in a man in his forties wearing low slung jeans. He had a mop of curly brown hair and an impish grin and was no more than five feet four inches tall. He held out a gnarled hand. 'Tony Pye,' he said. 'You must be Mrs Gunn. I've heard a lot about you from Jericho. We're friends. Drink at the same pub.'

'Right.' Martha swallowed a smile at the thought of Jericho Palfreyman and Tony sharing a couple of pints down at the local. She could just imagine Jericho leaking the latest drama that he was supposed to keep secret.

Incorrigible.

'Shall we look at the room?'

Tony took a long, critical look at the half-painted walls, the thick layer of gloss paint on the skirting board, the moulded ceiling, the French windows, the splashes of paint on the floor where she and Sam had finally given up the effort. He gave his verdict: 'Lovely room. What exactly did you have in mind?' Like Jericho he was another one with a pleasant Shropshire burr. Shrewsbury born and bred.

'Plain emulsioned walls, the skirting board and ceiling stripped and repainted.'

'Did you want to get the paint yourself?'

'I know the colour I have in mind. A sort of jersey cream with sage walls.'

'I can get you a couple of shade cards,' he said. 'I'll drop them off. Much cheaper if I get the paint.' He grinned. 'I get it trade price.'

'Well that's that then,' she said. 'How much?'

She'd already decided that he was going to do it.

He gave her a price roughly what she'd had in mind.

'And when can you start?'

'Next week.'

EIGHT

Friday

Alex wanted to put some questions to Alice Sedgewick alone. He didn't want her husband aggressively taking over the entire interview, threatening and generally being obstructive. He wanted to get to the bottom of the entire affair and quickly but, like most experienced detectives, Alex Randall knew that investigations could and would not be hurried. The facts would tease themselves out bit by bit.

He had a think about how best to solve this problem and finally decided to ring Acantha Palk and request that she bring her client down to the station.

'We'll only keep her an hour or so,' he said. 'I just want to ask her a few questions. Clarify a couple of points. That's all.' He kept his voice deliberately casual.

She agreed readily and Alex gained the impression that she was as curious as he was to get to the bottom of this very odd affair, which involved her friend.

They arrived at ten and Alex quickly realized something else. Right in front of his eyes Alice Sedgewick was changing. Morphing into something else. Today she was wearing a very smart tweed woollen suit with high-heeled boots and looked more confident than he had seen her before. It was as though she was plucking some inner strength from deep within her own resources.

'Inspector,' she said with a warm smile, holding out her hand.

Acantha Palk too greeted him with smiling confidence.

The two women had patently come to some sort of agreement, an impasse, he decided.

He addressed Alice. 'I hope you don't mind, Mrs Sedgewick, but I'd like to clear up one or two things that are puzzling me.'

She appeared quite composed. She leaned forward. 'But you do acknowledge, inspector, that I can have had nothing to do with the death of that little baby?'

Randall was prepared. 'It would seem so,' he said cautiously.

Alice Sedgewick leaned back in her chair. 'Good,' she said. 'I very much wanted to clear that up.'

'Quite,' Alex said. 'But nevertheless the discovery made you do certain things.'

Instantly Alice looked wary. She gave a swift glance at her friend. Alex continued smoothly. 'You undressed the baby.'

'No, I didn't,' Alice insisted. 'The baby was wrapped in a shawl. It was in tatters. As I pulled it out the shawl simply fell away.'

Acantha Palk gave him a triumphant look.

'You didn't notice what sex the child was?'

Alice shook her head slowly. 'I can tell you, inspector, that was the last thing on my mind.'

It was a reasonable answer.

Acantha's fine eyes were fixed on his face. She was trying to read whether the detective believed her client or not.

Alex kept his face impassive. 'Mrs Sedgewick,' he said. 'Who is Poppy?'

She didn't even hesitate. 'My grandmother. Didn't I tell you that? I meant to. My grandmother was named Poppy Eastley.'

Acantha gave her a friend a startled look.

Alex ploughed on. 'Why did you call the *child* Poppy?'

The evasive look was back. Alice Sedgewick's mouth opened a little. Her eyes dropped to the floor, flickering from side to side. 'I'm not sure,' she said uncertainly. Then, from somewhere, she found an answer. 'The baby, so stiff and still, limbs stuck together,' she said, 'reminded me of the dolls in the doll's houses. The Frozen Charlottes. Poppy's House.'

She didn't even expect to be believed, Alex thought with a shock.

'Is there anything else, inspector?' Acantha Palk asked with icy politeness.

'Yes,' he said, looking not at the solicitor but at Alice. 'I wonder if you'd mind,' he said, with formal politeness, 'going through the events of last Saturday night?'

She looked startled. 'Again? Why?'

Alex leaned forward. 'It's surprising,' he said, in a friendly manner, 'how often one forgets a small detail, the sort of detail which appears insignificant. Unimportant. Sometimes, just sometimes –' he gave her a pleasant, bland smile – 'that little detail –' he held up his forefinger and thumb in a pincer movement – 'can be the very one which cracks the case.'

Acantha Palk looked guarded and suspicious. 'Is this really necessary, inspector? Isn't it simply going to cause Mrs Sedgewick further suffering?'

Alex held up his hand. 'Humour me, Mrs Palk.'

Acantha Palk folded her arms and raised no more objections.

'Take it from about – say – six o'clock?'

'Well – I had some tea.'

Randall didn't interrupt.

'Just one of those nasty supermarket takeaways,' she continued, speaking very quickly now. 'I was going to watch the TV but it was all celebrity dancing and stuff like that. The films were rubbish. I'd seen them all before – the ones I wanted to, anyway. I got fidgety. So I poured myself a glass of wine and tried to settle down to a book.' She looked straight at him and continued in the quick, breathless voice. 'It was a thriller but I couldn't get into that either. So I started drawing plans for the loft conversion.' She met his eyes, challenging him. 'The trouble was that however I tried to draw the plans the hot water tank kept getting in the way and I couldn't see where else it could go in the house. I didn't want to move it down to the bathroom and the place is too big for one of those Combi-boilers. I wanted the extra guest rooms to have their own bathrooms and I wondered if I could have a sewing room up there too.' She looked at him carefully and pressed on with her story. Because Alex felt that it was that – a story. 'Just for curtains and cushion covers and things. I also wondered exactly how the staircase would fit in so I thought I'd go up and measure etcetera.' Again she smiled. 'I hate going up that metallic extending ladder. I hate the noise, you know, and never quite feel safe on it.'

Particularly clutching a dead infant, Alex thought.

'But I managed it with a tape measure and stuff and I started writing down the measurements but the wretched tank was always in the way and I couldn't understand why it had been boarded in like that. I mean it wasn't as though I could use it as an airing cupboard. Tanks these days are really well insulated. It seemed unnecessary, so I started pulling the planking off. Then I found what I thought was wadding and pulled at that too. It all seemed pretty old to me. Then I felt something hard, papery, dry and then I pulled it out.' Her hands flew up to her face. 'I didn't know what it was, at first, inspector. I thought it might be a dead cat or something. Then I realized.' She gave a convulsive shudder. 'I felt little legs. A head. It was horrible, inspector, horrible. The blanket fell away. Then I could see it was a baby. I didn't know what to do with it. So I brought it down the ladder.'

For the first time, Alex interrupted. 'You switched the light off?'

She hadn't expected this. 'Sorry?' she said politely.

'Did you switch the light off or was there somebody else in the house that night or the following morning?'

She frowned. 'I was on my own,' she said.

'So the light?'

'I don't know. I haven't a clue whether I switched the light off. I was just holding this . . .' She gave another shudder. 'Thing in my arms and . . .'

Alex waited.

'I went into . . .' She stopped herself. 'I went into one of the bedrooms and found a little blanket to wrap the baby in. And then I drove.' She closed her eyes. 'I drove and drove and then I saw the sign to the hospital A&E in red. I just went in there. I thought they would know what to do.'

'OK,' Alex said, 'but once there?'

'I just sat.'

Alex thought quickly. 'Where did you live before you moved to The Mount?'

'Bayston Hill.'

It was a suburb off the A49 to the south of Shrewsbury, just outside the ring road. 'The address, please?'

Acantha Palk looked as though she was about to raise another objection but she settled back in her seat without interrupting.

Alice gave the address and Alex thanked her.

'You haven't really explained,' he said, scratching the top of his head, 'why you named the child apparently after your grandmother.'

Alice Sedgewick shrugged and gave him an endearing smile,

offering him no further explanation at all. She met his eyes with sharp intelligence and he knew that she was aware of this too.

'Are there any more questions,' Acantha Palk asked crisply.

'Only one.'

Both women waited. 'You don't have any grandchildren, Mrs Sedgewick, do you?'

'No. My daughter is a career woman and Gregory . . . Well – Gregory's gay, so it's pretty unlikely.'

'Do any children come and stay with you? Nephews, nieces, children or friends' children?'

She stared at him. She knew exactly what he was asking.

What is the secret of Poppy's room?

And she wasn't going to answer. So Alex Randall smiled and stood up. 'That's all for now, thank you.'

Acantha Palk turned as she left the room after her client. 'And how are your investigations going, inspector?'

He didn't even attempt to answer the question. She would have seen right through him and know they were not really getting anywhere. He was on the point of dropping the enquiry. But . . .

When the two women had left Alex sat back and remembered talking to a junior officer about interrogating a suspect. He had analogized the answer to each question to waves moving on the shore, some crashing down with drama and noise, a huge visual experience, which seemed to flood the beach. Others simply slid over the sand, insignificant and quiet. But whatever the size or depth or volume of a wave the tide still came in relentlessly, crawling, creeping, moving up the beach. Investigations moved forward at varying rates and with varying drama, but move forward they did in *almost* every single case.

The talk had been a few years ago and the junior detective he had been teaching had been Sergeant Paul Talith.

So what had he learned by this interview?

Most importantly of all he had shared Alice's state of mind when she had discovered the corpse. She had not, however, confided in him the secret of the child's room. And there was a secret, Alex Randall was certain of it. She was hiding something and he wasn't absolutely certain that even her friend and solicitor knew what it was. He had read the same doubts and confusion that he felt mirrored in Acantha's face.

An hour later he had a further unpleasant experience. It began with a phone call from the desk sergeant who sounded grim and pessimistic. 'Got someone here called Sedgewick,' he said. 'Rosie Sedgewick. Says she's . . .'

'I know who she is,' Alex said wearily. He was heartily sick of the Sedgewick clan. 'Send her in.'

Rosie Sedgewick was one of those very thin women who appear to have been born with angular features and a sharp, disapproving expression. She'd also been cursed with her father's hooked nose. The effect was not beautiful.

In addition she had a harsh rasping voice that probably stood her in good stead in the courtroom but grated on the detective. 'Are you Detective Inspector Randall?'

He winced.

'I'm Rosie Sedgewick,' she announced. 'I'd better warn you that I am a barrister. Now this –' she sat down – 'is an informal talk. I want to know why you are continually hounding my mother over this affair.'

'It's obvious, isn't it?'

'I know the facts,' Rosie said, 'but my mother was simply the person who stumbled on the body. Why are you still questioning her?'

'There were a few anomalies in her statement.'

Rosie drew in a deep, sighing breath. 'Come on, inspector.' It was a failed attempt at pallyness 'I'm a lawyer, for goodness sake. Give me one statement that doesn't have the odd anomaly in it. My mother was very shocked by the discovery and has been very upset at your continued intrusion. I understand you still have your team of bloodhounds at the house and questioned her *again* only this morning.'

'That's correct,' Alex said. 'And she appeared well and in full control of herself. The interview did not distress her in any way.'

'As I understand it,' Rosie continued, 'you're going to be pursuing another line of investigation – the people who lived in number 41 *before* my parents moved there.'

'Certainly – that's correct,' Alex said.

'Well, please leave my mother out of this,' Rosie said. 'She can be quite vulnerable. It could have a very bad effect on her.'

Randall was surprised at Rosie Sedgewick. If she was a

lawyer she couldn't possibly think that this appeal would cut any ice. It was positively naive. 'I'm afraid,' he said carefully, 'that I can't promise that.'

'She has been under a psychiatrist, you know, for depression.'

'Oh?' It was news to him and Acantha had not mentioned this.

'Oh, well.' Rosie Sedgewick shrugged. 'Don't say I haven't warned you.'

'Thank you for that.'

They stood up, shook hands and the woman left, leaving Randall staring at the closed door. After a minute he sat back down, calmer. The girl was only trying to protect her mother whom she saw as vulnerable. He must excuse her on those grounds.

He sat at his desk for a while, tapping his fingers against the telephone, trying to come to a decision. Then he decided. He placed a call through to the Spanish police. They were able to provide him with the address and telephone number of Mr and Mrs Godfrey. 'They have built a lovely hacienda in the hills behind Malaga,' the policeman, Juan Gonzalez said. 'A beautiful place. One of our cars drove past earlier on today and there were vehicles outside and signs that they were at home. I have not alerted them in case they do a flit.' He gave a great belly laugh at his own English colloquialism.

'Many thanks, señor,' Alex said politely. 'I intend coming over to interview them myself this weekend.'

'You need a car, a police escort?' Gonzalez sounded eager to be in on the action.

'No, no. Don't worry. I'll hire a car from the airport,' Alex said. 'I don't anticipate any trouble but thanks for your help.'

'My pleasure, Señor Randall.'

He rang the number Gonzalez had given him and it was quickly answered by a Spanish female.

'*Senora Godfrey?*' she responded to his enquiry. '*Si, es acqui.* You want speak?'

'*Por favor,*' Randall said in his very best holiday Spanish accent. He heard the sound of heels clacking across a wooden floor then the phone was picked up.

'Yeah, who is it?'

He hadn't been prepared for someone sounding so bored

and pissed off. They were in the land of Rioja and sunshine after all. He introduced himself and explained that he was investigating the discovery of a baby's body in the house they had previously occupied. He left out the facts of the state of the body and that it had been there for a greater number of years than had the Sedgewicks.

'You can't think it's got anything to do with us.' The woman was sounding indignant but a little less pissed off. The drama had at least roused her from her boredom.

'I'm sure it hasn't,' Alex said smoothly, 'but we have to pursue enquiries. I'm sure you understand.'

'Not sure I do, mate.'

'Well,' Alex said, 'I'm proposing flying to Spain this weekend with another officer for the sole purpose of inter-viewing you and your husband. It would be a great shame for us to have a wasted journey.'

There was a long sigh as though whatever he proposed she would find it tiresome. 'We'll be around 'ere most of Saturday. Got a few friends coming over in the evening. It'll entertain them, I suppose, couple of coppers lurking.'

She sounded so utterly uninterested in the whole process that Alex became irritated. He could have shaken this woman. Behind the discovery of the baby must surely lie some tragic story and she couldn't have cared less? It made him angry and her next comment was no less infuriating.

'You come if you want to, mate.'

'Your husband – will he be there?'

'Where else would he be? Nothing much to do this time of year except hang around here. The whole place is dead.'

'Shall we say ten o'clock tomorrow – Saturday – morning then,' Alex asked.

'Bit bloody early, mate. Better make it midday.' There was a throaty chuckle. 'I just might be up by then. Hangover gone. Know what I mean?'

'Right. Midday it is then, Mrs Godfrey. Thank you.' She was hardly going to pick on his heavy sarcasm over the telephone but he felt all the better for it anyway.

He put the phone down still feeling angry with the woman. It was only two p.m. and already he'd dealt with Alice Sedgewick, her daughter and this creature who could barely manage to be civil. All he needed now was . . .'

Right on cue the phone rang and he was informed that Gregory Sedgewick was on the phone from Turkey.

The voice didn't even sound distant.

'Inspector Randall?'

Alex replied in the affirmative.

'My father asked me to ring and speak to you about my mother's involvement in this business.' He managed to make the investigation sound both unnecessary and distasteful.

Alex decided to flush him out. 'So what's your problem?'

'I don't know really.' Gregory Sedgewick sounded vague, rather weak. Nothing like his father. 'I just think Dad thought if we – me and my sister – harassed you enough you'd drop the case, leave Mum out of it. She's had enough to put up with, poor old thing.'

He sounded fond of his mother. More so than either Alice's husband or her daughter. There was real affection in his voice. 'She gets a bit upset, you know. Dad kind of bullies her – bamboozles her into doing all sorts of things.' Randall's ears pricked up. *What sorts of things?*

'She's not up to these sorts of games, you know.'

Alex felt his neck tense up. 'We don't play games, Mr Sedgewick. An investigation into the death of this child will proceed whatever your father wants.'

'Yeah. I thought that.' Gregory didn't sound too bothered either way. 'It's just that the old man – you know? He's used to controlling things.'

'I see. Where do you live – just for the record?'

'Bit south of Istanbul.'

'Have you lived there long?'

'Six years. I work in a bank here. I don't come over to the UK much. Me and the old man, you know. He's none too happy about his only son being gay. Doesn't mind too much if his daughter's as butch as they make them. It's just me, you know. But Mum comes over here once a year. She stays for a week or two with me and Harry, my partner. We all get on pretty well, you know. She's not a bad old stick. A bit under the pater's thumb, if you know what I mean. If Dad said she was to put her hand in boiling water I have the awful feeling . . .'He stopped abruptly. 'Sorry,' he said. 'Babbling too much. Promised Dad I would ring and so I have. Done my duty now.'

'OK. Thanks for the call,' Alex said, wondering why on earth Gregory had really rung and why, in all that 'babble' he had the feeling that Gregory had said something of significance, pointed him in a new direction.

However he had no time to ponder all this now. He picked up the phone and asked if PC Roberts was in the station. When he got hold of him he made his invitation.

'Fancy a trip to Spain, Roberts?'

NINE

Saturday

Gethin Roberts was feeling disgruntled.

It wasn't anything like he'd imagined. Having told Flora, his girlfriend, that he was off to Spain for the weekend on a trip (top secret) connected with the current investigation, and watching her eyes grow satisfyingly round, he was now sitting on a lumpy bed in a dingy room in a scabby pension that was more like a block of council flats. To cap it all it wasn't even quiet. It was on a main road, right on a traffic island and there was no swimming pool, let alone the imagined bathing beauties, strutting their stuff in skimpy bikinis. And it wasn't even hot. The girls around were all muffled up in coats, boots, scarves and woolly hats. They'd been held up for hours at the airport because of ice and fog and then, to top it all, when they had landed, his suitcase had burst open on the carousel, scattering hastily and carelessly packed clothes and he was sure people were making jibes about his dingy underwear in whispered Spanish. Not a good experience. PC Roberts decided there and then that next time he flew he would put a band around his suitcase. He and the inspector had had a very late and indigestible dinner of some tough meat and a bottle of Spanish wine between them. The wine had been the only thing that had lived up to expectations. Then Randall had told him the Godfrey's house was four hours drive away and they would have to make an early start.

Roberts was wondering what he had given his weekend up for, but then he remembered Flora's wide-eyed excitement and pride. He could embellish the drama. He bit his tongue and commented only that it wasn't quite how he'd expected it.

Randall looked at him kindly. 'Nothing ever is, Sonny Jim,' he said, resting his hand for a moment on the young constable's shoulder.

* * *

There was only one way to describe *chez* Godfrey. Opulent. In a hired Seat Ibiza they drove up a winding road that was in places single track, meeting farmers on the way herding goats. The tinkle of bells would always remind them both of this expedition and recall their mixed feelings.

Near the end of the road they were faced with huge gates and a plaque announcing *El Hacienda*. Very unoriginal. Randall glanced at Roberts whose mouth had dropped open as he took in the pink palace. 'In your dreams, Roberts,' he said kindly. 'Or else a bit of luck with the lottery.'

Gethin Roberts managed a half-hearted smile. 'First I'll have to do it, as they say.'

'Quite,' Alex said drily.

There was an electronic voice receiver in the wall. Randall climbed out of the car, pressed the button and announced their arrival.

He got the same bored voice that he'd met on the telephone and the gates swung open, lazily, as though they too had got the message, *mañana*.

They circled round the front of the house which had the most amazing views right over mountains and valleys, rooftops and a small forest, all the way down to the sea, sparkling far off in the distance. Roberts's mouth dropped open even wider. He was already practising the story he would relate to Flora, his 'intended', as his family called her. To him the word sounded just a bit sinister. But then he was a policeman.

'Sir,' he said urgently.

A woman was descending a curved flight of steps – carefully – as she was wearing skyscraper heels and a floating dress of many colours even though it was decidedly chilly up here with an almost arctic breeze. Even from this distance they could both see that she was wearing lashings of make-up. Thick, dark, greasy brown foundation and a lot of black around her eyes. Curiously, instead of making her appear youthful, this made her look like a very old woman. Something like Bette Davis in *Whatever Happened to Baby Jane*. An ancient parody of herself. Yet judging from her figure and strong, shapely legs, neither man would have put her at much over forty.

'Inspector Randall, I presume, and his sidekick?' She had impossibly white teeth, and close up a face stretched taut, probably by a plastic surgeon. She was dangling a pink cigarette from her fingers. She was, both men decided, again mirroring each other's thoughts, theatrical.

Randall introduced themselves.

'Oh cut the formalities and come in,' she said with a weary sigh. 'I'd guessed who you are. We don't get many visitors this far out. And it's freezing out here.'

She scanned the beautiful view with something approaching loathing. Then turning around as she ascended the steps again, she said, 'I absolutely don't have a clue what you hope to achieve by coming here. Still, I suppose it's a bit more entertaining for me than the usual Saturday morning cocktail party. And you've got a free weekend in the Costa del Sol. Though where the bloody *sol* is I don't know. It appears to have buggered off for the entire winter.' Again they both got the impression that however beautiful El Hacienda was Mrs Godfrey disliked it. No. Hated it.

Randall tried to flush her out a little. 'It's a lovely place, Mrs Godfrey.'

She turned around and gave Alex Randall a film star smile. 'Petula. Please.' She was quite an actress, swiftly replacing the apathy for a perfectly charming hostess.

Petula pushed open the door at the top of the stairs and led them into a conservatory which was jungle-hot and made full use of the view which spread out before them in a panoramic picture. The room was long and narrow and contained an assortment of cane furniture and a large, cream, leather sofa against the back wall. There were various brightly coloured canvases of modern art but the real star of the show was the view outside, of classical Spain.

Petula reclined across the sofa, legs stretched out in front of her, and waved a hand vaguely. 'Take a seat,' she said. 'Anywhere.'

Both men sat down opposite her, reluctantly facing the modern art rather than the picture through the glass wall.

'Now then,' she said. 'What's all this about?'

'I don't know how much you know,' Alex began, 'but the body of a child was found in the loft in number 41, The Mount, the house you occupied until five years ago. It had apparently been there for some time. The present owners deny any knowledge of it.' He looked at her questioningly, waiting for confirmation.

Petula had obviously decided to play this scene archly. 'And you think I put it there, inspector? You think I buried dead babies up in the loft of my old house?'

She had made it sound silly enough to match her burst of harsh, mocking laughter.

'A dead baby,' Alex said unsmiling. 'One male child, newly born. Now can you help us?'

'Of course I bloody can't.' Petula's face was pink with anger. 'What do you think I am?'

'Do you have any children?'

Petula looked away. 'I haven't, as a matter of fact. Not blessed – or looking at my friends' nasty little blighters perhaps cursed would be a more appropriate word – with them.'

'And Mr Godfrey?'

'Vince and I have been together since he was seventeen years old and he walked into my dad's hardware shop to buy some screws,' she said with a cackle. '*He* hasn't got any kids either. Even Vincey boy wasn't up to infidelity when he was seventeen.'

There was a bitterness in both her face and her voice which escaped neither of the police officers.

'You lived in the house for . . . ?'

'Almost four years,' Petula said, guarded now as though the joke had gone. Dried up.

'We bought the house off an old biddy,' she continued. 'Stripped it down, did the whole place up. Made a nice job of it.'

'Did you do any work in the loft?'

'I don't know. You'll have to ask Vince about that.'

'Where is your husband?'

'Playing golf,' she said. 'It's all right for the blokes here. They get to play golf practically every day. It's different for the women. Unless they join the golf boys, which isn't quite my cup of tea. Too damned hearty and horrible clothes.'

Randall smiled for the first time at the vision of Petula in peaked cap and checked plus fours.

'We women just get bored. And drunk,' she added in a sad challenge.

Alex shifted in his seat, the cane making a painful squeak. 'What time will your husband be back?'

'In an hour or so. Don't worry, inspector. He knows you're coming.'

She treated them to another film star smile. 'Well?' Her glance drifted across to Gethin Roberts who flushed and said nothing.

'Drink,' she ordered, wafting long, horrendously manicured nails that reminded Alex of harpies, towards a half-empty wine bottle. 'Well?' she said again, suddenly defensive. 'There isn't a lot else to do out here. Especially when the weather's this foul.' There was deep resentment in her voice. 'What do you want to drink?' Without waiting for their answer she said, 'I suppose you want a coffee. On duty and all that.'

'That would be lovely.'

'Graciela,' she screamed.

'*Si.*'

'Come here, you lazy cow.' A young Spanish girl, plainly dressed in a loose-fitting black dress and flat shoes scurried into the room.

'Make our guests some coffee and you can get me another bloody bottle of wine.'

The girl scuttled out again.

'Next question?' she snapped.

'Did anyone come to the house who was pregnant?'

Petula frowned. 'What a stupid question,' she said. 'I can't remember that. Possibly. Possibly not. I really haven't got a clue. I take it the baby wasn't premature or something?'

'No. It was full term.'

'So I would have noticed a bump, wouldn't I?'

'I would have thought so.'

'I mean you can't hide a bump that bloody big, can you?'

'Indeed not.'

'Who lived with you in the house?'

Petula rolled her eyes. 'It gets worse, don't it? Just me and my old man, sunshine.'

'So just the two of you,' Alex asked carefully.

'We had a bit of help in the house. Can't expect me to do the scrubbing and such like.'

'What sort of help?'

'I don't know. Enough to make sure the everyday things were completed.'

'What sort of help?' Alex repeated.

'A couple of maids. They never stay long. Greedy little things. Want money for nothing and then bugger off when they're bored.

'Anyone else?'

'A daily, a gardener. You know – the usual.'

'The maids?' Alex questioned delicately.

'None of *them* was pregnant. I'd soon have got shot of them if they were. What use would a pregnant maid be,' she chortled.

There was no answer to that but Alex persisted with the subject.

'What country were they from?'

'I don't know.'

'So how did you acquire them?'

'Can't remember,' she said dismissively. 'Probably through an agency.'

Alex held up a finger as though to make absolutely sure he had the facts so far clear in his mind. 'So as far as you know you are unable to help me establish the identity of the dead child.'

Petula stubbed her cigarette out in her wine glass. 'Correct,' she said.

They were distracted by a man in his forties in light coloured trousers and a pale sweater walking into the room. He looked jaunty and bent down to kiss Petula. 'Hello, ducky,' he said before extending a hand first to Alex and then to Roberts. 'I assume you're the two policemen from Shrewsbury.'

Alex nodded.

'Rum business. Well, I don't know how I can help you.' He waved a decanter around. 'Drink anyone?'

His wife sighed. 'Not whisky, Vince.' She glanced around her. 'Where's that bloody girl?'

She gave a loud annoyed sigh and addressed her husband. 'Nice game, dear?' There was something a little more than weary in her tone which told them all, including Vince, that she didn't give a monkey's rear end whether he had had a nice game or had knocked the ball to the bottom of a pond and not bothered to retrieve it. There was both resentment and a certain reproof in her voice.

Vince Godfrey poured himself a whisky, and flung himself

down in one of the cane chairs. It too creaked a little in protestation as though it was a living entity and resented his weight.

'Now then,' he said cheerily, leaning back and crossing his legs at the ankles. 'Fire away.'

'I understand from your wife that you did some extensive refurbishment of the house in Shrewsbury?'

'That's right. Made a lovely job of the place though I understand from various mutual friends that they've done it up all over again. Hah.'

'Yes. You refurbished the entire house?'

'Top to bottom.'

'It's more the top than the bottom that we're interested in.'

'The bedrooms?'

'No. To put it bluntly the hot water tank where we found the infant's body was in the loft. It had been boxed in. Did you do that, Mr Godfrey?'

'I might have done. I can't really remember. We did a lot of electrics up there, trailing wires and such but I can't think we would have bothered to box in a hot water tank. I mean, you're not going to have an airing cupboard all the way up there, are you? Accessible only by an extending loft ladder. And all cylinders these days are encased in foam so they're pretty well insulated. Can't you tell by the age of the wood that was used?'

'Not conclusively,' Alex said.

'Well,' Vince Godfrey said, draining his glass. 'Pet and I don't know anything about it. Can't help you there, inspector.' He spoke the words politely but firmly. As far as the Godfreys were concerned they had nothing to add.

'Sorry you've had a bit of a wasted journey – all this way.'

'Yes,' Alex said, making no move to leave.

The couple exchanged a swift glance, more disturbed by Alex's lack of movement than he would have expected.

'Did you notice any smell up there ever?'

Mark Sullivan had pointed out that because the child's body had desiccated rather than decayed there would in all probability have been no smell, but it didn't hurt to ask.

Oddly enough the Godfreys didn't seem to know how to answer the question. Simple enough, Alex thought. Yes or no.

Instead Vince asked something, 'How long do you think the body had been there?'

Again Alex was deliberately vague. 'It's hard to say. Somewhere around the time that you bought the property. Which is eight or nine years ago. By the way which estate agents did you use?'

Again the Godfreys looked at each other. Gethin Roberts gave his boss a quick, puzzled look but Randall's face was impassive. Petula frowned and nibbled her finger. Then her husband tapped the side of his head. He had seen the light. Remembered. 'Victor Plumley,' he said. 'Quite a small estate agents in Grope Lane in the old part of town. Love that name.' He leered. 'Grope Lane. Conjures up all sorts of naughty images.'

His wife gave him a frosty look but then the coffee arrived with some tiny petit fours which Gethin Roberts eyed greedily. He was working up quite an appetite. It was all set out very nicely by Graciela but Petula Godfrey wasn't pleased. 'Took your bloody time, didn't you?'

'*Lo siento*,' the girl whispered.

'And speak in bloody English, will you?'

'*Si.*'

They waited while the coffee was poured and handed around by Graciela. Alex waited until she had left the room before continuing the questioning.

'The lady you bought the house from,' he enquired delicately.

Vince gave a hollow guffaw. 'I can't see her doing much,' he said. 'When we bought number 41 she went to live with her son and daughter-in-law.'

'Where?'

'Somewhere in Birmingham, I think. Goodness. She was well into her eighties. Half demented from what I saw of her. The son and daughter-in-law were always there when we viewed. They were the ones who dealt with us rather than her. The place was quite rundown. She hardly used the upstairs. I suppose . . .' He thought for a minute. 'There *was* a bit of a fusty smell around the place but I just put that down to an old lady living there.'

'I see,' Alex said aware that it was a very neat answer.

'Mr Godfrey,' he said, 'I wonder if it would be possible to have a quick word with you – alone.' He gave a swift glance at Petula who was lighting up another cigarette and took no notice.

'Sure,' Godfrey said. 'Shall we go into my study?'

Leaving Roberts to be entertained by Petula, Randall was led out of the conservatory into a large hallway and then through an archway into a dark room at the back of the house. The windows had grills over them, he noticed, and wondered why. Was Godfrey worried about intruders? There was a huge desk in the centre of the room with a computer and other paraphernalia scattered over the top.

'Sanctum,' Godfrey said 'I don't let Pet or Graciela in here. This is *my* place.' As though to emphasize the point he banged the door shut and sat behind the desk. Alex took a leather armchair.

'I can guess what you want to ask me,' Vince said. 'And the answer is yes. I haven't exactly been a good little boy throughout our marriage but there's never ever been anyone serious. Pet knows that. She's the only one for me but when these women make a play for you.' He gave a cynical grimace. 'Women like money,' he said, sharing the information with Randall. 'Especially the young gorgeous-looking ones. They think they only have to stick with you for a couple of years and if they get fed up with you they can scarper and take a couple of million with them without having you hanging round their greedy little necks. Not bloody likely, inspector.' He examined his fingernails closely. 'I can honestly say, Pet's the one for me. And she knows it.' His face clouded. 'She does like to get her own way though. That's the only thing I can say against her. If she sets her heart on something, that's it.'

Alex nodded. The words seemed logical and sounded honest and Petula Godfrey had appeared like that to him. A realist. But at one point when Vince Godfrey had been speaking there had passed over his face a look of intense pain. At some point in his life, for all his bravado, some woman had hurt this man.

There was a moment's silence between the two men. Randall was watching Godfrey's face, searching, waiting for some other clue. But the man's face was wooden now.

He broke the silence.

'Was there anything else, inspector?'

'No, Mr Godfrey. That's fine.'

'You know. I've been thinking. The tank. It *was* already boxed in. I can remember now. I never touched it. I thought if it needed replacing I'd take it apart then. Maybe put a new one in. Otherwise – well to be truthful I was getting a bit fed up with doing the place up. Know what I mean?' he gave a bland, pleasant smile.

Alex nodded. 'OK,' he said carefully. 'Thanks very much. We'll be going now.'

The relief in the man's face was tangible but Alex reflected as they made their way back to the conservatory, that Vince was the sort of man who was probably always nervous around the police. A man like that who had made this amount of money was practically never completely above board. There was almost certainly a guilty secret lurking somewhere beneath the jaunty manner but it might have nothing to do with the case at all.

Just as they reached the doorway to the conservatory Vince Godfrey turned to face Alex. 'Look,' he said. 'This is rather upsetting for my wife.' He hesitated. 'Go easy on her.'

Alex Randall didn't reply.

Gethin Roberts looked relieved to see them return. He gave Randall a wry smile.

'One more question,' Alex said, 'before we go. Does the name Poppy mean anything to you?'

Both Godfreys looked completely blank.

'OK then,' he said. 'I think that's all. Thank you both very much for your cooperation.' He shook hands with each in turn. 'If I have any more questions I shall telephone.'

He had the impression that Vince Godfrey would have liked to say something more but nothing was said and they climbed back into the car ready for the journey back to the hotel. The sun had, at last, come out and to the winter-weary pair it felt almost warm.

Alex rolled down the car window and took a deep breath in. 'What say we stop at one of these lovely roadside inns and have some lunch?'

Gethin Roberts felt his spirits soar.

Martha was even in a temper deciding what to wear. She didn't want to play mediator between her friend's widower and his sugar babe. She felt middle-aged and rejected outfit after outfit. In the end she elected for jeans, high-heeled boots and a turquoise top, over which she knotted a tight-fitting turquoise cardigan. She dumbed down her make-up, brushed back her hair hard, almost seeing Vernon Grubb, her macho hairdresser, wincing as she did so. He was always telling her off for not treating her hair with the respect to which it was due. Sometimes she thought he should have opted for professional rugby where he could have taken his aggression out on the opposing side rather than women in their middle years whom he bullied mercilessly about their hair.

They met at Richmond's, a newly opened bistro in the town. Neutral ground. Martha was surprised at Simon's choice. He was more likely to eat in one of the many ancient restaurants or coffee houses which sprinkled this medieval town than here. It was ultra modern, spanking white with echoing marble floors and a long counter where you queued for food. It was too bright white, not the sort of place Simon would ever have chosen for himself. Then as she sat down and looked around her she felt pity. It was peopled with earnest and self-conscious teenagers. Simon would feel like a fish out of water. She picked up a menu. Nouvelle cuisine, no more than twenty calories a portion. Lots of rocket and basil. She waited for an anxious twenty minutes worrying that she had come to the wrong place. She was on the verge of ringing his mobile phone when he arrived. And again this was unlike Simon. He was a stickler for time. Never late.

He spotted her straight away and waved. His clothes too were different. A leather jacket, chinos, an open-necked yellow shirt. Not the sober-suited man she knew. In fact she realized that she didn't know this man. On his arm clung a girl. Martha couldn't have called her anything else. She was not a woman but a girl with long straight blonde hair and a fringe, which she had to distractingly blink out of her large cornflower blue eyes every few minutes. She was slim to the point of emaciation and looked vulnerable in tight jeans, high-heeled boots, an anorak with a brown fur collar, little make-up and beautifully manicured long nails.

'Sorry we're late.' Simon bent and kissed her cheek. 'We couldn't find anywhere to park and had to hoof it through the town. Not easy with Chrissi's heels.'

'Martha,' he said unnecessarily and with a flourish, 'this is Chrissi.'

Chrissi smiled, her eyes holding an expression of mute appeal. Shocked, Martha realized the girl desperately wanted her to like her, approve of her. Why? What on earth did she matter? She was merely a friend of Simon's dead wife and here to mediate between Simon's daughters and this 'child'.

But there was no doubt about it, Christabel did want Martha to like her.

So her pity swung from Simon, who was trying to pretend he was thirty years younger than he was, to a girl who must know that all his friends, family and acquaintances and in particular his two very bright, very energetic and very opinionated daughters, would disapprove of this relationship.

Martha held out her hand. 'Hello, Christabel,' she said. 'Do most people call you that or do they call you Chrissi?'

The girl nodded. 'Either.' She sat down. 'I've heard a lot about you,' she said in a breathless whisper. Then with a loving look at Simon she added unnecessarily, 'From Simon.'

'Always a bit worrying,' Martha said brightly. 'Shall we get some food?

'You two choose,' Simon said. 'I'll go and get it.'

Great, she thought. Give us a chance to get to know each other. And what if I don't want to?

Chrissi watched Simon practically all the time he queued and bought the food. Martha limited her questions to ones she could comfortably address to a profile. Where had they met? At work – she was his (cliché, cliché) secretary. She lived with her mother and brother. (She didn't mention the father). They 'really, really' liked Simon. Wasn't he handsome?

Errm.

He didn't look his age, did he?

Errm.

Simon returned.

As she'd suspected, even with the nouvelle cuisine that was on offer Chrissi didn't eat real food, merely played with bits around her plate, nibbling prettily as a rabbit on her rocket. And she let Simon lead the conversation.

'How's Sam doing?' he asked heartily.

'OK,' she said. 'At least he's off the injury list and back playing. He might – just might – be coming home and playing for Stoke – on a lend,' she added, explaining to Chrissi. 'He's a footballer,' she said, 'with the Liverpool Academy. He's almost fifteen. One of a twin.' Then she gave Simon a bright look which was meant to put him at his ease because he looked so terribly uncomfortable. 'You haven't heard the best. Sukey has decided she wants to become an actress.'

'Goodness.' He looked startled. 'Little Suks? What on earth would Martin have said, I wonder?'

'He was always one to let his children choose their own path.'

'Ye-es. But acting.'

The conversation stopped and she felt suddenly cross. What right did Simon have to drag her into this uncomfortable and untenable position? He should sort this out himself with his daughters. Not bring her in as mediator, no doubt to plead this child's cause.

Chrissi spoke. 'You were a friend of Simon's first wife?' She lifted her eyes to Martha's, beseeching, *Make this easier for me, please?*

'Yes,' Martha said. 'You haven't met Armenia and Jocasta yet?'

'Tomorrow. We're having lunch together. We hoped –' she put her hand in Simon's – 'that you would come along too. It would make it easier for me.'

'Of course.'

Martha risked a glance at Simon. He was looking away, frowning and she thought she could read his mind.

This was not going to work. He knew it and she knew it too.

But then Chrissi swallowed a mouthful of salad and gulped. 'You must be wondering what Evelyn would have thought of this,' she said, putting her hand in Simon's.

'Evelyn isn't alive,' Martha said quietly. 'If she was you wouldn't be here, would you?'

The blue eyes met hers with some understanding and Martha felt relief that she had spoken what had been in her mind from the beginning of lunch when she had recognized the incongruity of this relationship.

'I'm dreading tomorrow,' Chrissi said miserably. 'I know Simon's daughters won't like me.' Her voice trailed away.

'They're grown women,' Martha said firmly. 'They must adjust.'

Simon's arm stole around Chrissi's thin shoulders. 'Take heart, my darling,' he said quietly. 'Be brave.'

Chrissi was not the only one dreading tomorrow.

The rest of the lunch was equally perfunctory and Martha left the soulless restaurant at three.

Depressed and a little tired she decided to walk back down to the car park, towards the English Bridge, passing Finton Cley's antiques shop halfway down Wyle Cop. She glanced in the window and had a shock.

It sported a huge sign. 'Meet Martha Gunn'. Below it was a female Toby jug with the three plumes of the Prince of Wales on her hat.

Finton had mocked her before about her name. For ages she had not understood why. One day she had asked him. 'Why do you always smirk when you say my name?'

He'd looked smug, a public schoolboy who had a secret. 'I can't believe you've lived all your life and don't know the significance of your name? Your parents never told you?'

She'd shaken her head. 'They might not have known either.'

'Well that would be a coincidence.'

She'd waited, knowing he would tell her. 'She was a Brighton bathing attendant,' he'd said finally, 'in the early nineteenth century and reputed to have attended the Prince Regent. One version of events has her actually throwing him into the sea. A risky thing. Look.' He'd shown her the three feathers on her hat.

Martha looked through the window. And now here was the original Martha Gunn herself.

She pushed open the door. Cley was sitting down, reading a book. Although the shop bell jangled he did not look up but continued reading. She cleared her throat. He inserted a bookmark, closed the book and finally turned round. 'Martha,' he said. 'I've been expecting you. Somehow I thought that little jug would tempt even you inside.' He stood up. 'How are you?'

'I'm fine. You?'

He looked at her searchingly. 'You seem a bit . . . on edge.'

'It's been a difficult day,' she said. 'And I expect more of the same tomorrow.'

She smiled and walked across to the window, picking the Martha Gunn jug up. It had a price tag of £1,800 on it. 'An expensive lady,' she said.

'I can manage a small reduction,' Cley said smoothly, playing the antiques dealer to perfection.

She turned. 'How much of a reduction?'

'It depends.'

'On what?'

'On whether you understand.'

She stared at him. He was a charismatic character, with long, curling hair, too long for current fashion, one pirate earring swinging against his ear lobe. He was in his early thirties and had a very public school accent. He puzzled her, seeming to always have a secret message. She had thought it was simply her name but now she realized there was more to it than just that. Still holding the jug she sat down. 'Why don't you stop playing games, Finton,' she asked softly. 'It is you, isn't it?'

'What do you mean?'

'Message for Martha,' she said.

He eyed her for a moment as though wondering. 'Why don't I stop playing games,' he repeated softly. 'Why don't I? Why don't I tell you the truth, Martha? I'll tell you why, shall I?'

She waited, starting to see things more clearly now, as though frosted glass had suddenly become clear.

When he spoke again it was both soft and hard. 'You like stories, Martha Gunn?'

He drew in a deep breath. 'So why don't you sit down? Have a cup of tea and listen to the story I have to tell.'

He began. 'My father's name was William. William Cley.' He looked at her curiously. 'Does the name mean anything to you?'

'I don't know,' she said. 'I don't think so. And yet . . .' She paused. 'I have heard it before but I don't know in what connection.' She hazarded a guess. 'Work?'

'Interesting, isn't it,' Cley said. 'The name means practically nothing to you and yet you virtually destroyed his family.'

'What?'

'My father died twelve years ago. Unfortunately he had left a note stating his intention.' Cley met her eyes without flinching. 'His life insurance specifically excluded suicide so my mother and sister were left without any money. I had been at public school so of course I had to leave and was bullied fairly mercilessly at state school for my posh accent and eccentric clothes. My mother, you may be interested to know, went to pieces. She's dead now and my sister became very depressed and an alcoholic. There was no money for me to go to university. I could have become a lawyer or a doctor, just like you, but instead I had to support my family, both financially and mentally. That was what happened to William Cley's family after you brought in a verdict of suicide, Martha Gunn.' Then quite suddenly he erupted. 'Why didn't you simply say accidental death?'

'If he left a note,' she said quietly, 'I had no choice. Your father would have known what he was doing and the consequence of his actions.'

Cley's face crumpled. 'I know that,' he said. 'It doesn't make me feel any better.'

'Finton, I'm sorry about your father,' she said, 'but I was simply doing my job. You can't blame me.'

He did not reply but stared ahead of him, his dark eyes sad.

She bought the jug anyway.

TEN

Sunday

The lunch invitation had been extended to Sukey and Agnetha so they drove in Martha's car out towards the black and white half-timbered manor house where Simon had lived with Evelyn. Armenia and Jocasta had never really lived there as it had been bought after they had left home. Martha didn't know if Simon had ever realized, but Evelyn had never really liked it. Bought as a status symbol, Evelyn had found it spooky and too big even with an army of cleaners and gardeners.

The place was immaculate. They drove down the gravelled drive, taking in the manicured lawns bordered by topiary yew bushes and beyond that the little stone archway which led to Evelyn's favourite spot – the rose garden. Martha couldn't see Christabel having much of an interest in roses. Still – you never knew. She pulled up outside the oak door and tugged at the bell.

Armenia opened the door, rolling her eyes. 'What a bloody . . .' she exploded then remembered her manners. 'Hello, Martha. Lovely to see you. Sorry you've been dragged into all this.'

She was her mother in some ways, slim and elegant, but she lacked Evelyn's soft warmth. Armenia was as brittle as glass. She was, though she would have denied it hotly, a clone of her father. Tough, stubborn, very determined, she was a force to be reckoned with.

She looked past Martha and gave a shriek. 'Sukey Gunn,' she said. 'You've quite grown up. Right behind my back.' She gave her a hug and Agnetha too. 'Thank goodness you're here,' she said. 'It's been dire. My father. Oh.' She threw her hands up in the air. 'It's ridiculous. I'm ashamed of him. Bloody little gold-digger. Thinks we can't see right through her? Come on into the lions' den.'

Martha followed her into the panelled hallway hung with a few ancient portraits. Nothing to do with Simon – he had come from humble beginnings – and they weren't anything to do with Evelyn either. They had been bought at various salerooms up and down the country. Simon had a friend who was a clever and knowledgeable art dealer and he had purchased most of these through him. But the portraits had the desired effect. They made the house look like an old family seat which was the look Simon wanted.

Armenia was joined by her sister, Jocasta, who looked every bit as fed up as her sister. 'Hi,' she said gloomily. 'Join the happy family – I don't think.' She led them into the sitting room.

Simon and Chrissi were sitting side by side on the sofa and frankly Chrissi looked terrified. Simon shot Martha a despairing look and stood up. 'Glad you're here,' he said.

Chrissi gave her a swift smile. 'Hello again,' she said in her little girl's voice.

Simon had a housekeeper, Hannah Scholz, a woman in her thirties who had come from what had once been East Germany. She had been a real find, very tidy and organized, a terrific cook and it seemed to Martha that she did the work of three women, keeping the house immaculate. She was also blessed with common sense and looked after Simon as she had looked after Evelyn right up until her end, adding nurse to all her other roles.

Hannah called them in to Sunday lunch, roast beef with all the trimmings. The distraction of serving food and eating, plus the usual conversation, did lighten the atmosphere at the table. Hannah kept her gaze away from Martha which probably meant that she did not want to join in on the condemnation of Christabel.

Afterwards they sat and talked and Martha began to see Christabel not as a young lovely woman or even a gold-digger but as a person, and she decided then that she would ring Simon later in the week and talk to him. She had a few thoughts to share with him.

DI Randall and PC Roberts had a couple of hours to walk around Malaga, which proved to be an interestingly ancient and historic city. Then they made their way back to the airport and boarded the plane. They spoke a little about their meeting with the Godfreys but Alex was anxious to speak to Martha.

One phrase that Vince Godfrey said had stuck uncomfortably in his mind. *'What my wife wants she gets.'* For all the fact that Vince had protested he loved his wife there had been some bitterness – resentment – in his words.

But Petula had not had all she had wanted – if a husband's fidelity counted for anything. So how would a woman like that respond to a husband who broke his wedding vows and was unfaithful? Might she feel he owed her something?

They had no children. Neither had expressed any regret over this but had stated the fact baldly, without inviting sympathy. Perhaps a truly selfish person was better off having no children.

Alex winced. Personally he would love to have had children.

Alex had the feeling that Vince had said more than he had meant. If he consulted Martha and related the conversations, he argued, he might have a woman's take on it. Maybe.

He rang Martha first thing Monday morning and wasted no time on preamble, stating bluntly, 'I wonder if I might come over and discuss this case with you?'

'Of course, Alex. You know you're always welcome to talk about cases with me. How was Spain?'

'Not hot but we did see a little sunshine and enjoyed walking round Malaga. And of course we simply had to visit a bar for some *tapas*. I'll come straight over if it's all right with you.'

'Fine. I've got something to tell you too,' she said.

'I forgot. Sorry. How was your weekend with your friend's husband?'

'Dire,' she said. 'Even worse than I'd expected. Civil war in the Pendlebury household, I'm afraid.'

'Oh dear.'

He was round in less than half an hour before she'd really got stuck in to her morning's work. Jericho let him in with a sour, grouchy look. Alex took no notice but went straight into Martha's office.

'Not much of a tan,' she teased.

'No.'

'Now what can I do for you?'

He sat down in the chair, stretching his long legs out in front of him. 'At some point, Martha,' he said, 'we're going to have to decide whether to pursue this case or drop it.'

'Ye-es,' she said. 'I realize that. But you know I always want to find out what the truth is. It doesn't help that Mark Sullivan can't be absolutely certain of "a" how long ago the child died, and "b" whether it was born alive and "c" whether it died from natural causes.' She hesitated. 'I take it the visit to the Godfreys wasn't an out and out success then?'

'Not really,' he said. 'They certainly didn't admit to anything.'

'What were they like?'

'He's obviously made a lot of money. Money he doesn't quite know what to do with. I wouldn't like to say how exactly he made so much money. It might simply be hard work but he seemed a shifty sort of guy to me. He was certainly relieved to see us leave. They have no children and he practically admitted that he had been unfaithful to his wife.'

'Oh dear,' Martha said. 'And before they lived in number 41?'

'An elderly lady well into her eighties lived in the house before the Godfreys. She'd lived there for years and by the end was fairly incapacitated so obviously didn't go into the loft in the last few years. If, say, one of her carers was pregnant, she could have hidden the baby up there without the old lady being aware. It's possible. Vince Godfrey said she was demented by the time her relatives took her to live with them.' He shifted in his seat. 'Then there are the Godfreys themselves. Though they both said they had carried out extensive renovation to the property Vince Godfrey says he was not the one to box in the immersion tank. If Petula Godfrey had become pregnant there would have been no need and no point in concealing either the pregnancy or the baby. If she really hadn't wanted a baby she could have had an abortion and if she was intending to keep the child she would have had proper antenatal care.'

He chewed his lip, frowning. 'She admitted to having a couple of maids but denied that any one of them had become pregnant. She said she would have fired them.' He stopped. 'If one of her maids or one of her husband's mistresses had become pregnant . . . ?'

'That's a very sinister scenario,' Martha said. 'Do you really think? Are they capable of . . . ?' She looked at him. 'You've met them,' she said. 'What do you think? That she murdered one of his mistresses and the baby too?'

'It does seem incredible.'

'Is there another body there? Or did the mistress escape leaving the baby behind? Surely not?'

'I know, Martha, none if it does make sense but the fact is *someone* hid that body in the house.'

'The Godfreys seem unlikely, surely?'

'Ye-es except that I thought that Vince – Mr Godfrey – was trying to convey something to me when he said how determined his wife was, that she had to have what she wanted. He was telling me something, Martha.'

She was silent, unable to think of anything helpful to contribute.

'Anyway. Enough of that. Tell me about your weekend. How did dinner with the vamp go?'

'OK,' she said. 'She isn't really a vamp. Just seems very young. She was much as I'd expected but no worse. Truth is I don't think she's a bad kid. Just not for Simon. That's all. She's wrong for him.'

'Because she's not like Evie?'

'Give me some credit, Alex. No, not just because of that. It's because she's the wrong age, the wrong outlook, the wrong intellect. Even the wrong class. Everything's wrong.'

'You think she is a gold-digger?'

'Not in the usual sense. I'm sure she doesn't think of it like that. It's more that she might love him now but when he's older, more vulnerable, he won't be the same man. Anyway, that wasn't what I had to tell you. Alex. I know about the Message to Martha.'

'What? You've solved it on your own?'

'Not really. My stalker wanted me to know who he was and why.'

'I am intrigued.'

'Thought you would be.'

'Go on then.'

She related Finton Cley's story, finishing: 'Quite simply he blames me.'

'That's ridiculous.'

'We-ell. His point is that I put the family through a lot of unnecessary pain. He thinks I should have suppressed the letter and put in a verdict of misadventure. Then there would have been an insurance payout; he could have stayed at public school.' She recalled Finton's face. *'I might even have become a lawyer or a doctor, like you.'*

She carried on with the story. 'His mother wouldn't have been flung into penury and presumably his sister, in spite of her father's suicide, would not have descended into depression and alcoholism.'

'Very neat,' Alex said, 'but if there was a note and you had suppressed it you could, presumably, have been accused of insurance fraud.'

'That's right. I had no choice. I pointed this out to Finton but he was fairly unforgiving. His mother has since died and his sister has alcoholic cirrhosis of the liver. It's a sad story.'

Alex touched her hand. 'You're not responsible, Martha.'

'I keep telling myself that but a little voice inside me listens to Finton's arguments and I do feel responsible.'

'You are not responsible,' he repeated, louder this time.

'No, I know that. I don't really see how I could have acted any differently but it is one of the difficult and sore points of the job.'

'Is he going to leave you alone from now on?'

She nodded. 'I think so.'

'It's a grim business. Talk about something else.'

Afterwards she could have bitten her tongue off but she'd said it by then anyway. 'Did your wife mind you going away for the weekend?'

His face seemed to freeze and she knew she'd said something gauche. He said nothing but the look of anguish that passed across his face was grey and chilly. He opened his mouth and still said nothing. Then he looked away from her.

'I would dearly like to confide in you one day, Martha,' he said softly, 'but now is not the time. My wife is not a well woman.' He met her eyes very briefly and she nodded and smiled.

'When you're ready to talk, Alex,' she said, 'I will be ready to listen.'

He met her eyes, then: 'Thanks,' he said. 'I shan't forget.'

She changed the subject. 'Mark Sullivan seems better.'

A tinge of humour touched Alex's face. 'A little bird told me that Dr Sullivan has somehow managed to curb his drinking.'

'That was the conclusion I came to and I'm so glad. So very glad. He's clever and talented and it was a rotten waste.'

'He's also left his wife, so the same little bird told me, and is living alone in a small rented bungalow.'

'Another one with a much younger girlfriend?'

'I don't think so, at least, not that the little bird has told me. I think it were *the drink that done it*.' Alex stood up. 'Thanks for listening, Martha. I appreciate it.'

'Keep me informed,' she said. 'What's your next move?'

'Get someone to talk to the estate agents who sold number 41 to the Godfreys, see if I can interview the relatives of the old lady, just in case they have anything to add – maybe about carers or something, take some sniffer dogs over to the house the Sedgewicks lived in before they moved just in case they did bring the body with them to number 41.'

'But,' Martha protested, 'there are still the questions about Mrs Sedgewick's very odd behaviour, the shrine of the children's room, the name Poppy. There's something funny about Alice Sedgewick and from what you've told me the family form a wall around her. They are abnormally protective of her. Why?'

ELEVEN

Holmes and Watson were a pair of springer spaniels trained as sniffer dogs and their relish for detection was about as great as that of the great Sherlock himself. Their trainer was a police sergeant named Shotton and he too did his work with great gusto and loved the dogs almost more than his wife (though he wouldn't have dared tell her so). The three of them worked as a beautiful team.

Holmes and Watson's particular speciality was the sniffing out of decayed corpses. In their time they had unearthed quite a few and as Shotton put them in the back of his van and looked at their eager faces, tongues hanging out, already panting in anticipation, he wondered if today's mission would bring more success.

He had his orders: first of all to take the dogs to 41 The Mount and see if they found any sign of a second body. If the site proved negative he was to move on to Bayston Hill, to the house the Sedgewicks had previously occupied and do the same there.

Anticipating opposition he had telephoned the Sedgewick's house to forewarn them. Aaron Sedgewick was absolutely livid.

'I don't know what you think you're doing in this police state,' he said.

Yeah, yeah, Shotton thought. Police state when they don't like what we do, but powerless and ineffectual when it is they who want us.

'Merely trying to find out the truth, sir. I'll be round with the dogs in half an hour.'

Sedgewick was no more friendly when Shotton arrived at number 41, the dogs straining at their leashes.

Aaron Sedgewick stood, stony-faced, in the middle of the lounge, as the dogs, noses burying in the carpets, began their frantic search handled by Shotton who took absolutely no notice at all of the furious man.

Holmes and Watson covered every single corner of the

house, even managing to scamper up the ladder into the loft. Apart from interest in the area around the water tank they found nothing.

When Shotton had loaded up the dogs back into the van he returned to the house.

'Thank you, sir,' he said. 'Your cooperation was much appreciated.'

Sedgewick snorted and gave him a look of pure loathing.

Of his wife there was no sign.

He had a very different reception when it came to the house in Bayston Hill. Occupied by a lively and elderly widow who was, of course, not implicated in the case at all, she thoroughly enjoyed the search. Her name, appropriately enough, was Alexandra Mistery and she heard his sketchy explanation with incredulous eyes.

'Yes,' she said excitedly. 'I read about it in the paper.' She frowned. 'It was a bizarre case. I couldn't make head nor tail of it.'

Neither, Shotton thought, could the police.

'But then the newspapers don't always get it right, do they?' She waited, hoping he would volunteer more information, adding, 'And the lady who went to the hospital was the same one who sold us the house. We-ell.'

She made a great fuss of the dogs, made Shotton a cup of tea, sat at the table and chatted on and on. He found it difficult not to give the game away as she was so curious.

'I'm a big fan of crime fiction,' she said. 'I love Andrew Taylor and Val McDermid. Oh, they have such wicked minds.' Her eyes gleamed at the memory of some of the plots. 'And you think . . . you really think there might possibly be a dead body here?' Her eyes shone with ghoulish glee. 'Oh, what a thing. That would be amazing.' She clasped her hands together. 'Another cup of tea, sergeant?'

'No. Thank you. I'd better get on.'

The house was the neat, orderly abode of a middle-aged woman who lived alone. The only thing that interested Shotton was the pile of paperbacks stacked up by the side of the bed. A bookshelf downstairs was full of the same sort of titles. For Holmes and Watson, sniffing their way enthusiastically from room to room, there was nothing to interest them at all except a dead mouse they found at the bottom of the airing cupboard.

Mrs Mistery followed him around from room to room, enjoying herself, tut tutting at the dead mouse and practising what she would tell her friends.

'The police. They thought . . . another body. Dogs . . . murder. Just like one of my books. And the dogs – all over the place. Scampering up and down the stairs, sniffing under the beds. All too thrilling.'

Like many people who live alone she made little comments to herself which left Shotton wondering whether he should join in the conversation or leave Mrs Mistery to carry on chatting to Mrs Mistery.

When he and the dogs had finished with the house she made another pot of tea and they sat and drank while she continued her attempted pumping of the officer. As soon as he had finished the first cup she offered him a second but Shotton stood up. 'Thank you, Mrs Mistery. You've been really kind but no. If you don't mind I'll just check around the garden and then all will be done.'

The garden was quite small with a rectangular lawn and a couple of young trees at the end. Nearer the house it had been largely paved over. Shotton stepped through the patio doors straight onto an area paved with pink and cream slabs. Immediately Holmes and Watson began to yelp excitedly, their noses right down on the paving slabs. Shotton's heart sank. It was so much easier to dig up a garden than lift a dozen or so concrete paving stones. But there was no doubt about it. The dogs were barking at something. And they expected their reward.

Through the patio doors the dogs' behaviour had not escaped the vigilant Mrs Mistery's attention. She rapped sharply on the glass, mouthing, 'Have they found something, sergeant? Is there something there?'

Her excitement at being part of a real live murder was so great that it hadn't occurred to her that this would mean the lifting of at least some of the patio slabs, disrupting her garden possibly for weeks. Shotton watched as both Holmes and Watson yelped and tried to stick their noses right into the crack between two of the slabs. He marked the spots then put the dogs in the back of the van, rewarding them for their skill. Then he returned to the house and the now wildly excited lady.

'Was it you who had the patio laid, Mrs Mistery?'

'Oh no,' she said, with relish. 'It was done before we came here. Clive, my husband, was already ill by the time we moved here to be nearer my daughter. Poor man, he wasn't up to laying a patio or any other building work for that matter.' Then her eyes widened. 'You think somebody is buried under there, don't you? That they laid the stones to conceal a body. Like that West chap. Oh yes, Sergeant Shotton, I have an interest in true crime as well as fictional works.'

Shotton couldn't think of a suitable reply. Far from being upset at the thought of a body lying underneath her patio since before she had moved in with her dying husband, Mrs Mistery was delighted. 'Oh how thrilling,' she said. 'Just wait till I tell my friends at the WI about this. They'll be so *jealous*. Who do you think it is, sergeant?' Her eyes swivelled towards the patio. 'Lying there all that time. The mother of the dead child?' she deduced. 'It has to be. This is amazing.' Her eyes still sparkled even when she added, 'I suppose you'll have to take the entire patio up. Put up one of those white tents like you see on CSI. It'll be in the papers. Reporters will be camping on my doorstep asking me for a statement.'

Shotton began to feel slightly alarmed. Mrs Mistery was jumping too far ahead. He tried to put the brakes on. 'Umm, Mrs Mistery . . .'

She took absolutely no notice. It was as though he had not spoken.

As each realization hit her she grew more and more excited. 'I'll have to take them out cups of tea like Mary Archer did. Oh my word.' Yet another idea landed. 'What if there's a second baby under there? What if there's a serial baby killer around?'

Shotton felt quite dizzy. 'Mrs Mistery,' he said carefully, 'let's keep all these ideas to ourselves for now, shall we? Let's not jump the gun and start making up stories. The dogs are trained to sniff out decayed bodies. Not necessarily *human* remains. But yes, we will have to dig up the patio but we'll put the slabs back too when we've found what's beneath them. Please don't start rumours and please, please don't worry.'

'Oh, I'm not worried,' said the lively widow.

He recalled the final words of the TV show as he said, 'And don't have nightmares.'

She looked at him. 'Nightmares? You must be joking. This is the most exciting thing that's happened to me since my husband died.'

Shotton was even more taken aback at this. He studied her, now thoroughly puzzled and confused. He might have a good relationship with dogs, he reflected, as he returned to his van and called in to the station, but he didn't get anywhere near understanding humans.

Grope Lane was a narrow passageway lined with shops near St Mary's Church and the Bear Steps. It was a pretty, historic part of the town and was reminiscent of a medieval alleyway where all sorts of skulduggery would have gone on. One could almost imagine the shout of '*Garde-loo*' and a bucket of slops being pitched out of one of the crooked casement windows in the thirteenth-century home of one Richard Stury, a successful merchant of Welsh wool.

WPC Delia Shaw walked over the cobbles to a shop halfway up called Victor Plumley's. She had been detailed to speak to the estate agents. Like many in the town, it was an old family business with a sign over the door which proclaimed that Victor Plumley had been an estate agent in this 'shoppe' for more than two hundred years. Delia smiled as she pushed the door open. This feeling of history underfoot was the very reason why she loved this town which so unashamedly and proudly flaunted its history and why she would never work anywhere else if she could help it.

A young man looked up as the doorbell jangled. His badge informed her that his name was David Plumley.

'Good afternoon,' he said politely, 'Can I help you?'

She flashed her ID card. 'I'm part of the team investigating the discovery of a child's body in number 41 The Mount. You may have read about the case in the papers.'

David Plumley frowned. 'Is that the lady who took a dead child to the hospital? About a week ago.'

'That's correct.'

'I really don't see how we can help you?'

'It's to do with the history of the house where the child was found,' she said. 'Number 41 The Mount. The people who are the current occupants bought the property from another couple. They, in turn, bought the property through you.'

'That must be years ago.'

'Eight years.'

David Plumley couldn't quite assimilate the information. 'I'm sorry,' he said, 'but I don't understand what this has to do with us.'

'Forensic evidence,' WPC Shaw said, 'indicates that the baby had been dead for a number of years. The pathologist is not absolutely sure how many. We're covering all possibilities.'

Plumley made an expression of distaste. 'How horrible. How gruesome. Are you telling me that the body could have been in the house for more eight years?'

'It appears so,' Delia said carefully.

David Plumley swallowed. 'I showed people over that p-property myself,' he stuttered. 'Are you telling me . . . ?' His voice trailed away and his colour changed to an odd shade of green.

'So you handled the sale yourself?'

'Well yes, partly. It's a lovely house. I remember it quite well. Not the usual run-of-the-mill place. Large, Victorian semi-detached, as I recall it. They're always popular. Sell very quickly as a rule. Particularly in such a good area. An old lady.' He narrowed his eyes. 'A Mrs Isaac was selling it. She was quite elderly and a wee bit muddled. She wasn't really up to showing people round the place so when her son and daughter-in-law couldn't get up here we showed prospective purchasers around ourselves. Subsequently she went to live with her family.' He frowned again. 'I can't remember where they were from.'

'Were you the only member of staff who showed people around?'

'No. I had an assistant at the time called Jenny. She did some of the viewings for me. There weren't that many. The Godfreys appeared fairly soon after the property had gone on the market. The Mount is a very popular area. Number 41 was only on the market for a couple of months as I remember.'

'When you showed people round was there any time when they were alone in the property?'

'Absolutely not,' David Plumley said. 'That would be totally against our rule book. Oh no. Quite definitely no one would ever have been ever left alone in the property.'

'Do you know whether Mrs Isaac had carers in?'

Plumley screwed up his face. 'I don't think so,' he said. 'I mean she wasn't that bad. Just a bit dotty and a bit frail. I don't think I remember any carers being there.'

'Does Jenny still work here?'

'No. She left a few years ago. Her husband got a job in Australia.'

'Are you still in touch with her?'

David Plumley coloured. 'No,' he said shortly. 'But I can vouch one hundred per cent that Jenny would not have left people alone in the house. It would be against all the rules in the book. They could have stolen something for a start and then we would be liable. Jenny was a professional.' He smiled and WPC Shaw wondered why the embarrassment? Plumley had mentioned a husband. An office affair?

'And the Godfreys?' she prompted.

'As far as I remember he was a bit of a wide boy while she was typical of a woman who wanted her own way. I remember she was saying she'd have this changed and that changed and she didn't like this. She was quite a picky person. She slightly irritated me. She seemed to want to change every-thing. Original fireplaces, central heating system, all the colour schemes, paint over the banisters. She would have spent a lot of money –' he gave a deep sigh – 'removing every single vestige of a period property. Ghastly woman. She should have had a newbuild.'

'She wasn't pregnant?'

'Not that I saw. I mean it's a long time ago and she could have been in early pregnancy without it showing but I know she wasn't obviously pregnant. I can't recall much detail now but as far as I remember this was how they struck me. Mr Godfrey had made a lot of money in a fairly short time and . . .' He laughed. 'His wife was going to make sure she spent it. He appeared . . .' He paused. 'Indulgent. Does that help you?'

'Yes. Thanks,' Delia said. 'You've been really helpful. I wonder if I might trouble you for the contact details of Mrs Isaac's family.'

'It'll take a while,' Plumley said. 'It was a few years ago. Can I ring you later?'

'That'll be fine.' WPC Shaw gave Plumley her card. 'These

are my contact details. If I'm not there just leave the names and addresses on the answerphone.'

'I will.' Plumley stood up and shook her hand.

As soon as he got the phone call from Sergeant Shotton, Alex Randall sent Paul Talith round to number 41 to talk to the Sedgewicks and tell them that they were following a lead at their previous house in Bayston Hill. He would be interested to note their reaction.

Talith broke the news to both Sedgewicks in the now familiar sitting room.

Alice appeared composed. In fact she didn't react at all, but sat, hands folded on her lap, a polite half-smile on her lips, looking around the room. Her husband, however, was incandescent.

'A lead,' he taunted. 'What lead?'

'I'm sorry but I'm not at liberty to reveal that, sir,' Talith said, watching the man's face carefully.

The careful politeness failed to improve Aaron Sedgewick's mood. 'That's right,' he flung back bitterly. 'Hide behind bureaucracy, why don't you?'

Talith didn't rise to the challenge.

Aaron thundered on. 'I don't know why you're hounding us in this way,' he shouted. 'My wife was simply the person who *found* this wretched body.' His eyes bulged as he spoke the word. There was no sympathy for a tragic death or even for the impact it might have had on his wife. Aaron Sedgewick was, Talith decided, an extremely self-centred man.

Sedgewick ranted on. 'There's nothing at all to connect my wife with the child's death. I shall speak to Acantha and demand that you stop persecuting us.'

Talith thought the word 'persecuting' a little strong but he kept his cool, a talent he was fast honing to perfection.

'We're being as quick and thorough as we can, Mr Sedgewick.'

'So why have you come round today?'

'Just to clarify some details.'

'Clarify? What details?'

'The patio, sir, that you constructed in the garden of your old house?'

'What about the patio?' Sedgewick responded irritably. 'This is quite ridiculous. It's just a patio.'

'We're only doing our job,' Talith said steadily. 'That's all. Now. The patio? Did you build it?'

'Yes I did,' Sedgewick admitted.

'Yourself, sir?'

'Yes. Well, I had some help from a firm of builders that I owned back then but I did most of the work. Want something doing and all that.'

'Can you remember exactly *when* you built the patio?'

'It would have been around 2003 or 4. I know it was some-time during the summer. It was really hot and then suddenly it turned wet. We had the devil of a job trying to drain the water off so we could lay the flagstones.' He eyed Talith. 'I admit I built a patio,' he said, mocking him. 'It's hardly a major crime. You don't even need planning permission. So what of it?'

Talith kept quiet and watched Sedgewick's eyes narrow as he stopped blustering and started to work out what was behind this trail of questions.

'Why are you interested in a small building project?'

'We've taken the sniffer dogs round there,' Talith said steadily. 'They are specially trained to detect long-decayed bodies.' He waited. His inspector had taught him the value of a pause of the right length and in the right place.

Aaron Sedgewick was scowling like a troll.

'Exactly what are you implying?'

Again Paul Talith waited for Aaron Sedgewick to realize where this was heading – which he finally did.

'You think my wife buried someone under the patio?'

Talith gave a swift glance at Alice. Even though her husband had just spoken the most outrageous of sentences which involved her she was still sitting, staring in front of her, a fixed smile on her face.

Talith felt a shiver. This woman was not quite right in the head.

He looked back at Aaron. And right in front of Talith's astonished eyes the colour drained out of Aaron Sedgewick's face. For a moment Talith even thought he would pass out. 'Sir,' he said urgently. 'Sir?'

Aaron stared right past him, as though seeing his own ghost.

He completely ignored the presence of his wife, muttering, 'My wife. My wife? My wife?'

Talith could see no point in pursuing the questions.

Half an hour later he was relating the result of the interview to Alex Randall.

'Honestly, sir,' he said. 'I thought he was going to drop in front of my very eyes. He looked completely shocked, as though he had suddenly realized something. All the fight was gone out of him.'

'Did he actually say anything?' Randall asked.

'He sort of muttered, "my wife, my wife, my wife", over and over again and she just sat there with this weird smile on her face. I've never seen anything like it. I was glad to get out of there.'

'What do you make of it?'

They looked at one another, possibilities streaming through their minds.

'Oh my word,' Alex said slowly.

Martha rang Simon that afternoon and he sounded clipped and strained.

'Hello, Martha,' he said glumly. 'How are you?'

'I'm well. Thank you, Simon. You?'

'The girls are making things very difficult,' he complained. 'They're hell. They won't even try and like Chrissi. They're being so unreasonable. Do they want me to be alone for ever?'

She thought he was being a little dramatic. 'Simon,' she said, 'hear me out.'

'You don't like her either,' he said glumly.

'I don't dislike Christabel,' she said. 'I think she's fine but lots of people find it hard when they're suddenly left on their own after being married for a long time.'

'And?' She could sense the hostility in his voice. He was guarded, negative, suspicious.

'Why not have her as a girlfriend. Why all this talk about being married? What's all the hurry?'

The other end of the line went quiet.

'It's because you haven't got used to the fact of being alone. I know, Simon, because I've been through it myself. You're simply rushing for a swift solution.' She paused. 'It's more likely to be a disaster than if you wait.'

More silence. Then: 'Have you not been tempted to marry again?'

'At first I desperately didn't want to be alone,' she said, 'rather than wanting to marry a specific person.'

'And now?'

'Mind your own business,' she said, laughing.

And after a brief pause Simon joined her. 'I shall listen to your voice,' he said.

Almost as soon as she had put the phone down Alex Randall rang her. 'Just keeping you informed, Martha,' he said. 'We're digging up the patio at Bayston Hill, the house the Sedgewicks lived in before they moved.'

'Why?' she asked bluntly.

'The sniffer dogs became frenzied there this morning – over one particular spot. They're rarely wrong, Martha.'

She tried to keep the pictures out of her mind, of a further body – or even bodies – being found in another property.

'Keep me informed, Alex,' was all she said, but he sensed that she was disturbed.

Tuesday morning

The team was assembled and arrived at the house in Bayston Hill at nine o'clock. To their relief there were no journalists and no more than a passing interest from the other inhabitants of the road. They'd offered to move Mrs Mistery to a hotel for a few days but she would have none of it. 'Absolutely not,' she said. 'Miss out on all the fun? This'll probably be the only murder investigation I'll ever be involved in. This is my moment of fame. Go to a hotel? You must be joking. I'm staying put and what's more, if some of my very dear friends want to come to tea, which I'm sure they will, I shall invite them.'

Hughes and his team looked at one another, shrugged and carried on with their work, certain that a steady stream of elderly ladies would be observing what they could through Mrs Mistery's patio doors.

Luckily the ground wasn't still frozen. The slabs of concrete were heavy and they stacked them neatly against the fence.

It took them all day to remove all the stones and underneath was a concrete level, which would take all the next day to take up with the help of a percussion hammer. Hughes swallowed a smile as he saw a rim of bird-like faces watching him through the window. See what the old biddies made of the noise of that. The building work, he noted, had been done very thoroughly. By four the light was going. They set up arc lights (another disturbance for the inquisitive women).

At six p.m. there was a briefing with plenty to report.

WPC Delia Shaw related the conversation she'd had with Plumley. 'I'm just waiting for his call back,' she said, 'with the address Mrs Isaac moved to when she left the house in The Mount. He absolutely insists that no one had an unaccompanied viewing at number 41,' she added.

Talith related the odd behaviour of Aaron Sedgewick at the Mount the previous afternoon, then Randall picked up the threads of the investigation of what lay underneath the patio stones in Bayston Hill. Could the baby have been kept there and moved? Were there other bodies?

'We'll know a bit more when we see what SOCO unearth,' he said. 'They're still lifting the patio as we speak.'

Plumley rang back just as Delia Shaw was putting her coat on. 'I've got the details you want.' He rattled off an address in Birmingham.

'Do you have a telephone number?'

There was the sound of papers rustling and Plumley gave her a Birmingham landline. She glanced at the phone. It was seven o'clock. She was already late.

She dialled the number anyway.

TWELVE

A man answered the phone and listened politely as she spoke. 'I see,' he said. 'I had read something about a child's body being found in a house in Shrewsbury but I had no idea that the house in question was my mother's.'

'Is there any possibility,' Delia suggested tentatively, 'that I could come down and speak to you about the property?'

'Of course,' he said, sounding surprised, 'though I can't see that I can help you in any way. You do know my mother died a couple of years ago?'

'I'm sorry,' she said.

'It's OK. She was elderly. She didn't suffer. Her last couple of years with us were happy. The children got to know her. No regrets. Anyway, I'm around tomorrow if that's any good.'

'Yes – that would be really convenient.'

'OK. I'll see you tomorrow then.' He sounded buoyant, unconcerned.

Innocent, she decided. 'About eleven?'

'That'll be fine.'

'Thank you,' she said and hung up.

At least, Delia Shaw thought, as she switched the light off and left the room, now she too would have some contribution to make to the case.

Maliciously Roddie Hughes started the noisy work digging up the concrete at seven a.m. the following morning and was rewarded by a sleepy looking Mrs Mistery drawing back the curtains and looking slightly less delighted at being at the centre of a crime drama. They had also spoilt her fun by erecting a screen right around the small patio which completely blocked her view. They did not want Mrs Mistery's geriatric gang of mates witnessing their activities, drinking cups of tea, pointing fingers and generally mischief-making.

He and the team worked steadily, lifting the concrete until they had exposed the underlying hardcore, finally exposing the soil.

They had almost finished this task when Shotton returned, bringing Holmes and Watson with him. As soon as they were out of the van, the dogs scampered towards the patio, eagerly pressing their noses to the newly exposed earth. They concentrated their attention over practically the same spot as before, yelping excitedly, wagging their tails and waiting for their reward. The SOCO team looked at one another.

They had a hit.

The M6 was its usual nightmare and WPC Delia Shaw worried that she would arrive late for her appointment with the Isaacs, but in the event, with the luck of a sudden clearing of the traffic and the aid of her Satnav she pulled up outside their house only a few minutes after eleven, having left a message at the station to let them know where she was going.

Mrs Isaac's son lived in a similar house to the one his mother had inhabited, a large detached Victorian property near the centre of Moseley Village, a stylish suburb two miles south of Birmingham's city centre. It was an area with its own character, a village green, shops and cafes, both bohemian and cosmopolitan, reminiscent of Greenwich Village, New York.

Two saloon cars stood in the driveway and the door was opened to her as soon as she knocked. The Isaacs were ready for her. They welcomed her warmly into a large, cosy kitchen, bright with cream bespoke units and amply warmed by an Aga. PC Shaw thanked them for seeing her and reassured them that no suspicion fell on either them or the late Mrs Isaac. They sat companionably around a kitchen table, a cafetière of coffee supplying the dual purpose of scenting the room and providing refreshment. Paul Isaac was a tall, dark-haired man in his fifties. Rebecca Isaac was quite a lot younger than her husband, maybe in her thirties, Delia noted. She was also heavily pregnant.

Paul Isaac spoke first. 'I really can't see how we can help you.'

PC Shaw gave them both a disarming smile. 'It's a very puzzling case and we feel we would like to get to the bottom of it,' she said. 'We haven't really got any substantial leads so we're clutching at straws.' Another of her wide smiles. 'Hence the trip down the M6 to see you. So anything – absolutely anything that you can think of – even if it appears irrelevant to the case, might just be the tip we need.' Her smile was returned by both of them.

Paul Isaac spoke first. 'It's difficult for us to think of anything that can possibly have any bearing on your case,' he said. 'It was about eight years ago now that we brought mother to live with us. She was getting a little forgetful, a bit frail and we thought it safer to keep her under our eye. The house in Shrewsbury is a big place. Far too big for her. She couldn't really manage it, even with help.'

'What help?' WPC Shaw asked sharply.

'She had a lady come in in the mornings for a couple of hours,' Rebecca said.

Delia Shaw drew out her notebook. 'Her name and address?'

'Maisie somebody,' Rebecca said vaguely. 'I can't remember her surname. She lived somewhere on Castlefields. I probably threw away her contact details years ago – after mother died.' She glanced quickly at her husband. 'But she can't have had anything to do with a baby. She was well into her fifties.' Her hands brushed her swollen stomach.

'How did your mother-in-law find her?'

Again it was Rebecca Isaac who answered. 'Through an advert in the *Shrewsbury Chronicle*. She advertised to do cleaning and mentioned that she was particularly happy to work with the elderly as she'd done some sort of nursing. She sounded ideal for Mother.' She gave another quick, puzzled look at her husband. 'She was wonderful. She did everything, cleaned and shopped and tidied up, did any errands, even drove Mother to the doctor's or the dentist's. She picked up her prescriptions and cooked her lunch. She did just about everything. She was a real treasure. A find. Mother was really fond of her. In fact, she was so good that when we finally brought Mother to live with us we gave her a cheque for two thousand pounds. In recognition of her help.'

'Very generous,' Delia commented.

'Well – we thought a lot of her. She was a lovely woman and she made Mother's life so much easier.' Paul Isaac seemed to think something more was expected and added to his wife's comments. 'She was pleasant too. Always friendly. When we visited she cooked us meals and generally made us welcome. To be honest, we couldn't have wanted anyone better.'

'What about her family?'

They looked at one another. 'I don't remember her mentioning a husband,' Paul Isaac said dubiously. 'And I haven't a clue whether she wore a wedding ring or not. She might have had a son or a daughter but I don't recall anything about them. She didn't talk about anything to do with her personal life. We certainly never met any relations of hers. It was all about Mother.'

'Do you know if a son or a daughter ever visited her at your mother's house?'

'Not that we know of.' They answered in unison without any consultation, Paul Isaac adding unnecessarily, 'If they visited when we weren't there we wouldn't have known anything about it, would we?'

'Quite. And the garden?'

Paul Isaac answered again. 'A firm of gardeners came round. Greenfingers they were called.' He chuckled. 'A very memorable name. They came round one morning a week, once a fortnight through the winter to tidy up. They did the lawns, the hedges, maintenance. They weren't cheap but they kept the grounds immaculate. Mother wasn't short of money and she would have been upset to have seen the place fall into neglect, so it was money well spent.'

Delia copied it all down religiously without a clue whether any of it would prove relevant. 'So you brought your mother to live with you in . . . ?' She looked up enquiringly.

'October 2002.'

'Why then?'

'She was getting older. Into her eighties. Oh, I don't know,' Rebecca Isaac said. 'The world suddenly seemed to have become a more dangerous place, people a little more vulnerable, families a little more precious. I lost a brother in the Twin Towers attack. He was my only brother. I have no sisters. My parents are both dead. We felt. We both felt,' she corrected, 'that we wanted what family we had near. Paul is an only child. The winter was coming. Travel can be tricky. The motorways . . . well.' Rebecca Isaac gave her a sudden smile. 'We don't need to tell you, Constable Shaw. You've come down it this morning. It's a nightmare. If there had been a sudden crisis we couldn't have been certain of arriving even using the M54. We didn't want her to go into a home even if Mother would have accepted that arrangement.' She waved her hands around vaguely. 'This is a big enough place. Plenty big enough. We wouldn't be on top of one another. Paul's children had both left school to go to university. We'd had some alterations done for her so she had her privacy and dignity, her own bed-sitting room and bathroom. I was more than happy to cook for her and make sure she ate properly.' She looked up. 'It seemed the obvious thing to do. We were all happy with the arrangement.' Paul Isaac glanced at his wife and they smiled at one other. The arrangement, it seemed, had worked for both of them.

Delia noted the term of affection Rebecca had used for her mother-in-law. She called her 'Mother'. This gave her a picture of the deceased Mrs Isaac, of a warm, independent person, dignified, loved and elderly. She could have had nothing to do with the concealment of a baby's body, surely? They belonged in different worlds.

She tried to retrieve something from the interview. 'I know this is a long shot but can you think of any circumstance that a child could have been secreted in the loft while your mother lived at number 41?'

Both of them shook their heads.

'No one ever went there with a baby,' Paul said, 'not that we remember. Or pregnant. Our friends and acquaintances would have gone to antenatal clinics and pre-birth exercises, parent classes. That's the sort of world we belong to, Constable Shaw – not concealing a pregnancy and then a child's body, being ashamed of it like that. It isn't our way. It's not civi-lized. Even if someone we knew was pregnant and didn't want to be they'd simply go and have a legal and safe termination on the National Health Service or privately in a clinic. None of our friends or acquaintances would go through the trauma of having a baby away from trained midwives, doctors, pain relief, a hospital, a paediatrician. It's too risky. But if by a long long stretch of imagination they had found themselves in this awful and frightening situation and the baby died they wouldn't just hide the body. They would want it buried, have a funeral, mourn. It's our culture, Constable Shaw. It wouldn't make any sense. It's just not the way we do things.'

WPC Shaw could see the absolute, unarguable logic behind his words. 'Excuse me asking,' she said, not even knowing why she was asking this, 'but how long have you been married?'

Paul Isaac answered very stiffly. 'Rebecca and I were married in 2000. If it's got anything to do with you.'

'I am expecting our first child,' Rebecca said gently, putting her hand over her husband's. 'Paul and his first wife were divorced in the late 1990s.'

'Thank you.' Delia Shaw knew she'd lost a bit of face with her last question but now she'd alienated the Isaacs she felt that she should try to retrieve something more tangible from the interview even if it was in a misguided direction and distanced them still further from the truth. 'Your mother's house was obviously worth a lot of money.'

The Isaacs waited, looking vaguely affronted at the bluntness of the comment and a little wary.

WPC Shaw felt she was in pursuit. 'What was the value of her estate when she died?'

It brought out the sting in both of them. Rebecca's mouth tightened and she gave a swift, worried glance at her husband.

'I can't see what that's got to do with your enquiry,' Paul Isaac said stiffly.

WPC Shaw waited.

'A little over two million in all.'

'That's a lot of money.'

Paul Isaac dipped his head.

Delia Shaw addressed her next question directly to him. 'Your father?'

'Died back in the 80s.'

'What did he do for a living?'

The Isaacs exchanged a strained look and appeared even more uneasy. Rebecca Isaac started rubbing her fingers together with a soft, dry, rasping sound.

'He was an undertaker,' Paul Isaac said reluctantly.

PC Shaw was taken aback. She hadn't expected this answer. She had a moment's hesitation while she wondered what to do next. She didn't want to go just yet. She felt she was on the verge of discovering something of potential significance. Perhaps she could still flush something useful out of this interview. She stood up, decision made. 'Would it be an awful nuisance if I took a look at the rooms your mother inhabited?'

'If you must,' Paul Isaac said reluctantly and WPC Shaw knew now that any pretence of friendliness was over.

They wanted her to go.

The Isaacs had converted two large, sunny rooms on the ground floor into a sitting room with an electric adjustable bed in one corner and a walk-in shower and bathroom, everything made easy for the elderly lady. It was clean and had obviously been scrubbed and tidied since the old lady's death, yet there was still that lingering scent of an elderly female. A little like fusty rose petals. Delia looked around for something which would give her a clue into the late Mrs Isaac's character. She scanned the room and finally found it in the bookshelves. The late Mrs Isaac had been an avid reader of crime fiction. She found plenty of classics, Sherlock Holmes and Agatha Christie as well as a few surprises, Patricia Cornwell and Michael Connolly. A Val McDermid.

'Thank you,' she said, turning to see Paul Isaac had dropped his arm around his wife's shoulder as though to comfort her. Both were looking upset. They didn't like being in this room. Through affection? Grief? Was there something else? Guilt, perhaps? Or was she simply being a suspicious policewoman?

'One last question,' PC Shaw said, 'and then I promise I'll leave you in peace.' She caught the relief in the dropping of their shoulder muscles and the release of tension in their faces. But they still braced themselves for this final query. 'What do *you* do for a living, Mr Isaac?'

It had not been the question they had feared and Paul Isaac answered easily enough. 'I'm in the family business,' he said. 'I'm an undertaker too.' He grinned. 'Not the most glamorous of occupations but it's recession proof. People are always dying and it provides us with a certain lifestyle.' Again he and his wife exchanged glances.

WPC Shaw shook hands with them both and climbed back into her car, noting that they were watching her from the doorway. They stood until she had turned the corner out of their drive. Either they were being polite or were simply glad to see the Law off their property. It could be either. She felt an unaccountable twitching in her toes. At the back of her mind was the Sherlock Holmes story of the disappearance of tall Lady Frances Fairfax being buried alive in a coffin which had been designed for only one small, dead, old lady. The coffin had been too big. Then, as she turned onto the Bristol Road she almost laughed at herself. That would have meant a complete reversal of this situation. Not a body being secreted somewhere and found years later. Even she could work out that an *undertaker* would have had no need to wall up a child's body. He could have hidden the tiny body in anyone's coffin whether the corpse was for cremation or burial.

Bugger, she thought.

There was still the question of money, she pondered next, as she sped along the Aston Expressway towards the M6. The Isaacs had definitely been sensitive on that point. But again she was barking up the wrong tree. They might have swindled Inland Revenue, even polished off the elderly mother, but even if they had committed both crimes it wasn't going to solve this case. They were investigating the death of someone right at the other end of life. An infant. Not a wealthy geriatric. All she'd really learned for definite was that the Isaacs were not short of money. And it was irrelevant. A red herring. Paul's mother could have been worth the entire National Debt and his father Vlad the Impaler, even Anubis, Egyptian God of mummification. It still wouldn't have had any bearing on this case. This was nothing to do with money or the Isaac's profession or Mrs Isaac herself. It had been a wasted journey; she'd learned nothing to move the case nearer solution. But she reminded herself of DI Randall's frequently uttered statement when an entire trail of investigation came to a blind ending. Nothing was ever really wasted.

Was it?

It was late in the morning, almost Thursday lunchtime, that after painstakingly sifting through the earth, guided by the dogs' noses, that the crime scene team unearthed a bone, then another bone. Both very small. Tiny in fact. Painstakingly they brushed the soil away until they had a perfect set. It was a very small pile of bones and the mood of the men quickly changed from concentrating on the work to one of sombre anticipation. Almost acceptance. It had been what they had half expected to find.

WPC Shaw made her report to Alex Randall and he listened without comment until she'd finished. 'You did well,' he said. 'It was a long shot but I agree with you. Get the report typed up and file it for now. It had to be done,' he added kindly.

'We have so little to go on in this case that we must explore all leads. Well done.'

He made a note that WPC Shaw might be suitable to move to the plain-clothes division if she could use initiative like this.

She'd barely gone when he received the call about the bones found in Bayston Hill.

Martha received his call at a little after four p.m., Alex's voice sounding grave and a little upset.

'We've found some bones,' he said.

'Where?'

'Under the patio of the house in Bayston Hill, the house the Sedgewicks lived in before they moved to The Mount.'

Even Martha felt chilled.

'It's a very small pile of bones,' he said. 'I'm just waiting for clarification from the forensic team whether they're human or not.'

'What do you think, Alex?'

'I'm not sure,' he said. 'I'm no expert. In my opinion the head's too small but if it had just been born, well . . .'

Microcephaly, Martha thought, with a shudder. Babies born with heads too tiny for life.

'A small head doesn't necessarily mean they aren't human,' she said.

'We'll have to wait and see,' Alex responded. 'If they are the bones of another child it probably means that the Sedgewicks are implicated in something grim, something . . . well, even I can't imagine. In any case we're going to have to speak to them again.' He paused, adding, 'I wish you could be there when we interview them, Martha. Sometimes,' he said, 'I think you have an insight – well, an instinct – that we police just don't have. I don't know. Maybe it's the medical training. But it's impossible for you to be there,' he added then fell silent. 'Unless . . .'

She waited.

'Maybe it could be arranged,' he said slowly, 'if we use the interview room with the one-way mirror. Unfortunately,' he added, 'the press have somehow got wind of this new develop-ment and are running a piece about the discovery of bones in tonight's paper. I would have done anything to keep this secret.

For a start if the Sedgewicks do have a connection it fore-warns them. But I don't want to interview them until I know for certain whether the bones are that of another child. If it's just a dog or a dead pet or something I'd look silly hotfooting it round there.' He paused. 'There's something else that's troubling me, Martha.'

'Go on.'

'Well – according to her daughter Alice Sedgewick is unstable, unpredictable. We know she's been treated for depression. There is the possibility that she might read of this new development. If she does . . .' His voice trailed away miserably. 'The trouble is that the story has attracted an awful lot of media interest. The press have been watching our every move.'

'What's your real concern here, Alex?'

He groaned. 'Oh, I don't know, Martha. The thought of there being a second child, worrying that Mrs Sedgewick is, frankly, unbalanced. All sorts of things. You know me, Martha.' He gave a short laugh and she could picture him running his hands through his hair. It was a familiar gesture when he was disturbed about something.

He continued, speaking frankly, 'I think it's the fear of the unknown.' He gave a short laugh. 'So much scarier than facing something tangible. I suppose at the back of my mind is a fear that somewhere, deep inside these gruesome facts, lies a shocking truth. If this is a second baby's body how crazy is Alice Sedgewick? And how many more are out there?'

'Alex,' she responded, concerned. 'This isn't like you, to start getting imaginative and unreal. Stop right there. You're letting this get to you.'

'Yes,' he said wearily. 'That as well.'

'It won't help, you know. Speaking as a friend, you need a break.'

He gave a sour laugh. 'My thoughts exactly. It would solve everything. Only it won't. It won't solve anything.'

She had never heard this bitter tone in Detective Inspector Randall before and it concerned her. He was an excellent police officer. It would be a disaster if he cracked, but she sensed he was not far from that. She also knew that this sudden vulnerability wasn't just because of the case. She knew now that it was compounded by a home life which she suspected, without knowing any real detail, was, for some hidden reason, equally nightmarish. He had said his wife wasn't well. In what way 'not well'? Mentally? Was she like Alice Sedgewick, unbalanced and unpredictable? Or was it something physical? Did she have some awful disease? Or was it possibly both?

She sat back in her chair and closed her eyes. In his own time he would, one day, she was convinced, confide in her. Until then she must ignore the sarcasm and innuendo in his voice and concentrate on her own role. It would not help him if he knew she was so aware of his fragile state and certainly not if she delved into a place where right now she was not wanted.

'I take it once you've photographed the bones in situ you will move them to the mortuary to have them examined?'

'That's what I'd intended,' he said, sounding more normal now. 'I thought I'd better run it past you first.'

'Fine,' she said briskly. 'Let me know the result of the analysis as soon as you can. Please. Whatever time it is.'

'I will.'

'Alex,' she said suddenly. And now it was she who was uncertain as she urged him on. 'There's a dark story behind all this. Find it. Otherwise . . .'

'Otherwise?' he prompted, surprised.

'This is something which will continue.'

'Why on earth do you say that?'

'I don't know,' she said, 'except that there is something malicious behind this case.'

He gave a dry laugh. 'Malicious? That's a strange word to use. I'm spooked enough already, Martha,' he said. 'You're usually the one to have your feet well on the ground. It isn't like you to get fanciful.'

'I know but I'm spooked too. Keep me informed, Alex. Day or night.'

'I will. Goodbye, Martha.'

She hung up then.

Randall was just about to head for the mortuary when Delia Shaw stopped him. 'Sir,' she said. 'I've been thinking.'

Alex Randall took in her intelligent brown eyes, her scrubbed, eager face. 'Yes?'

'It's something that the Isaacs pointed out, sir,' she said.

'Yes,' Randall said again.

'They said, "None of our friends would risk having a baby away from a hospital, doctors, a midwife, pain relief, that sort of thing".'

'Yes?' Alex couldn't see where this was leading.

Delia Shaw ploughed on. 'So the person who was delivered of the baby Alice Sedgewick brought to the hospital was outside these parameters.'

'Go on.'

'Someone not in that social strata. It made me focus on the baby's mother instead of on the baby, sir. She is from a damaged and deprived background, sir. Someone outside society.'

He looked at her. It was a new and interesting angle.

'The house in The Mount is valuable, sir, but our mother was someone alien, someone without funds or access to the NHS.'

Randall was silent. 'Anything more?' he asked gently.

Delia Shaw dropped her eyes. 'No, sir. I hadn't really thought beyond that.'

Randall put his hand on the WPC's shoulder. 'Thank you,' he said. 'You've been most helpful and I think I agree with you. Perhaps you'll consider being seconded to the plain-clothes department at some point?'

WPC Shaw coloured up. 'That'd be great, sir.'

THIRTEEN

Martha worried over the new development for half the evening. This case was haunting her more than any other. Was it simply because it was a baby who had died? Or was it to do with what she suspected lay behind the discovery. There was both wealth and poverty here, knowledge and ignorance, care and neglect. Behind every crime is a character, sometimes vulnerable, sometimes cruel. But behind this case she sensed someone who was so cold as to be devoid of any normal human emotion. We are all programmed to love babies, to want to care for them, protect them. They represent the ultimate vulnerability. So to discard one in this way shocked her.

She worried about Alex too. They had worked together on a number of cases and she had watched as life had twisted and turned for both of them. He had become a trusted colleague, though not a close friend. He was not someone who invited intimacies. Somewhere, she sensed, there was, carefully and deeply buried, some private tragedy in his life that made him keep people at arm's length. He struggled to conceal this secret from everybody and particularly her. She sighed. No one would call Randall a handsome man with his craggy, irregular features, lean, spare frame and a tendency to restlessness, but as so often happens, the odd collection of physical and mental characteristics made him attractive. He was also a very proud person and she sensed that to uncover his secret would be to leave him exposed and raw. He would do anything to preserve his facade. But real friends do not hide behind walls.

One of the things that puzzled her was that the concealment of a newborn's body was not necessary in these modern times. Ever since abortion had been legalized in 1967, there had been no need to give birth to an unwelcome baby, and if you did, there were plenty of willing arms to stretch out and adopt it.

So, why give birth in a house? Why hide a baby's body unless you had murdered it and – according to Mark Randall

– this could not be proved. She asked herself other questions. If this case wasn't solved would it have serious repercussions? Would it leave someone free to commit the same crime again – and again? Were there other babies hidden in various places, an attic, beneath a patio? She tried to put herself in the position of just having given birth, the baby dying, concealing it, and felt only an overwhelming sense of vulnerability. She gave up; it was all beyond her comprehension. Her feeling of unease wasn't helped by the headline in the evening paper.

Police find bones in suspect's house
Police have searched a second house connected with the woman who brought a child's body to the Royal Shrewsbury Hospital just over one week ago.

There was little else of substance but as she read through the text her heart sank. It was just what Alex had feared. She couldn't object to it. The article was factual but it was the omitted details which made it dangerous. The paper failed to mention that it had not been confirmed that the bones were human. As she read it through for a second time she wished that the paper had chosen some other lead story.

It could have repercussions.

Even switching the television on she couldn't escape the story. It was repeated by the local news correspondent, standing right outside number 41, The Mount. She studied the background and made a silent plea that Alice Sedgewick was not tuned in to the local news. She studied the background as the report was aired. There was no sign of life around the house. The curtains were drawn. There was one car in the drive and no movement at all.

What, she wondered, was going on inside?

She spent the evening fretting and unable to enjoy it even when Sukey, Agnetha and she sat and watched *Casino Royal* for the umpteenth time. It was a few years old now, but still one of their favourite films. But tonight even Daniel Craig couldn't lift her out of her concern.

She was still distracted when she got ready for bed and spent a fitful night, tormented by dreams of babies crying, tiny legs kicking, baby hands grasping.

Alex Randall too was having a troubled evening. As he had

been driving home he had been chewing over Delia Shaw's words and as though he had punched a hole through a paper wall, he saw the new dimension it would give to the case. So he forced himself to consider the case from this new and different angle and ask the right questions. What sort of woman would have had a child under these circumstances? Someone very young. Someone naive. Someone ignorant and vulnerable. Someone who could be exploited. Someone who had failed to access the very accessible National Health Service.

He turned into his drive, almost avoiding looking at his home, feeling the usual sinking sensation. He sat for a while in his car, reluctant to move and enter the house. Then the front door opened.

Friday

He rang her so early he broke into the tail end of yet another distorted and distressing dream, this time of a large bird hovering over a tombstone, squawking throatily and pecking at the moss that obscured the chiselled lettering on the stone. It was a very vivid dream. She could see all the detail of the bird, feathers stuck to its beak where it had pecked carrion, strands of pinkish flesh, the blue-black on its feathered wings. As it pecked she deciphered some of the words of the engraving: *In Loving Memory of Poppy, darling daughter*. A few more pecks and she would read more detail. But the bird stopped pecking and perched on the top of the stone, giving a harsh caw. And then the cawing translated into a telephone ringing. She picked up the receiver and couldn't stop herself from giving an enormous yawn into it.

'He-e-llo?'

She wasn't really surprised to hear Alex's voice. He had been so much in her thoughts, even through the nightmare.

'I'm sorry to ring you so early,' he said, speaking in a steady, controlled voice which didn't fool her for a moment, 'but I have both good news and bad news and you did ask me to keep you up to date,' he reminded her.

'I'm beginning to regret it,' she said, smiling. 'I'm not even properly awake yet. I saw the headlines last night, Alex,' she added. 'I wish they'd left it for a day or two. Anyway, you've interrupted a particularly unpleasant dream for which maybe I

should be grateful.' She reflected. 'Good or bad, you said. Well
. . . it's too early for bad news.' She sat up, awake now. 'So,
give me the good. Aaagh.' She gave another huge yawn.

'The good news is this,' he said. 'The bones are not human
but that of a small dog. It was confirmed by Dr Sullivan last
night. He took a quick look and had no doubt. Some time ago
someone must have buried a pet dog and then a year or two
later a patio was built over the grave.' He paused. 'There's nothing
suspicious about it and nothing else sinister in that area.'

'That is good news,' she said. 'And a relief, though it doesn't
explain why Aaron Sedgewick reacted in such a dramatic way
when he learned the patio was to be dug up, does it, Alex?
What did he suspect his wife had done? Not buried a family
pet, that's for certain. He'd have said.'

'I don't know, Martha. But we'll almost certainly get nothing
more out of him.'

'And her?'

'We'll never get *anything* more out of her, Martha,' he said
quietly. 'Alice Sedgewick committed suicide some time in the
night.'

'No? Oh no. Alex.' The worst of it was that she knew that
the dark shadow that both of them had sensed yesterday
evening had been exactly this, that Alice Sedgewick would
kill herself.

Alex repeated the news slowly and factually. 'I worried half
the night about her fragile state of mind and the story in the
newspaper. If only they'd kept it back just for twenty-four hours.
We could have released the fact that the bones were not human.
It would have made all the difference. I hoped she wouldn't
read it or hear it on the television but she obviously did.'

'You're certain it *was* suicide?'

'Pretty much so. Barbiturates and alcohol and she had a
history of mental instability. Just look at the way she behaved
last Saturday. Irrational.'

'Yes. So it would appear. Did she leave a note?'

'It appears not. At least none has been found.'

'Was her husband at home at the time?'

'No,' Alex said dryly, 'he was away on business yet again.
Not far away. Coventry this time. According to him he'd
planned to be away until the middle of next week. He tried
to ring her this morning and got no reply so he was worried.'

'It must have been very early,' she observed, glancing at her bedside alarm. It was seven fifteen.

'A friend rang him late last night, apparently, telling him about the newspaper article. He tried to ring his wife but got no reply. He imagined she was either watching television or had had a couple of drinks and gone to bed with some sleeping tablets so didn't worry too much. When he got no reply again this morning he asked Mrs Palk to call in and check that everything was all right. She has a key to the house.'

'Really?'

'Yes. I thought that. Anyway she let herself in and found Alice spreadeagled across the bed, fully clothed, bottle of barbiturates in her hand, a glass of water spilt on the floor. She said the body was cool to the touch which inclined us to think that she had died some time during the previous evening or the early part of the night. The police surgeon was called at six and pronounced her dead at seven a.m.'

He'd wasted no time in letting her know.

She was silent for a minute, gathering her thoughts. Then she spoke. 'Check it, Alex,' she urged. 'Check it all. Is there a newspaper at home? Was she in the habit of watching the local evening news on the television? Which friend called him, the hotel he's at. Log the calls to his home and to Mrs Palk. Check it,' she repeated. 'Check it all.'

Alex smiled. 'You wouldn't be trying to teach me my job, would you, Martha,' he murmured.

She laughed too. 'It might sound like it,' she said, 'but I know you would have done all these things anyway. I was simply encouraging you.'

Randall was quiet for a moment then he spoke softly. 'You're wasted being a coroner,' he murmured. 'You should have joined the force. You'd be a commander by now.'

She laughed out loud then. 'I don't think so,' she said. 'It's not the way I would liked to have gone. I enjoyed studying medicine and I wouldn't want to be anything but a coroner. But, oh dear, Alex,' she said with feeling. 'What a tragedy. That poor woman.'

'Exactly. Is it OK if we move it to the mortuary?'

'Yes,' she said. 'Move it.' She hesitated. 'No note, you say?'

'No.'

'Shame. It might have provided us with some answers.'

'Yes. And saved some time.'

'So who or what or when is in the frame now?'

He chuckled. 'Are you sure you're awake enough for this?'

'I am now.'

'Well, in the time frame we're talking about, i.e. the last five to eight or so years there are the three families involved. The Sedgewicks who are probably out of the picture unless they brought the baby's body with them when they moved house, which is unlikely. But if the baby had been kept in a warm, dry environment and the body was moved straight from one to the other, even possibly refrigerated during the move, it is possible. The most suspicious thing about them is Alice Sedgewick's odd behaviour. And now, of course, there is her suicide which points to an unsound mind.' He paused. 'I might suspect a guilty conscience if she hadn't thought the child was a girl. She didn't seem duplicit enough to use that to throw us off the scent.'

'Go on.'

'Then there are the Godfreys.'

'You haven't said much about them.'

'No, because apart from them being pretty objectionable people I can't really see where they could possibly fit into the greater picture. She says she's never been pregnant. They haven't got any children and don't appear to want any. She doesn't even like children.'

'And you think the person who did this to the newborn *liked* children, Alex?'

He was initially silent, but finally spoke. 'I see where you're coming from, Martha, but . . .' Then resuming his subject he added, 'And then there is old Mrs Isaac and her family who fit even less into the picture.'

She interrupted him then. 'Alex, it's a bit early. Do you know what time the post-mortem's scheduled for?'

'Not yet, Martha. I'm hoping Mark will fit it in some time today.'

'Hmm. I'm going to have to talk to Aaron Sedgewick,' she said. 'Preferably as soon as possible after the post-mortem.'

A suicide, she was thinking. Like Finton Cley's father. Only this time there was no note so the verdict could be questioned. That was why she was so insistent that Alex

Randall check on Aaron Sedgewick's movements the night
his wife died.

'Have *you* any plans to interview him?'

'At some point, yes. I'll have to, Martha.'

'You know,' she hesitated. 'If you want my advice you'll
do that sooner rather than later.'

'Thank you for that, Martha.' She knew he was smiling as
he spoke.

'And now having done half a day's work, I suppose I'd
better get out of bed,' she said. 'See you later.'

Alex rang Mark Sullivan as early as he could – at nine o'clock
– and asked whether the post-mortem on Alice Sedgewick could
be held first thing as he was anxious to proceed with the investigation. It was imperative that a police officer be present in
case samples were taken and, partly spurred on by Martha's
advice, Randall wanted to be absolutely certain that Alice had
died by her own hand. As he drove in he considered another
explanation. Mrs Sedgewick had come over to him as a vulnerable woman. Why, was more difficult to work out. She had two
children who seemed superficially to have done well. She was
married, had a lovely home and yet she was vulnerable and he
simply couldn't work out why. Alex Randall was a policeman
– perhaps more tuned in to people's feelings than most – but
still primarily a policeman. To him Mrs Sedgewick seemed
vulnerable enough for him to imagine her being coerced or
persuaded into taking her own life. She appeared someone who
would listen to a stronger voice. Alex frowned, his hands grip-
ping the steering wheel. Why did he have the feeling that he
had just expressed a significant statement of fact? He tried to
go over what he had just voiced but a silver Citroën cut him
up at the roundabout and he lost his train of thought.

Damn.

Mark Sullivan was already wearing his scrubs and long
waterproof apron when he arrived. 'Thought I'd save time,' he
said cheerily to Alex. 'I'll get Peter to wheel her in.'

As was the usual practice, Alice Sedgewick was still fully
clothed in a dark skirt and blouse, no shoes and no stock-
ings. There was the usual procedure of weighing the body
and the initial examination. Then Sullivan inserted a gloved
finger into her mouth. Even Alex could see the remains of

tablets semi-dissolved, still not swallowed. 'Apparently she had them on prescription from a private psychiatrist,' Sullivan said disapprovingly. 'She'd been treated for depression and intractable insomnia for a number of years.'

Alex looked up. 'How many years?'

'Three, four.' Sullivan was absorbed in removing Alice's clothes and dropping them into the bag Roddie Hughes was holding out for him.

'Who by?'

Mark Sullivan looked up. 'Sorry?'

'Who'd been treating her?'

'Oh, a private psychiatrist named Richmond. Alan Richmond. He's a very well thought of chap hereabouts. He's treated my own wife.'

'Really?'

Sullivan bent back over his work. 'With very limited success I have to say. But still – you can't win them all.'

'Indeed not.' They both looked at the sad figure of Alice Sedgewick, laid bare now and Randall added quietly, 'Especially as it would seem that it was he who prescribed the fatal medicine.'

Mentally he was tacking yet another thing to his list. Phone Dr Richmond. He was surprised the doctor hadn't come forward to offer some information about the dead woman. If he had she might not be dead now. He would almost certainly be called as a witness to the inquest.

Half an hour later Mark Sullivan gave him his initial findings. 'No marks at all on the body. Amylobarbitone is rapidly absorbed but I'd say she took a fatal dose of a barbiturate together with alcohol some time yesterday evening. He looked across. 'No note, you say?'

'No.'

'Shame that. It might have helped. Still my instinct is that this poor woman committed suicide.' He glanced across at the body. 'She probably saw the headlines in the newspaper and that was that. Whatever had gone on before it tipped her over the edge. You want me to phone Martha?'

'Don't worry – I'll do it. I suppose you'd better get on with the rest of your work now. Thanks, Mark.'

Sullivan smiled. 'Yes – like an undertaker – never short of customers.'

FOURTEEN

Randall rang Martha at home and gave her the results of the post-mortem.

'Much as we'd suspected,' she commented. 'There was no sign of trauma around her mouth, anywhere on her body?'

'No.'

'Was a copy of the newspaper found at the house?'

'I don't know,' he said. 'Obviously the team who originally attended the scene took a quick look round but as this didn't appear to be a suspicious death I haven't ordered a full blown forensic search.'

'That makes sense.'

'But even if she didn't have a newspaper, Martha, she could still have heard about the finding of the bones on the local news on the radio or the television or even seen it on a newspaper hoarding,' he pointed out. 'Or . . .' He stopped. 'Someone could have rung her.'

'That's true,' she said. 'Have you anyone in mind?'

'It'll be difficult to prove.'

'You know me, Alex,' she said. 'I like it neat and tidy. If someone had rung to tell Alice about the bones being found it would have been a malicious act. Someone who was not a friend.'

'Most definitely not,' he agreed.

'Anything else?'

Randall hesitated. 'I'm going to have to speak to Aaron Sedgewick at some point,' he said. 'I'd like you in on it. It might help you decide on your verdict,' he added by way of a sweetener.

'You know I can't attend in person, Alex,' she said. 'It would be considered prejudicial. But I can watch from behind the one-way mirror.'

'I'll see what I can do.' He paused. 'Of course with this being a suicide case I can't order him down to the station. I can only invite him.'

* * *

Alex Randall dreaded having to face Aaron Sedgewick again. He was convinced the man would hold him and the police investigation responsible for his wife's death. So when he connected with Sedgewick he was fully prepared for a battle. But to his surprise Sedgewick was relatively polite over the phone. Randall had fully expected that Aaron Sedgewick would want to be in control and had offered to interview him at his home but no, Sedgewick was adamant he would attend the police station. 'If you don't mind,' he said angrily, 'I've had quite enough of the police poking around my house. I can't see why you feel the need to speak to me at all, particularly when I am so obviously busy with my family problems but if you insist and it means I can bury my dearest wife . . .' There was a break in his voice which almost convinced Alex Randall that the man was genuinely grieving. Almost but not quite. It was the first time he had heard the man express any affection towards his wife. His main feeling towards her had seemed to be one of irritation.

'What time do you want me?'

'As soon as possible.' Randall paused. 'Let's get it over and done with, sir.'

'I'll be down within half an hour although I want it registered that I consider it a gross intrusion by the police at a very difficult time for me.'

Fine, Alex thought as he put the phone down. Just fine.

He rang Martha straightaway and was not surprised when she agreed to witness the interview from behind a one-way mirror. He was looking forward to hearing her observations.

It was six p.m. by the time the three of them were assembled, Martha stationed behind the one-way mirror. Randall found Aaron Sedgewick in more of a state of shock than he had expected. He arrived looking pinched and pale and very tired. Unexpectedly Alex felt some pity for him – an emotion he never would have thought he could have applied to Aaron Sedgewick. He sat him down in the interview room and offered him some coffee.

Once they were seated he explained the purpose of inviting him down. 'This is an informal interview,' he began. 'There are no charges. I simply need to explain to you the findings of the post-mortem and to clarify one or two points.' He met Sedgewick's eyes. 'I apologize for the intrusion but you must understand we, the police, have a job to do. Your wife's death is unexplained.' He paused. 'As yet.'

Immediately Sedgewick began to bluster. The détente was over. 'What do you mean, unexplained? It's obvious what happened. The police have been harassing her since she took that horrible thing up to the hospital. God knows why she did that but that is what she did. My wife . . .' He looked around hopelessly, crumpling before Randall's eyes. 'My wife is . . . was . . .' he corrected, 'a very fragile woman.'

'Why?' Randall asked bluntly.

'There is no why,' Sedgewick snapped. 'She just was. That's the only why. It was her mental make-up, if you like.'

'So you would not be surprised if she had committed suicide?'

'No.' Sedgewick frowned thoughtfully. 'Not really. Alice was a vulnerable woman.'

Randall pressed on. 'But you understand that without a letter of explanation we don't know exactly what happened, what state of mind she was in, what finally tipped her over the edge. After all – it's a week since her visit to the Royal Shrewsbury and she seemed to be coping well.'

Sedgewick leaned forward, a fire burning in his eyes. 'Isn't it bloody obvious what tipped her over the edge? This ridiculous hounding of our old property. Yesterday you found some bones.'

Alex felt himself grow hot with embarrassment. 'They were animal bones.'

'Right.' If anything, Aaron Sedgewick's eyes blazed even more furiously. 'You are telling me,' he said speaking very slowly and deliberately, 'that my wife probably committed suicide over a few *animal* bones?'

'If that's why she did it,' Randall admitted. 'We can't know for sure, Mr Sedgewick, without a note.' Alex had put the ball neatly right back into Mr Sedgewick's court but Aaron wasn't about to give up. 'Why on earth did you have to dig up that wretched patio?'

'It was a necessary part of our investigation.'

'But why make it public?'

Randall felt bound to defend himself. 'We didn't, deliberately. Unfortunately the story leaked out and we had no control over what was printed.'

'If you say so,' Sedgewick said wearily.

'You know a post-mortem was performed on your wife this morning?'

Sedgewick winced.

Alex ploughed on. 'I'm sorry to have to inform you that it appears your wife took her own life using a mixture of barbiturates, which she had been prescribed by a doctor, along with alcohol. Did she give you any clue that this was her intention?'

'No. Not when I last saw her.'

'Which was? Just for the record?'

'I left for Leicester on Tuesday night,' he said. 'She seemed quiet, a little withdrawn but I wasn't worried about her.' He looked up. 'If I had been I would not have gone on a business trip. You understand?'

Alex nodded. 'Your wife has appeared extremely disturbed by recent events.'

'Well – wouldn't your wife be just a little troubled by this?'

Alex's face darkened. Had Sedgewick been observant he would have seen the inspector's face twist with pain. But Aaron Sedgewick was noticing nothing. Martha, however, didn't miss it. She watched Alex Randall as he regained control of himself and continued.

'When did you last speak to your wife, Mr Sedgewick?'

Martha leaned forward to catch Sedgewick's words.

'Yesterday morning. She sounded well. And Acantha keeps an eye on her, of course.'

'And you haven't found a note somewhere in the house?'

'No.'

There had been, Martha thought, the very slightest of hesitations. To such a simple question?

It seemed Alex had picked up on something too because he went over the point again, carefully. 'Not addressed to you or your daughter – or your son – or even Mrs Palk? The two seemed close.'

'No,' Sedgewick said, deliberately aggressive. 'I said no. That's the truth. If she did, as you say, deliberately take a fatal dose of her tablets, she must have done it on impulse.' He frowned and looked up. 'How can you know she did it deliberately? It's pure supposition on your part. You can't possibly know. It could have been an accident.' His face changed, became softer. 'Maybe she had a bit to drink and forgot how many tablets she'd already taken.' He obviously liked this explanation. His face relaxed.

But Alex was not going to let him off the hook. 'Did your wife have a drink problem?'

Sedgewick wasn't quite sure how to answer this question. 'Not a drink problem,' he said slowly. 'But sometimes she had a little more than was wise. It made her rather emotional. Shall we leave it at that?' With an effort he lifted his eyes up to meet Alex's. Martha knew that this admission had cost Sedgewick something.

Randall thought for a minute then nodded his head slowly. 'Without a note I have no option but to agree.' He met Sedgewick's eyes. 'Had there been a note it might have provided some explanation of her actions last week. I suppose it's possible that your wife did not mean to kill herself. In which case we can discuss the circumstances with the coroner and possibly have an accidental death verdict. We may even be asked to look into the impact of our investigation, together with the effect the newspaper story would have had on her already fragile mental state.'

Martha smiled. Randall was well used to her advising him on his job. This was the first time he had directed her. She concentrated on listening to the interview.

'Do you know whether your wife knew about the discovery of the bones at Bayston Hill?'

'I don't know,' Sedgewick said, 'but I would have thought it highly probable. It was even on the TV.' Then as suddenly as a flash of lightning Sedgewick found his temper again. 'Why didn't you just leave things alone, inspector? Why did you have to go digging up the past, searching for something you were never going to find, digging up the patio of our old house, making us look so guilty when you must have known we can't have had anything to do with the death of that thing?'

Alex leaned forward, his face steely. 'We have to investigate the death of the child, Mr Sedgewick.'

'But it had nothing to do with us. My wife simply came across the body.'

'Right.' Alex Randall shuffled some papers. 'Well, I'll share with you some of the anomalies which have bothered us and made us suspicious of you. Can you explain the presence, in your house, of a room specifically decorated for a child when you have no children, no grandchildren and, according to Mrs Sedgewick's previous statement, no children stay with you? Why have a room for a child that doesn't exist?'

Sedgewick had his answer polished and ready. 'She was one of those women who looked forward to the day when she would have grandchildren. And of course, she had an *interest* in the doll's house.'

He hadn't used any adjective to describe his wife's interest in doll's houses but Randall had the feeling if he had he would have used the word 'sad' or 'pathetic'. There was something demeaning in his tone.

Behind the mirror Martha had noted the same point. Whatever Aaron Sedgewick said about his wife, he had despised her, she decided. Alice Sedgewick had not counted. She sat and thought about this, feeling that this was somehow significant but unsure how it fitted into the wider picture. This case was like one of those apparently simple Chinese Puzzles which can frustrate you for days on end. The more uncomplicated they appear the more complex the solution.

'And you still can't explain your wife's behaviour on taking the baby's body to the hospital?'

'No.' The answer came quickly; the explanation took only a minute longer. 'Shock,' he said firmly.

'And you insist you know nothing about the baby's body?'

Sedgewick's face was thunderous now. 'No,' he said.

'And you don't know why she called the little boy Poppy?'

'No,' he shouted again. 'I don't know anything about the wretched child or why my wife should have behaved in such an illogical way unless it's simply another part of wanting to be a grandmother.' He shrugged. 'I don't know. And I haven't the faintest idea why she should commit suicide unless it was the obvious suspicion you people have had of her.' The affectation of care had dropped. He now sounded angry – both with the police and his recently dead wife. 'You've hounded a vulnerable woman. I shall speak to Mrs Palk about it.'

'Ah yes.' Alex picked up on the point. 'Mrs Palk. Why did she have a key to your house?'

Martha practically rubbed her hands together. Alex Randall was asking all the *right* questions.

'She used to check up on the house when we were away,' Sedgewick said. 'That's all.'

It was a logical reason but Alex felt the need to probe a little further. 'It was nothing to do with checking up on your wife while you were on business trips?'

'No.' Said tightly.

'And yet,' Alex said with a smile, 'that was what finally happened, wasn't it, Mr Sedgewick?'

Sedgewick nodded, thought for a moment then said, 'You need to be looking for someone different, inspector.'

'Explain.'

'It's a class thing,' Sedgewick said angrily. 'You need to be looking for some vulnerable young woman who didn't want a child. Not amongst people like myself and my wife. It's a class thing,' he repeated.

Alex stood up and proffered his hand. 'Thank you very much, Mr Sedgewick. You've been a great help.' Sedgewick failed to pick up on the fact that the inspector's voice was heavy with sarcasm.

The man reluctantly shook his hand and Alex ushered him out of the interview room.

Minutes later he was speaking to Martha. 'Well,' he said. 'What did you make of that?'

'Two things,' she said slowly. 'He did put his finger on the pulse about it being a class thing but I've got a feeling we're looking at this from the wrong angle. Let me think about it, Alex.'

'And the other thing?' Alex asked curiously.

'He's quite disdainful of family life,' she said. 'And again I'm wondering what bearing that can have had on this.'

'Not very helpful, Martha,' Alex said, smiling.

'No,' she agreed. 'You know, Alex . . .' She paused. 'I still think he's hiding something from you.'

He nodded in agreement.

'Well, I shall have to speak to him myself later. I'll get Jericho to give him a ring on Monday morning. What's your next step?'

'Speak to Dr Richmond,' he said, 'and I'm not looking forward to it. I think he'll be a slippery customer – and on the defensive.'

'Well. Time to go home for me,' she said, 'and hope Agnetha's cooked the tea.'

Randall's face clouded. 'Yes.'

She picked her coat up off the chair. 'Keep in touch, Alex.'

'I will.'

She smiled. 'Good luck,' she said and left.

There was no point trying to get hold of Dr Richmond on a Friday evening, so Alex had to leave it to the Monday morning. He tracked his telephone number down easily enough in his private clinic and found him, as expected, in a defensive mood. 'Dr Richmond, I believe you treated the late Alice Sedgewick?'

'Late?' the doctor queried sharply.

'Yes. It appears she committed suicide on Thursday evening with a combination of alcohol and a fatal dose of barbiturates, tablets I believe you had prescribed for her.'

'It's correct,' the doctor said stiffly. 'I did prescribe barbiturates for her. She suffered from intractable insomnia and severe depression and as the NICE guidelines recommend benzodiazepines for this condition I prescribed them.' He paused, mid flow. 'I gave her strict instructions about dosing and told her that she was not to take them with alcohol.'

'What was the cause of her depression?'

'Come on, inspector,' he said testily. 'You know I can't divulge that.'

'You can with permission from the Medical Defence Union when it's in the patient's interest.' He waited but the doctor was not offering anything more.

'It's possible the coroner might ask you further questions. I'm surprised that knowing of our involvement in this case you didn't come forward and at least tell us she was vulnerable and having treatment from you.'

'That too would have been divulging information.'

'Did you consider her a suicide risk?'

Dr Richmond took a long time considering this question. 'Not really,' he finally said.

'Even with the added stress of recent events?'

'I haven't seen her for a few weeks, inspector.' He was being a little more polite now.

'This is a private service. If she had *asked* to see me I would have seen her but she didn't.'

'Does that surprise you?'

For once Dr Richmond showed his human side. 'Nothing my patients do surprises me,' he said. 'Patients are patients. Frequently unpredictable.'

'Did she suffer from delusions?'

'No.' The doctor was insistent. 'She was not psychotic – merely depressed.'

'Thank you, doctor. 'We'll be in touch and you'll be summoned to appear at the inquest, so might I suggest that you clarify things with your defence union.'

The phone was banged down. Alex listened to the dialling tone then rang the coroner's office.

The first thing Martha had done when she arrived on Monday morning was to ask Jericho to contact Aaron Sedgewick. 'I take it you heard that Mrs Sedgewick committed suicide on Thursday night?'

Jericho's eyes brightened. 'I did,' he said. 'It was on the local radio. Poor woman. First she ends up at the hospital with a dead baby. Next she tops herself.' He risked a look at Martha. 'Whatever will happen next, I wonder.'

'Quite,' she said dryly.

Martha had not been looking forward to this interview but it was unavoidable. Alice Sedgewick had apparently committed suicide and she needed to speak to her next of kin to ascertain the dead woman's state of mind. She anticipated that considering his frequent business trips Mr Sedgewick would not be an easy person to speak to but he agreed to come to her office at 3 p.m. that afternoon. He was having a busy day, she reflected.

As was her custom she began the interview by offering her condolences. Sedgewick eyed her suspiciously but thanked her and sat down.

'The evidence appears to indicate that your wife took her own life deliberately,' she said.

As expected Sedgewick was immediately on the defensive. 'You can't know that,' he said.

'No,' Martha agreed. 'Without a note it's difficult to know what goes on in a person's mind, whether they simply want to sleep.' She eyed Sedgewick thoughtfully. 'Did your wife have difficulty sleeping, Mr Sedgewick?'

He appeared uncertain how to answer this question. 'Sometimes,' he said. 'Yes – no.'

'You know you'll be expected to give evidence at the inquest speaking about your wife's state of mind.'

'Is that really necessary?'

'Yes, considering she did not leave a suicide note which is the usual case. We need an explanation, Mr Sedgewick. At the moment we have none.'

Sedgewick's temper burst through then. 'All this has been stirred up by your lot.'

Martha leaned forward, her face firm. 'Mr Sedgewick,' she said, 'get this clear. I am not the police. I am a coroner. It is my job simply to ascertain who has died, where they died and how they died. If this is not clear I shall have to give an open verdict. This is my policy when there is no suicide note and the death does not appear suspicious.' She recalled Finton Cley's words about the impact the suicide verdict had had on his family. 'As far as is possible we would want to avoid an open verdict. It lacks clarity and finality. But neither myself or the police started this. It all began when your wife, for some reason still unknown to us, walked into the hospital with a dead child in her arms. A child who had been dead for a number of years and whose body had been concealed in your house. You understand that I must hold an inquest for the dead child too. It is another of my responsibilities, so I would like closure on that too. Now though we are fairly sure your wife was not responsible for the baby's death, we obviously wonder what her state of mind was that she did this rather strange thing. Why didn't she simply call the police? What was she doing up there anyway in the attic?'

'She told you,' he said furiously, 'or at least the police. I was thinking of doing a loft conversion. She was simply inspecting the proposed site. That's all. There is nothing in the least bit suspicious in that.'

'No. But there is in the way she subsequently acted, Mr Sedgewick,' she said and repeated herself. 'I am not the police and they are not me. My role is simply to find out the circumstances surrounding the death of an unknown infant and subsequent death of your wife.'

'You're linking them together,' he accused.

'Naturally we are. What I want to know is what is this link?'

Sedgewick looked crushed and she continued, 'Mr Sedgewick, we are truly sorry for your loss and regret recent events but you cannot blame us for this situation. We are simply trying to find out the truth. Do you understand?' She met his eyes.

'Yes.'

Martha consulted her notes. 'According to the police your wife called this child Poppy.' She looked up. 'Do you know why?'

'It was her grandmother's name. It's on her doll's house.'

'But why call a dead little boy after your presumably long-dead grandmother?'

'Not a bloody clue,' he said.

'Further, she wrapped the infant up in a pink blanket.'

He frowned at her, his anger leaking into his eyes. 'Pink. Blue. Has the world gone mad to focus on such things?'

Not the world, she thought.

A very disgruntled man left her offices soon after. She heard his car roar away just as Jericho appeared with a mug of coffee and a plate of chocolate biscuits. She smiled at him. Chocolate biscuits – on a china plate. He must know she was having a difficult Monday.

She was glad to finish work and drive home, even more pleased that Sukey and Agnetha had cooked that ultimate comfort food, shepherd's pie. She teased Agnetha about making Swedish shepherd's pie served with lingonberry jam which Sukey insisted tasted just like cranberry sauce.

Cranberry sauce? With shepherd's pie?

Over tea Sukey eyed her and fidgeted and Martha knew she wanted to ask her something. 'Go on,' she said, finally putting her fork down. 'Spit it out.'

'They do a summer school in acting,' Sukey said hesitantly. 'It's a bit expensive but apparently they start teaching you all sorts of useful things.'

'What sorts of things?' Like many people not in the profession Martha imagined one simply acted. How could you be taught it? It was surely simply a talent one either had or did not have. 'Who are they?' she asked. 'Where is it?' She wanted to ask, 'and how much does it cost?' but felt this was going a little too far in the interrogation and that her daughter would find it discouraging.

'It's a really good springboard, Mum.'

'How long is it?'

'A month – over the summer.'

'And what do they teach you?'

'I don't know.' She gave her mother a wide smile. 'I haven't done it yet. Methods, I suppose.'

'Well, Suks,' she said, 'it seems to me that you'd better go to this school and find out.' She smiled at her daughter, loving her enthusiasm. 'Get me the details. Print them off the Internet and we'll look into it together. What do you think, Agnetha?'

'I think Sukey will make a wonderful actress,' Agnetha said loyally. 'She is a girl of so many talents.' They smiled at one another.

'Oh, Agnetha, we're going to miss you when you go,' Martha said. 'You're one of the family. How can you bear to leave us?'

Agnetha flicked her long pale hair behind her shoulders. 'I want to be married, Mrs Gunn,' she said. 'I want to have children of my own and I hope very much that I have a daughter like yours one day.'

'I'll raise a glass to that, Agnetha,' Martha said. 'Well, here's to you and your future, both of you.'

Agnetha and Sukey exchanged glances. 'And yours, Mrs Gunn,' the au pair said steadily. 'What will be your future?'

It was a question Martha was unable to answer so she ducked it with a: 'We'll have to wait and see.'

It didn't help that Simon rang very late that night. It was almost ten o'clock and he sounded upset. 'Christabel's finished with me,' he said.

Martha switched the sound down. She had been about to watch the ten o'clock news. 'Finished with you? Why?'

'Can't you guess?'

Unfortunately she could – and was proved right.

'She couldn't stand the hostility of the girls. Selfish little bitches.'

This one sure knew how to divide a family, Martha thought. Privately she felt that Christabel could have held back, bided her time. What was the hurry anyway? Simon had been widowed for a year. Why on earth did he feel he had to rush into *marriage*? The two girls had lost their mother not so very long ago. She couldn't blame them for taking against another

woman who was their age – and half of their father's. Surely
if she had really cared for Simon she would have waited and
hoped that one day Simon's daughters would accept her –
even if the process might have been slow.

A thought struck her. 'Simon,' she said. 'Whose idea was it
to be married?'

'Hers,' he said shortly. 'She'd had a boyfriend she was
engaged to and he cheated on her. She said she felt insecure
unless she was married. He persistently refused to marry her.
I wasn't going to tell you this, Martha, but she got pregnant,
hoping he would marry her. He not only refused to but insisted
if they were to stay together that she should have an abortion, poor girl. She was devastated. At about the time that I
was feeling so vulnerable so was she. It was inevitable we
should get together and comfort one another. The poor child.'

Something stirred in Martha, the smallest of understandings
of a situation.

But she said nothing except: 'Are you all right? Do you
want to come round here? Drown your sorrows? You can stay
if you want.'

He heaved a great big sad sigh. 'Yes – no. I don't know.'

She allowed him to be silent for a while.

'No, I'd better not. I've already had a couple of whiskies.
I'm probably over the limit. The last thing I want is to lose
my driving licence. It'd be the last straw. I'd better stay here.'

She would have offered to drive across herself but it was
late. She was tired and she didn't want to push her attentions
on him. Not for the first time she wished Martin was around.
He would have jumped in the car, shared a 'jar' or two with
his pal, talked over 'varsity days' and seen his friend through
this dark hour which Martha believed would be shorter than
Simon imagined.

He continued speaking, sounding quite sorry for himself.
'I suppose at the back of my mind I suspected that it would
prove a temporary thing but when she wanted to get married
. . .' His voice trailed away. 'I needed someone to need me.
And you must admit it, Martha, she's very beautiful.'

'Mmm,' she said conscious that acknowledging a much
younger woman's 'beauty' was just a little too large of a horse
pill for her to swallow.

Simon gave a bitter laugh. 'I know what you're going to

say, Martha,' he said. 'I was trying to recapture my youth. I don't know. Maybe I was. Maybe it was just loneliness or lust.' He gave another mirthless, bitter laugh. 'I don't know but I can't ever forgive the girls for putting their own prejudices before my happiness.'

Martha knew she must tread very carefully but she could not see Simon make such a sweeping statement of alienation of his daughters without defending them on Evelyn's behalf.

'Maybe it was less to do with them wanting to block your happiness,' she said tentatively, 'and more to do with them seeing you as vulnerable, wanting to protect you from hurt. Perhaps they didn't think this relationship was right for you, that it would not lead to happiness. At least not long term. They've lost their mother, Simon, and although I admit I didn't really know Christabel, certainly not well enough to make a judgement on her character, she appeared very different from Evelyn.'

'But Evelyn's dead,' he said. 'However nice, however beautiful, however lovely, warm, comfortable and loving she was, she is not here for me now.'

His words struck her. He had never expressed this selfish grief before.

'No, Simon,' she said, very softly. 'Evelyn is not here. Not through her own choice. You perhaps need to allow your grief to come out a little longer before you can form another relationship.'

'But, Martha, I hate it,' he said viciously. 'I hate these long evenings alone. No one to holiday with or come home to at the end of a day. I hate it.'

'Be careful, Simon,' she said. 'You're a very wealthy man in a very vulnerable state. Be very careful.'

'Thanks for the advice,' he said. 'I'm going to have one more whisky and then take one of Evelyn's sleeping tablets and go to bed.'

'Good night,' she said, struggling not to sound cross with him.

When he had hung up she sat and stared at the silent, moving pictures on the television screen. Simon had said something that had a bearing on the case. There was the obvious connection of Alice in an equally disturbed state finding oblivion through alcohol and sleeping tablets. Yes, there was that. But there was something else too. It was the reference to what lay people call an abortion but medics call a termination. Terminations of pregnancy are not legal after 24 weeks unless there is a specific and serious medical defect in the foetus. She knew that as a medic.

But the child who had been brought to the hospital would have shown no sign of a medical defect until it was born. And it had been a full term foetus. Not an abortion. So why did she feel instinctively that it had a bearing on the case?

She went to sleep with the question still buzzing around inside her.

FIFTEEN

Simon rang again first thing Tuesday morning making it the second morning she had been awakened by the telephone. At this rate she wouldn't even need an alarm clock, she thought, stretching out a hand for the receiver.

'I've rung to apologize, Martha,' he said, speaking in a short, abrupt manner. 'I feel such a fool. I should have remembered that whisky makes me maudlin. It really wasn't a good idea to dump it all on you. I was in my cups last night and have the headache this morning to prove it. Again – I apologize –' he laughed – 'most humbly. You're going to think I'm an idiot,' he continued, 'or worse a prat, but I sort of needed to do something stupid. I feel much better for it this morning. And,' he said grandly, 'to prove how very sorry I am for dumping all that on your lovely shoulders I want to take you out for dinner.' He paused for a second. 'If we're still friends, that is.'

'Of course,' she said, smiling at his penitent humility – not his usual attitude. 'Although neither the apology nor the dinner is necessary. I consider it a compliment that you chose to speak to me.' She smiled to herself. 'Even if you were pissed. It's a mark of true friendship, Simon. Anyone is willing to share happiness but it's true friends who confide in you in their hour of adversity and expose their vulnerability as you did. Besides – I really owe you a dinner.'

'How so?'

'You've given me insight into one of my current cases.'

'Which one?'

'I can't tell you, Simon. It'll probably all come out in the end and then I promise I will explain all.' She hesitated. 'I'm sorry to be so mysterious but I'm a bit tied up at the moment so can we hang back on the dinner until this case has come to court? Then I can really look forward to the evening.'

'Fine,' he said. 'You'll ring me?'

'I will, Simon,' she said. 'I promise.'

'Until then, Martha.'

As she put the phone down she reflected on Simon Pendlebury and his mysterious past, both recent and distant. He had been at university with Martin and they had been unlikely friends. Different both in personality and in their looks. Simon had been the good looking one while Martin . . . well, Martin had had the personality. Simon had initially been shy but had grown into a tall, handsome man who had married the gentlest of women, Evelyn. Martha had known Evelyn Pendlebury for almost as long as Simon and she had never heard her say an unkind or unpleasant word about anybody. Which could have made her appear bland, insincere, shallow even, when she was anything but. Evelyn had explained her lack of malice in typical humble and honest fashion. She had said to Martha that she simply 'didn't bother' with anyone about whom she would want to say anything unpleasant. 'I select my friends very, very carefully,' she had said.

So how come Evelyn had married Simon? Simon who had clawed his way up – somehow – from an emotionally and physically deprived background, left behind his scarred working-class roots via a scholarship – but to all that wealth? Huge house, cars, housekeeper, swimming pool, daughters educated at one of the top 'ladies' establishments, and was now talking about buying a black-and-white, Grade I listed house attached to something like a thousand acres. Worth millions. Where did all the money come from? Where had all the money come from?

It was something she and Martin had puzzled over for years. Nothing legal had been their final conclusion but what made this unlikely was Evelyn's personality. Martha could not imagine her friend being married to a man who was less than honest. And Evelyn was too bright to turn a blind eye to an unpleasant truth. So she and Martin had argued the point round and round, never coming to a sensible conclusion until they had dropped the subject completely but unsatisfactorily.

Evelyn's death from 'the silent killer', ovarian cancer, the year before had been a tragedy for all who had known her.

Martha lay back against her pillows, her mind racing, firstly thinking about Simon and Evelyn but then progressing to this strange case. Her thought processes were slow at first but as she became more awake they speeded up.

Sukey was the next person to intrude into her bedroom, in

pink pyjamas, dressing gown and fluffy slippers, carefully carrying a mug of coffee which she handed to her mother. 'Morning, Mum,' she said, climbing onto the bed.

Martha took the coffee from her, inhaling the scent. It was fresh coffee. 'Is this a thank you for allowing you to go to acting school?'

Sukey nodded, unabashed that her strategy had been penetrated. 'I'm so excited, Mum,' she confided, giving her a hug, almost splashing coffee on the starched white duvet cover. She opened her blue eyes wide. 'I've just got this feeling that I'm born to be very, very lucky.'

Martha could have warned her enthusiastic daughter that a career in acting was at best precarious, quoted the mantra that many were called but few chosen and told her that even successful actresses had periods of inactivity. She might have added that they had no contacts in the media world, no famous relations who might be able to ease Sukey's way into a role or two. But she had gone along a similar path with Sam, warning him about choosing football as a career. And look where he was now. The Liverpool Academy. With her twin brother so successful it was no wonder that Sukey was aiming high, convinced she would share his good fortune. Martha wondered if Sam would secure the Stoke deal and superstitiously crossed her fingers. Her twins, she was fast realizing, were a very unusual and unique pair. It made it more of a shame that their father could not witness their successes and perhaps be there to comfort them through their downfalls. But if Sam could play in a Premier League team why should not Sukey star in a soap or a film or go on the stage, whatever Noël Coward warned Mrs Worthington. Martha put her arm round her daughter, breathed in the soapy, lemony smell of her hair, drank her coffee and tried to find the right words to say, not to discourage but to encourage without raising false hopes.

In the end she kissed the top of her daughter's head. 'Go for it, Suks,' she said. 'Life's too short to sit back, suddenly arrive at middle age and wonder what would have happened if you had followed your dream.'

Sukey flicked her long blonde hair behind her shoulders and looked into her mother's face, frowning. 'What parts do you think I could play, Mum?' She was already sounding self-absorbed.

'Just about anything.'

Sukey's frown deepened. 'I wanted you to say something more specific,' she said grumpily. 'Not soft soap me.'

'What would you like to play? Classical stuff? Jane Austen?'

Sukey made a face. 'I wouldn't want to be one of those simpering wretches like in *Pride and Prejudice*,' she said. 'I'd want to be someone more like Vesper Lynd in *Casino Royale*.' Her chin was jutting out.

'Wouldn't we all,' Martha muttered. 'Come on, Suks, climb off your cloud. Time to get up and go to work and school.'

Martha felt very happy that morning. Tuesday had started well, with the brief chat with her daughter and the telephone call from Simon Pendlebury which had been so pleasant and friendly. As she showered, she reflected that she had neither liked nor trusted him while Evelyn had been alive but since she'd died they had become friends. She smiled to herself and dressed in a black Betty Jackson suit worn over a pink silk blouse. One of the downsides to her job was that dealing so much with death on a day-to-day basis she was almost always forced to wear, if only for decency's sake, sober colours. Most days she had face-to-face meetings with grieving relatives. But she felt she could risk a pink blouse today. She wore high-heeled patent shoes for a small touch of glamour.

To her surprise when she reached her office Jericho Palfreyman opened the door to her, his eyes bright with inquisitiveness. 'Morning,' he said, looking pleased with himself. 'Detective Inspector Randall's already here to see you, ma'am. I let him into your office.'

She hung up her coat. The weather was still freezing, especially in the early morning; she'd had to scrape the ice off the car which had delayed her by five minutes. But it was still only ten to nine. 'It's a bit early for a visit from him, isn't it?'

'It is.' His words were heavy with meaning. He was dying for her to ask *why* DI Randall had called in so early.

She gave in. 'Do you know what it's about, Jericho? Did he say?'

'No, ma'am, but he looks . . . ' Jericho fished around in his head for an appropriate word. 'Restless. I think he's worried about something.'

'Right.' She pushed the door open. Alex was silhouetted

against the window, staring out at the snowscape. He turned round as she entered. 'Alex,' she greeted him warmly. 'It's nice to see you.'

'I had to come, Martha.'

Jericho was right, she thought. Alex Randall was positively agitated.

'Sit down,' she invited.

He folded his long, spare frame into the armchair and leaned forward, his hands on his knees. 'I'm going round and round in circles,' he confessed. 'Going mad and not getting anywhere very satisfactory which is why I've come here to talk to you.' He smiled. 'The voice of reason.'

She sat down too, not behind her desk but in the chair to his side. 'You think I can help?'

'I damn well hope so.'

She leaned back. 'OK,' she said. 'Shoot.'

'I need a clue, Martha. A direction. Something – anything to give me a focus.'

She thought for a minute then spoke slowly. 'This probably hasn't got anything to do with it,' she said, 'but a friend of mine rang me late last night.'

Randall looked at her, patently wondering where this was leading.

'He mentioned a friend of his who'd had a termination. A medical abortion,' she explained.

Randall stared at her as though he thought she was stark staring mad. 'That was not exactly what I'd expected.'

She met his eyes and he gave his head a faint shake. 'I'm sorry,' he said. 'I can't see what that can possibly have to do with this case.' His eyes were on her face as though he was searching for something. 'I simply can't see it, Martha,' he said finally. 'We're talking about a baby here, not an abortion.'

'I know that,' she said stiffly. Then she smiled. 'Stick with me, Alex,' she said. 'Be patient. Initially I wondered about Alice's daughter, Rosie, if she had got pregnant. Could the baby possibly be hers? Then I decided no. If she had had an unwanted pregnancy she would have had a legal termination. Not gone to full term and then hidden the baby's body. Rosie Sedgewick is simply too bright,' she said. 'And besides, from what you've told me she's also too strong a personality. She doesn't fit the profile I've built up of the child's mother.' She smiled at him mischievously. 'I'm not being very helpful, am I?'

Randall waited, hoping she was about to say something a little more illuminating.

Martha knew she needed to reassure him. 'All this, I feel, does have some bearing on the case.'

Alex thought but he still couldn't see it. 'Any other thoughts?'

'I was planning to interview Mrs Palk,' Martha said.

'Whatever for?' Randall was bemused.

'Because she was the one who found Alice Sedgewick's body. She had a key to number 41,' she reminded him.

'And?' He felt a little more interested now. His pulse quickened as Martha leaned forward. He caught a waft of a very light, spicy, clean perfume and wondered what it was. He diverted his attention from her perfume to the light which gleamed in her long green eyes. 'Even so,' he said steadily, 'Why would you want to speak to Acantha Palk?'

'Because I have some questions for her.'

Alex stretched out his long legs and spoke in a casual tone. 'You wouldn't care to tell me what these questions are?'

Like a spring, Martha thought, he was uncoiling. 'Not at the moment, Alex,' she said. 'If I get any answers then I'll tell you.' She touched his hand and looked straight into his face. 'I promise.'

She paused for a moment then looked away. 'Tell me a bit more about the Godfreys,' she said, catching him completely unawares.

'I'd almost forgotten about them,' he admitted. 'They're surely right out of the picture?'

'You think?'

Alex looked at her suspiciously but Martha Gunn, Shropshire coroner, had never looked more innocent. 'Sometimes,' he said, 'I can't follow your line of reasoning.'

She gave him a cheeky grin. 'That's what makes you come here for help and discussion,' she said.

He narrowed his eyes, half closing them in thought. 'I might just be curious about your methods one of these days, Martha,' he said. Then he added quite unexpectedly, 'Who is this friend, anyway, the one who was talking about an abortion?'

Annoyingly she felt herself blush. 'Just a friend,' she said shortly. If Detective Inspector Alex Randall could keep his private life private then so could she. They might have known each other for a good few years but they had never quite crossed the boundary from colleague to friend, however narrow it had sometimes become. Maybe they never would. Alex Randall was a very private person. Not open about his personal life at all. She knew little about him other than that he was married though he had never talked directly about Mrs Randall. Children? She didn't know that either. Where did he live? Something else to add to the list of 'things she didn't know about Alex'. He was, in fact, a complete enigma. A mystery.

She looked up to see him watching her and returned to safer ground. 'There is another thing, Alex,' she said. 'Did you say one of your WPCs interviewed the Isaac family who, if I remember rightly, lived in Number 41 before the Godfreys?'

'Well – Mrs Isaac did. She's dead now. WPC Shaw visited her son and daughter-in-law.' Again he was both surprised and puzzled at the direction her questions were moving in.

'Did she feel there was something – well – suspicious there?'

Alex shifted uncomfortably in his chair. 'Not exactly.'

'So, what?'

'WPC Shaw felt they didn't like her probing into their finances. It was just an impression that they were reluctant and less happy to focus on that topic. Apparently they appear to be worth a packet, those two. And . . .' In spite of himself Alex Randall smiled. 'Personally I think WPC Shaw simply took against the fact that Mr Isaac is an undertaker. As was his father before him.'

'Really?' Martha said briskly. 'Well, Alex.' She stood up, squared up a sheaf of papers on her desk. 'Time for us both to get on. I'm sure you've plenty to do.'

He looked at her and caught the faintest touch of a smile. 'Thank you for your time, Martha,' he said, 'though what help you've been I'm not quite sure.'

'And thank you for yours, Alex.' She paused and couldn't suppress a wide grin. 'I haven't helped you at all, have I?'

'No,' he said. 'Or more truthfully perhaps I'm not quite sure. But thanks anyway.' He turned to go but before he moved his guard was down. She read something in the drop of his face, some glimpse of a deep sludge of sadness that must permeate throughout his entire life. She almost – almost –

stretched out her hand and asked him what it was, how she could help, why he needed to suffer like this and keep it to himself. But as clearly as she read the emotion she read too the Keep Out sign planted firmly in front of it and knew instinctively that now was not the right time. She must draw back and wait. He would not welcome her crossing this invisible but tangible line drawn in the sand. In fact she could never cross this boundary without a clear and unambiguous invitation. So she held out her hand. 'I'm sorry I couldn't be of more help.' She paused. 'I hope, however, that I have planted some seeds and that they bear fruit.' She gave him a warm smile. 'Goodbye, Alex,'

'Goodbye.' He held her eyes for a split second too long – long enough for her to read even more clearly this truly terrible pain that he locked inside himself. She watched him go with a feeling of frustration.

When she had heard his footsteps patter down the stairs, she wandered outside her room to speak to Jericho. He was someone who knew everything and everyone. A great source of information – even if he did get his facts muddled up on some occasions and embellish the truth on others. He was also an incredible gossip and had antennae which picked up on any whiff of scandal as tall as a mobile phone mast. But he was also very intuitive and would know why she was being so curious so she must be careful how she posed her questions. 'Tell me, Jericho,' she said casually, 'What do you make of Detective Inspector Randall?'

Her assistant pursed his lips. 'Don't rightly know,' he said.

'Does he live in Shrewsbury?'

'Don't know that neither. I've never seen him around the town.'

'No.' She frowned. This was not proving informative at all. 'He is,' she commented, 'an enigma.'

'He is that,' Jericho agreed.

'Is he married, do you know?'

Her assistant shrugged. 'Don't know that neither, Mrs Gunn.' He was unsuspicious – so far. Best retreat before his curiosity went into overdrive.

'Now then, what sandwiches will you be wanting for lunch?'

'Oh, Jericho,' she said laughing. 'Do you ever think of anything but food?'

He considered the question literally, as was his way, his face impassive. 'As your assistant, ma'am,' he said severely, 'I have to consider your wellbeing at all times. Part of that duty is to make sure you have proper meals at decent intervals.'

She smiled at him. 'Well, at least Dr Sullivan seems very happy and contented these days.'

'I've heard two things there,' Jericho said, his eyes bright with the gossip.

And in spite of herself Martha didn't stop him.

'Divorce and Alcoholics Anonymous,' Jericho announced, touching the side of his nose significantly. 'Transformed him, so I've heard.'

'He does look and appear better,' Martha said cautiously. 'But divorce *and* AA? Where on earth do you get all your titbits from?'

'Here and there,' Jericho said, deliberately mysterious.

It was time to end this conversation and get on with some real work. 'Can you get me Mrs Acantha Palk on the telephone, please, Jericho,' she said. 'She's a solicitor connected to the Sedgewick case. Also a friend of the dead woman.'

It didn't take Jericho long to track her down. He was practised at his work of Coroner's Officer. Less than four minutes later Martha found herself addressing the deep and formidable voice of Mrs Acantha Palk.

'What can I do for you, coroner?' Clearly Mrs Palk was in polite mode. Coroners and solicitors do not always have the happiest of relationships.

'I wonder if you would mind dropping by my office some time,' Martha said casually. 'As you can probably guess it's connected with the death of your . . .' She hesitated. 'Friend and client, Mrs Alice Sedgewick.'

'Can you tell me why?' Acantha Palk's voice was guarded.

'I'd rather speak to you face-to-face, if you wouldn't mind.' Martha waited a second or two before adding, 'At three o'clock, this afternoon?'

Acantha Palk must know she did not really have much choice. 'Yes, ma'am,' she said, notes of resentment and resignation making her voice sound sulky. 'At your office?'

'Yes, please,' Martha said.

*   *   *

Alex, in the meantime, was chewing over Martha's words. For all they seemed to him to be leading him round and round the mulberry bush, or worse, in the wrong direction, he had watched her arrive at correct solutions too many times to dismiss her thoughts out of hand. To that end he caught up with WPC Delia Shaw in the corridor. 'Have you got a minute?'

'Yes, sir.' She followed him into his office.

'Shut the door, would you?' She did as he asked and faced him, her eyes questioning.

Alex dived in. 'The coroner, Mrs Gunn, has suggested that the Isaacs have some criminal activity to hide. Did you get that impression?'

Slowly Delia Shaw nodded. 'I did, sir.'

Randall frowned. 'But in what connection?'

'I don't think it's anything to do with the case, sir,' she said. 'They seemed perfectly at ease when I questioned them about the house, the baby, that sort of stuff. No . . .' She thought for a minute, recalling the exchange of tense glances as she had looked round the elderly Mrs Isaac's converted 'sickroom'. 'It was more when I asked them about old Mrs Isaac, sir. And her money. I just got the feeling that there was something there, something they didn't want me to probe into. It was just an impression, sir,' she added quickly, 'but having been quite happy for me to visit them and question them about the dead child, they were very relieved to see me go.'

'Sometimes,' Alex said grimly, 'impressions direct us towards the facts. Unfortunately sometimes it isn't logic but instinct which solves cases, Shaw. And then we have to search for hard evidence which will stand up in court to support our thesis.' He smiled at her. 'Thank you. Was there anything else that struck you?'

'No, sir.'

'OK, you can go.' He paused for a minute then added, just as she reached the door, 'Have you thought any more about going into plain clothes?'

Her eyes lit up. 'I'd love to, sir,' she said.

Alex sat in his office and pondered the WPC's observations of the Isaac family. He would be happy to ask the Birmingham police to investigate them, but he couldn't see how whatever they found would help solve his case. He eyed the phone, tempted to pick it up and dial the coroner's office. He wondered whether Martha had made contact with Acantha Palk yet.

She had.

In fact at that very moment Martha Gunn was sitting right opposite her.

She had had a shock when Jericho had ushered the solicitor in. So tall, deep voiced, such an overbearing presence.

'Mrs Palk,' she said. 'Thank you for coming. Do sit down.'

Acantha Palk looked enquiringly at her. 'Mrs Gunn,' she said formally, making no attempt to keep the irritation out of her voice.

Martha put her chin on her hand and stared straight at the solicitor. 'What did you do with the note?' she asked politely.

As Martha had expected Acantha Palk looked affronted. 'What note?' she asked angrily. 'What on earth are you talking about?'

Martha didn't explain. She simply kept her eyes on Acantha Palk's large frame and repeated her question in exactly the same tone. 'What have you done with the note?'

Acantha Palk glared at her and pressed her lips together. 'You've been told that there wasn't one,' she said eventually.

'I know what I've been told.'

The two women faced each other. It was a battle of character.

'You were first on the scene,' Martha said, 'and Alice Sedgewick was your friend. You might think you are protecting her reputation. Again, I ask you. Where is the note? What have you done with it?' She held on to the woman's gaze. 'I do hope you haven't destroyed it.' She waited. But Acantha Palk was a tough nut to crack. She simply stared back, her face displaying little emotion except anger.

'OK,' Martha said slowly. 'Let me ask you another question. Did you ring your friend, Alice, the night before she killed herself?'

Acantha Palk leaned forward and barked at her, 'I assume you have access to police records?'

Martha dipped her head.

'Then you will know that I did ring Alice. Aaron had asked me to keep an eye on her while he was away. He was worried about her.' Her dark eyes met Martha's fearlessly as she continued. 'However unless that telephone was bugged you have absolutely no idea what I said to Alice.'

'That's true,' Martha agreed, not dropping her eyes, 'though I can guess. You told her about the bones being found in Bayston Hill, didn't you?'

Acantha Palk pressed her lips together tighter and looked furious, finally spitting out, 'Pure conjecture.'

Martha continued calmly, 'Unless you have something even more sinister to hide, Mrs Palk, than suppressing evidence I suggest that you . . .' She rolled her eyes theatrically towards the ceiling. 'What is that lovely and appropriate Americanism? Ah yes. "Come clean" with me.' She was finding it hard to conceal her enjoyment at this small drama.

Mrs Palk interlocked her fingers. 'Coroner,' she said, 'I am a solicitor. This is a serious allegation. I know—'

Martha interrupted impatiently. 'Yes, yes, your rights. We all have rights. Alice wrote that note to speak for her after her death. That is her right. It is what she wanted to be heard. As coroner *I* have the right to know why that poor woman killed herself. The baby sparked something off, didn't it?'

Acantha Palk was hardly breathing as she absorbed Martha's words. 'It was explained in the note, wasn't it? You were supposed to be her very best friend, Mrs Palk. Practically the only friend she had.' She fixed her gaze on the woman. 'That was why she addressed the note to you, wasn't it?'

Acantha Palk was beginning to visibly wilt and Martha ploughed on mercilessly. 'I suggest if you have the letter with you, you hand it over now. And if you do not have it you arrange for it to be delivered to me at the earliest possible opportunity.' She paused. Acantha's eyes were practically boiling with rage. 'As you are a solicitor, Mrs Palk, you prob-ably know that it is an offence to suppress any information which is pertinent to an unexpected, unexplained. suspicious death. My powers and my position demand that you put this information into my hand as soon as possible or I shall have to accuse you of concealment and inform the police.'

After a short, tight-lipped pause Acantha Palk spoke. 'How did you know?' she asked. 'How could you possibly have known that Alice left a note? Suicides don't always.'

'People work in certain predictable ways,' Martha responded. 'I did not believe that Alice Sedgewick would elect to leave this world without explaining to her family why she was doing it.'

Acantha Palk stared.

'It *was* addressed to you wasn't it?'

Acantha Palk nodded.

'Do you have it with you?'

'No.'

'Where is it?'

'At home.'

'Did you tell Mr Sedgewick that his wife had, in fact, left a suicide note?'

Acantha Palk nodded. 'It was he who told me to destroy it.'

'Aaah,' Martha said.

The vaguest, faintest smile crossed Acantha Palk's face. 'Much as it would have been more convenient and better for everybody if the note was burnt, as a solicitor, it went against the grain to destroy evidence.'

'Alice Sedgewick is dead,' Martha said, leaning forward. 'These were her last words. It was her explanation, sent to you because she trusted you. You could not betray that trust. You could not deny your friend this last, plaintive voice, could you? Or her relatives the satisfaction of knowing why?'

'No. Not really.'

'Then would you mind?'

Half an hour later Martha had read through the letter. And part of the story unfolded.

> Dear Canthie,
>
> By the time you read this I will be dead but I had to set the slate right by you. I want you to speak to Gregory, to explain. He has been such a devoted son, loving and caring as much as he could when his father was so – well – difficult. As you know Aaron is the stronger of us two and can be a little . . . just a little, overbearing.
>
> My behaviour must have seemed inexplicable to you as perhaps other things might have struck you in the past. But you have said nothing. Ten years ago, I un-expectedly found that I was pregnant. I was very confused. Gregory and Rosie were grown up. I had not expected to have another child so late in life. I was in

my forties. Then as I made certain that I was not mistaken
I was thrilled. Absolutely ecstatic, if you want to know.
It seemed like a gift. A great gift. From above. I had
loved being a mother and missed my children, in particular when Gregory left home. I hated the boarding-school
years. This child, I vowed, I would keep close to me.
But Aaron put all sorts of objections in my way. He
worried the child would be deformed. You know how he
likes things his way and hates what he sees as imper-
fections. In fact he was livid that I was pregnant. At first
he accused me of being simply careless but as I got more
excited about the child he started accusing me firstly of
having deliberately tried to get pregnant and then that it
was not his child but a lover's. Acantha, I never had a
lover. It was undoubtedly his child. But he would not
accept it. He insisted. Absolutely insisted that I have an
abortion. I tried everything to persuade him that it was
our child, pointed out how close he was, in particular,
to Rosie and that this could perhaps be a second daughter
but he became violent and said, quite cruelly, that it
might be another son. I am so sorry and guilty now.
When I went to the doctor and said I did not want this
child, I was lying. Since then I have lived with the conse-
quences of that lie. That child has stayed in my mind
ever since. I called her Poppy. Every day I hear her cry.
I see her face. I nurse her. I play with her. Aaron thought
if we moved house it would make me forget. But I made
a room for her in the new place and Aaron finally lost
his temper. He made an appointment for me to see a
psychiatrist and told him I was mad. I wanted to tell Dr
Richmond but Aaron sat in with me and I could say
nothing of the truth. Dr Richmond diagnosed me with
depression. So I allowed myself to be drugged and treated
for an illness I did not have. I was simply grieving for
my lost daughter. Acantha, you must have wondered why
I decorated a bedroom in children's wallpaper. I did it
for Poppy. I bought her clothes, a cot, blankets, toys.
When I found the baby in the attic I believed it was
her, that somehow she had not been aborted but had lived
and died – somewhere. I took the old blanket away from
her. I nursed her. I wrapped her in a new blanket and

took her back to the hospital so she would not haunt me
any more. But I was wrong. She has. She has not left
me. Poppy is still here with me and now we must go
together. Please explain to Gregory. Tell him I will miss
my visits to him. Thank him for the happiness he has
given me. Thank you, dear friend, for all you've done.
Give my love to my family. Tell Aaron I am with Poppy.
One last wish: I wish to be cremated and my ashes scattered somewhere near the hospital. I believe they have
a garden there for such purposes. Goodbye, my darling.
I am happy.

Martha looked up. 'You couldn't have suppressed this,' she
said. 'Not her last words to her son. Her dying wishes.'
  'Well, I didn't, did I?'
  There was no remorse coming from Mrs Palk. She was on
the defensive. Martha leaned forward. 'I shall put this letter
in the hands of the police,' she said. 'It's up to them whether
they charge you. It will find its way to Gregory Sedgewick.
I think,' she said, fingering the sheet of paper, 'that it's one
of the most poignant notes I've ever read.'

SIXTEEN

As soon as Acantha Palk had left, Martha rang Alex Randall. 'I have something for you,' she said, deliberately not telling him what it was. 'I was wondering whether to bring it over.' She looked out of her window. The winter sunshine had set the snow sparkling. She felt a yearning to be out there, in the brightness and the cold.

'Does it help us with our case?'

'I think it might.'

'What is it?'

She laughed. 'Don't deny me my moment of drama, Alex,' she said. 'You'll find out in fifteen minutes.'

Alex was in his office when she arrived. Without a word she handed him the note. He read it through and she watched his expression change from pity to sorrow, through grief, finally landing at anger. He looked up. 'Are you going to tell me where you got this from?'

'Have a guess,' she teased.

He steepled his fingers together and met her eyes. 'Mrs Palk,' he suggested.

She nodded.

'And I would think,' he added, 'that it was probably Aaron Sedgewick who asked her to—'

'Destroy it,' she finished for him. 'He wouldn't think of anyone but himself. He would have read it through and realized that it accused him, threw him in a bad light. So . . .'

Alex glanced down at the sheet of paper. 'I can see why.'

'You might see why, Alex, but I take a very dim view of this.'

'But Mrs Palk didn't destroy it, did she?'

'Thank goodness,' she said. 'She would have. But she didn't. And I wonder why not. Out of loyalty to her friend, a sense of justice? Or I just wonder. It put her in a very powerful position over Aaron Sedgewick.' She looked at Alex. 'She might even have intended to blackmail him.'

'You, Martha Gunn,' Alex said, his lips twitching, 'have a very nasty mind.'

She was unabashed. 'So I believe. And in this job it has developed. But this does answer all your questions about Alice Sedgewick and her state of mind when she took the infant to the hospital.'

'It certainly does,' he said. Then paused. 'I hate to put a dampener on this, Martha,' he said, 'but while it does explain all about Mrs Sedgewick, her state of mind, the attitude of her family, the pink blanket, the name Poppy, the fact that she returned to the hospital where she had "lost" her baby, it still doesn't tell us anything about the identity of the dead child or how it came to be concealed in the attic of number 41 The Mount for somewhere between five and ten years. We know it can't have been the baby that Alice lost. There never was any possibility that the newborn infant was Alice's child. Not poor old Alice. With this letter we know that her pregnancy was terminated, something she was cruelly coerced into from which she never recovered. Certainly not her mental health.' He stopped speaking, his face frozen and serious. 'Is it possible that Alice abducted a substitute child which subsequently died?'

'It's possible,' Martha agreed, 'given her mental state. However I don't really think that's what happened.'

Alex was tempted to ask her again what was her verdict on the affair. What did she think had happened? Instead he forced himself to ask questions with more factual answers. 'How did Acantha Palk appear to feel about her friend's plight?'

'Oddly enough I don't really know,' Martha said, frowning. 'I don't even know whether this was a surprise to her or she already knew that Alice had had a pregnancy terminated. Strange, isn't it?'

'Yes.' He was silent for a moment then murmured, almost to himself, 'So where does that leave us with this case? Whose was the baby?' He searched her face, as though he would find the answer there.

Martha returned Alex's long hard stare with one of her own. 'You already know the answer in your heart, don't you,' she asked softly.

He laughed. 'Do I? I don't think so.'

'Oh yes you do. What was it Holmes said?' She smiled. 'I don't mean PC Shotton's sniffer dog but the real McCoy. "When you have eliminated the impossible, whatever remains, however improbable, must be the truth".'

'Go on, Martha,' Alex prompted steadily.

'Put it like this. It was never going to be anything to do with the Isaac family, was it? Apart from one tenuous connection. They already had their own children and didn't live in The Mount anyway. They were on the edge of this but never part of it. I have a feeling that if you really delve into them money will be at their hearts. They strike me as avaricious people. You will find them guilty of some crime. They took their wealthy mother to live with them. No.' She held up her hand. 'I don't think they would murder. It isn't their style. It'll be something maybe to do with duties or property. There will be some irregularity which your WPC picked up on, clever girl. Besides, look at it from another angle. An undertaker would never leave a body in an attic. Particularly such a tiny body. He would have ample opportunity for concealing a child in, say, a coffin due for cremation. It can't be them and it isn't them. The baby is not Poppy. Neither is it anything to do with the Isaacs.'

'I agree.'

'And now we know all about Alice and why she behaved as she did. Her mind was not robust after she was forced into having a termination when she had already built a bond with the child. It must have been terrible for her.'

Alex Randall looked at her intently. 'What exactly are you saying, Martha?'

'It's a class thing,' she said cryptically. 'Now who was it who said that? It struck me as an interesting comment at the time. Now I see they couldn't have been more right. It *is* a class thing.'

Alex was getting irritated. 'You're being just a mite too mysterious, Martha. I'm simply not with you.'

'We took that comment the wrong way, didn't we?'

DI Randall continued to be mystified.

'It's a little like when you look down the wrong end of a telescope. Instead of things appearing larger, they appear smaller. That's what's happened here. We were looking at the discovery of an infant's body from the wrong end. Our little baby was not an *unwanted* infant. He was a very much wanted infant. But he wasn't perfect so he died, probably very soon after birth. There was ignorance here, yes. But it came about through callous and cynical exploitation. Put it all together, Alex,' she urged, 'and you will have arrived at the truth. And by the way,' she

added, 'when Mark Sullivan rang me with the findings of the
post-mortem on Alice Sedgewick I did ask him if he would
look up something else on the hospital computer.'
'Anything I should know about?'
'I think so.'
Baldly she related dates, times, details.
Alex took it all in without comment. Then he cleared his
throat. 'You mentioned I should have a holiday,' he said.
'Perhaps I should go to Spain – again?'
'Sounds like a good idea to me,' Martha said.
He grinned at her, looking like a hopeful monkey. 'I don't
suppose we could stretch the rules and you join me?'
'Not this time,' Martha said. 'But perhaps before you go to
Spain you might want to send someone round to pay a visit
on . . . Now what was her name?'
Alex smiled.

As Alex had expected Petula Godfrey was not in the least bit
pleased to hear that he had a few more questions to ask her.
'What sort of questions? I've answered enough already,'
she grumbled.
'I prefer to meet up with you face-to-face,' he said calmly.
'Look mate,' she said tightly and now he could hear, almost
taste, the panic in her voice, 'this dead baby thing, it ain't
nothin' to do with us. I haven't got any kids. I have nothin'
to do with them. I hate the bloody things. I don't like kids.'
'We've been assuming, Mrs Godfrey, that the person who hid
the baby's body, also "didn't like kids".' Alex remarked drily.
She came back quickly then. 'When I say I don't like 'em
I don't mean I'd bloody kill 'em. I know what's legal, you
know.'
'Do you?'
There was silence from the other end of the phone. It was
left to Alex Randall to wind up the conversation. 'Well, thank
you, Mrs Godfrey,' he said. 'We'll be over some time tomorrow
morning. Would you like to attend at Malaga police station
or shall we come up to the house?'
'The house,' she snapped. 'I'm not going to some ruddy
Spanish cop shop.'
'Till tomorrow then,' Alex said politely.
When he got back to the station he spoke to WPC Delia

Shaw. 'I have a job for you,' he said. She listened carefully, her eyes intelligent and understanding. 'Yes, sir. And then . . .'

This time DI Randall did not take Gethin Roberts with him but Sergeant Paul Talith. He needed his thoughtful intelligence rather than Roberts' obvious distraction with the flight delays, the poor accommodation and late food. Besides PC Gethin Roberts had an important job to do.

On the way over Talith was curious. 'So why are you going over again, sir?'

'Well,' Randall said, stretching out his legs as far as he could. 'We've excluded the Isaacs and Mrs Sedgewick is now dead which leaves Mr and Mrs Godfrey. They fit the time zone best anyway so we'll focus our investigation with them.'

Talith thought for a moment then said, 'I just don't see how they can possibly fit in,' he said. 'They don't fit the profile at all.'

'And what is the profile?'

'I don't know.' Talith frowned. 'Some ignorant young girl, I suppose. I mean from what you said Petula Godfrey's street-wise. She's the sort who'd have an abortion in her lunch break and get back to work in the afternoon without giving a backward glance. That's the sort of woman she is, sir.'

Alex said nothing but remained silent and thoughtful.

The phone call couldn't have been better timed. Delia Shaw rang just as Alex switched his phone on at the luggage carousel at Malaga airport. Randall listened then gave out some more instructions.

Chez Godfrey looked just as opulent this time around as it had a fortnight ago but this time Alex Randall thought it looked a bit tacky. Talith was well impressed though. He whistled through his teeth as they approached the tall gates. 'Must be worth a packet,' he observed, 'especially over here.'

Petula was distinctly on edge to see them for the second time. Wearing skintight jeans, spiky heels and a pink sweater she met them at the foot of the stairs and gave Alex a hard, hostile stare. 'I don't know why you've come back,' she said. 'You're wastin' your bloody time. I would have thought you would have realized you'll get no help from us. We don't know nothin' about no dead baby.'

'I think you do,' Alex said steadily, 'and that's why we've come back.'

Petula Godfrey wobbled on the steps and clutched at the handrail but she had lost none of her fighting spirit. 'You better watch what you're sayin',' she said. 'My husband has an evil 'abit of takin' people to court if he thinks they're spreadin' rumours.'

'It's only rumours if it isn't the truth,' Alex said mildly. 'You may not like it, but the truth is the truth, isn't it?'

Vince Godfrey was standing in the doorway, his face thunderous. He must have been a very scary guy in the school playground, Talith thought, as they reached him.

'What's goin' on here,' Godfrey said, bunching up his fists, ready for a sparring match. 'Why have you come troublin' us innocent people?'

'I simply want some answers,' Alex said, deliberately low key.

'What kind of answers? How can we answer stuff we don't know nothin' about? It's so obvious, plod,'

Godfrey continued. 'This ain't somethin' we know anythin' about.' He gave a heavy, theatrical sigh.

'Just answer my questions.'

'Well keep it clean then. Don't go makin' wild accusations unless you can prove them.' Vince couldn't resist tacking on a threat: 'Or you'll regret it.'

This time Randall and Talith were shown into a more formal sitting room, carpeted and plush with two large red sofas facing each other.

The Godfreys sat very close together on one, the two police officers a little less close on the other.

'Graciela,' Petula screamed. The maid scuttled in.

Randall took a good look. It was more obvious on this visit.

Petula rapped out some orders to the maid who scuttled back across the passageway. 'Right, fire away,' Vince Godfrey said, 'and as I said, watch what you're sayin'.'

Alex reflected that litigation had made policing twenty times more difficult.

'Now what's all this about?' Godfrey was suddenly urbane.

'Children,' Alex said without preamble or explanation. 'It's about children.'

'We haven't got any,' Vince replied truculently.

'Why not?' Alex asked mildly.

''Cos we don't bloody well want 'em.' It was Petula who had supplied the answer. She leaned forward, lit a cigarette and blinked.

'You don't want them or you don't have them?'

'We don't want them.'

The maid came in, carrying a tray of cups and saucers, a big round teapot.

'And yet,' Alex said heavily, 'you went to great trouble and expense in a clinic to have multiple courses of IVF which failed and also other procedures, I believe.' He did not look at either of the Godfreys.

Vince Godfrey was quick off the mark. 'Where do you get your information from?'

Alex didn't answer.

Petula pinned him with a stare.

Graciela poured out the tea, her face wooden and impassive.

Alex drew in a deep sigh. 'From 1994 to 2001 you underwent extensive investigations and procedures because you badly wanted a family,' he said. 'But the treatments were unsuccessful and in the end the doctors advised you to consider adoption which can take a long time.'

Vince Godfrey cleared his throat noisily.

'Shall I continue?'

Petula Godfrey was watching his face, mesmerized, as she lifted the teacup to her lips.

'How am I doing?'

The question remained unanswered so Alex continued, 'In 2002 in response to an advertisement you placed on the Internet a young lady from Poland came to live with you. Her name is Celestyna Zawadzki. She was seventeen years old.' Alex kept his eyes on Petula Godfrey. She had gone chalk-white. In contrast her husband, he noticed with interest, had gone a deep, dusky red.

'The reason that you couldn't have children was to do with your wife, wasn't it? You were OK. You'd been told that.' Randall made an inspired guess. 'You have a child from another relationship, don't you?'

Without looking at his wife Vince gave a heavy nod.

Randall continued. 'So you impregnated Celestyna Zawadzki; she bore your child. You were to pay her money.'

Vince had almost shrunk into his chair.

'The trouble was that you were worried the authorities would home in on you, accuse you of coercion and so you neglected to take Celestyna to antenatal clinics or for any medical check-ups at all. But even there you struck lucky, didn't you? You'd kept on Maisie Stokes who had nursed the old Mrs Isaac and Maisie Stokes had worked for a few years as a midwife. For a small consideration she was perfectly happy to supervise Celestyna's antenatal care and perform the delivery. Celestyna was an ignorant girl. As far as she was concerned she was getting Rolls Royce treatment.' He looked at Petula. 'One of my WPCs has taken a statement from Maisie Stokes this very day, Mrs Godfrey. There isn't any point you denying it. We knew someone like that had to be the mother of that little boy. What we didn't understand was that there was also exploitation of the most wicked and callous kind.'

'I don't . . .' Vince started and stopped abruptly, seeing the disgust on the detective's face.

'You kept Celestyna a virtual prisoner at your house and when she went into labour you gave her no medical attention. Unfortunately for you – and for her finances – the baby was not perfect.' He gave Petula a quick glance. 'I can't see you pushing a Silver Cross pram around with the baby inside who had a harelip.' He gave her a straight stare. 'And so the baby died, didn't it?'

'I'm sayin' nothin',' Vince said.

Graciela scuttled in with a second pot of tea. Alex gave her a sharp scrutiny.

'Now you were left in a dilemma, weren't you? You had a dead baby, a boy whom you just wanted to get rid of and still no child of your own. And of course Petula likes to get her own way. She still wanted a baby. So you sent Celestyna Zawadzki back to Poland, telling her she hadn't fulfilled her end of the bargain. You paid her fare and you hid the body of the baby upstairs, in the loft.'

Vince and Petula watched, frozen.

'And then,' Alex said, 'you came to Spain.'

SEVENTEEN

He rang Martha from the airport. 'We got the name of the girl from Maisie Stokes,' he said. 'Celestyna Zawadzki. But all she could tell us was that she was from Poland. Tracking Celestyna down might be a little more difficult.' He chuckled. 'This is turning into an international affair,' he said. 'I just might get a trip to Poland out of it too.'

'Good luck,' she said. She didn't dare add, So what now?

Interpol agreed to help search for Celestyna and using passport controls and work permits they finally found her living in a small town just north of Krakow. Initially Alex rang her up. Her English was good but she wanted nothing to do with what had been an unhappy episode in her life. 'They told me the child would not live,' she said, 'that it's mouth was somehow not normal and it would not be able to feed. They told me this.'

Who knew what the truth was.

'I am married now with a child of my own. My husband knows nothing of my past or of my baby who died.'

'He was born alive?'

'With a weak cry. I knew at once that something was wrong.'

Alex related the conversation back to Martha. 'I feel I should speak to her myself,' she said.

Celestyna was a little more amenable to Martha once she had explained who she was and why she was ringing.

'We'll be holding an inquest on your son.'

'I would prefer not to attend,' Celestyna said quickly. 'I do not want to return to England, ever. I did not like it there – or the people.'

'That's all right,' Martha said. 'You do not have to attend but sometimes people want to. Would you like to give your child a name rather than the inquest be held on an anonymous infant?'

Celestyna was horrified. 'No,' she said. 'It will make him a real person. Please no.'

'Did you have an idea of a name?'

'Of course not,' Celestyna said bluntly. 'He could never

have been my child. There was no point in my thinking of a name for him.'

'I would like to call him something,' Martha said. 'What is the name of your father?'

'Martyn,' the girl said. 'We spell it with a "y" in Polish.'

'Then he shall be called Martyn Zawadzki.'

It was three weeks later that Alex arrived at her office to talk. The inquest on Alice Sedgewick had been held the week before. Martha had returned a verdict of suicide and had read out the letter. It had been her revenge on Aaron Sedgewick. She had enjoyed watching him squirm right through the slow, deliberate reading which Jericho Palfreyman had elected to do. Somehow his ponderous voice, combined with his lank grey locks had seemed appropriately grave.

And though the forensic evidence was not strong enough to return anything but an open verdict the inquest was held on Martyn Zawadzki and in a rare gesture of generosity Aaron Sedgewick offered to have the baby cremated with his wife. Maisie Stokes gave her evidence. They would have struck her off the midwives' register but she had long since retired so Martha merely admonished her.

'So, Alex.' Martha wondered what had brought him to her office on this clear, cold February day. 'I thought you'd want to know,' he said, 'The Birmingham police have found out something about the Isaacs.'

'Ah,' Martha said wisely.

'It's to do with inheritance, as you thought. Mrs Isaac had a large and very valuable collection of Chinese porcelain. We looked into her old house contents insurance at The Mount. The collection was worth in excess of half a million pounds.'

'Good gracious,' Martha said.

'The money they gave to the charlady was, in fact, hush money,' Alex said. 'When Mrs Isaac's estate was valued for probate—'

'It had disappeared?'

'Correct.'

'What happened to it?'

'It was sold – for cash – to a Dutch dealer. Isaac has been busily laundering the money ever since, with little buys here and there.'

Martha nodded.

'We've made a charge against them and the Inland Revenue will be sending them a not-so-small bill,' Alex said with satisfaction. 'They're lucky to have escaped prosecution. Inland Revenue can be quite ruthless at pursuing their debtors.'

'And the Godfreys?'

'It's going to be difficult to know what charge we can make stick without a statement from either Maisie Stokes or Miss Zawadzki. And she's not going to play ball, I can promise you. She wants nothing to do with us.' He paused. 'Which would have left us with concealment of a body except . . .'

She waited.

'Their present maid, Graciela, is four months pregnant. They were trying the same thing again.'

Martha frowned. 'There's been quite a gap.'

'After what happened they didn't dare try anything again in the UK so they lay low in Spain. It's more difficult now to recruit a surrogate mother via the Internet. There are stops put on it so they had to wait for a suitable Spanish girl, someone from the villages.'

'And now?'

'Graciela seems to want to go through with it,' Alex said. 'It isn't illegal for money to change hands along with a child. Their suitability as parents might be called into question but as Vince Godfrey is the biological father it rather looks as though the child might end up with them anyway. They're desperate to have a child, Martha.'

'Desperate people. Desperate measures.'

'Quite.'

He'd finished all he had to say but DI Alex Randall didn't move. He smiled at Martha. 'This isn't the first time you've helped me out,' he said. 'I'm really grateful.'

'My pleasure.'

She had thought he might say more but he didn't. He simply smiled, shook her hand and left.

She sat for a minute or two then picked up the telephone. Perhaps it was time she had a little bit of fun in her life. Being a coroner was interesting. As was being a mother but her life was slipping away all too fast. No one is more aware of the swift flow of the sands of time than a coroner. She'd been promised dinner. Why not?

She dialled the number and was soon connected.

AUTHOR'S NOTE

When I was a child I inherited my grandmother's doll's house. Called Nora's Villa, dated 1894, my usual Saturday job was to clean and tidy it out. It was fully furnished with some lovely furniture and had a lead fireplace, even an ebony piano. My aunt had had it before me but had only sons so I inherited it. Coincidentally I too had sons so it went to my nieces, Lucinda and Alicia.

In the house were porcelain dolls. Two of these I felt particularly sorry for. Porcelain, made from one piece, unable to move either their legs or their arms. These dolls, I was to learn, are known as Frozen Charlottes. As always, a story leads to yet another story. Surfing the Internet, I discovered that Frozen Charlottes are named after Fair Charlotte, the unwise heroine of a poem by Seba Smith, a Maine humorist (1792–1868). Fair Charlotte, setting out for a New Year's Eve Ball elected to travel in a silken cloak. By the time she reached the ball she was frozen solid! A warning to young ladies who put glamour ahead of warmth on snowy nights.

We've all done it!